IN A VAST AND SAVAGE LAND
HUMAN PASSIONS REFUSED TO BE TAMED.

MICHAEL CONNOR—Handsome, reckless, proud, he fought to free Ireland from the hated British rule. With him, Mary knew the rapturous heights of love, the wrenching depths of tragedy.

JONATHAN GARRETT—Powerful, brooding, consumed by outrage and need, he was determined to build a new life in the harsh wilderness—and to share that life with Mary Mulvane.

DINNY O'BYRNE—Dashingly seductive, he was a fierce man who would rather die with honor than live a slave.

MAURICE GREVILLE—Charming, corrupt, infuriated by Mary's refusal to become his mistress, he swore to have his revenge.

LOUISA WILTSHIRE—The ambitious, amoral wife of a wealthy landowner, inflamed by jealousy, she vowed to destroy her only rival—Mary Mulvane.

Yet, Freedom! yet thy banner, torn but flying,
Streams like the thunder-storm *against* the wind!

George Gordon, Lord Byron:
Childe Harold's Pilgrimage, Canto IV.

AGAINST THE WIND

Richard Butler

A DELL BOOK

Published by
Dell Publishing Co., Inc.
1 Dag Hammarskjold Plaza
New York, New York 10017

This work was first published in Australia by Corgi Books,
Transworld Publishers Ltd.

Dell ® TM 681510, Dell Publishing Co., Inc.

ISBN: 0-440-10249-9

Printed in the United States of America
First U.S. printing—September 1979

CHAPTER ONE

The lake lay like a sheet of slate under the October sky, sheltered from the west wind by hills lifting in green slopes of turf that glowed with pools of emerald where they were touched by slowly-moving shafts of sunlight. Beside the lake, where the road to Rathcurran curved in from the east, a fringe of reed-beds reflected waveringly in the water and a heron stalked among the stones in the shallows. Abruptly, he lifted his head. Then, as the rhythmic tramp of boots and the clink of metal on metal grew louder, he flew off with slow wing-beats, his trailing feet leaving an arrow-head of ripples that gleamed like quicksilver in the cool morning light before they died.

A damn pretty prospect, the ensign said to himself. Peaceful. Not what he'd been led to expect at all, by God. In Dublin, they'd told him that this autumn of 1796 was going to be damned difficult down here in County Cork, and a fellow might expect a damned rebellious Irishman behind every bush. With the French War in progress these three years now and His Gracious Majesty King George III seized with bouts of sickness—raving lunacy, some said—England's grip on her Irish possessions had eased somewhat and the Papist rabble, instead of showing gratitude for the vote they'd been granted, seemed now hell-bent on stirring up the kind of mischief he'd been sent to put down—burning barns, tearing down fences and the like. But, here by the lake, it seemed tranquil enough.

Immaculate in his blood-red coat and his mirror-polished boots, he reined in his mount to permit his men to take a stand-easy. 'How much further', he asked in his high-pitched English voice, 'to this village, Sergeant?'

The sergeant, squat, bull-necked and with a pock-marked face that looked as if it had been fashioned out of saddle-leather, lifted his right hand. The metronomic crunch-crunch of boots and the clink of musket-swivels behind him cut off sharply as the file of six men came to a halt. With a smooth economy of movement, he swung the hand across his body, slapped the pole of his pike and brought the nine-foot weapon down from his left shoulder. 'Oh, I reckon on another two or three miles, sir.' Out of the habit of fifteen years' non-commissioned service, he half-turned to check his men. Belts all lying straight. No neck-bands undone. Aye, a good turnout.

The chestnut stallion tossed its head with a chink of harness in the silence. The young officer gentled him, then said, 'What manner of—well, reception do you think we'll get?'

The sergeant picked up the slight hesitation as his gaze swung back to the smooth pink face beneath the wig and cocked hat. Reception? Why, damme, what kind of reception did the lad expect? This was occupied territory, wasn't it? Enemy territory. He grinned, his broken teeth yellow against the deeply-tanned face. 'Bless your heart, sir, they'll be snapping and snarling at us like a pack of half-starved curs. Your Irishman's a surly devil at the best o' times. But, when they're bent on mischief like they are in this county—well, I'd feel more welcome in a bear-pit.'

Damnation! Exactly what they'd said in Dublin. The ensign suppressed a twinge of uneasiness by wrinkling his forehead sternly and trying to put something of his Colonel's rasp into his voice. 'We'll have to be ready for trouble, then.'

'Aye, sir.' The sergeant's grin broadened. 'And, if we don't find trouble, why, we'll have to make some, won't we?' The smile faded as he saw the uncertainty in the officer's face. In God's name, why didn't they teach these babes-in-arms something other than how to ogle a woman and pass the bloody port? His steel-grey eyes hardened as he said, 'Tis the only way to deal with these damned insurgents.' For that's what they were, these bastard Irish. Insurgents and traitors to a man. Worse than the French who, at least, had the grace to fight in the open. But this parcel of bog-trotters formed secret gangs like the White-boys who wore white masks and went out by night to do their devil's work, maiming cattle and performing all manner of villainy. In life, as in the Army, a man had to know his station. You took your orders from above without question, as he himself had always done. But, nowadays, the world was going to the devil, with first the American rebels and then the French bare-arsed peasants all yelling for liberty, and every Jack claiming to be as good as his master. Only one way to deal with that, by thunder! 'Push them', he said grimly. 'Prod them a little.' He stood as if on parade, tough and formidable in his weather-faded scarlet coat, his boots gripping the ground, the pike held at exactly the correct angle. 'Get them out into the open. Then you've got something to shoot at.'

The young officer stroked his horse's neck absently as he stared at the sweet tranquillity of the lake, at the cloud-dappled hills luminous with that soft moist light-quality that is to be found only in Ireland. A whitewashed cottage, small with distance, stood at the head of the lake, a thread of peat-smoke rising from its stubby chimney. A tiny figure moved down the slope of a hill that was patched with stone-walled fields. A girl, from the way she walked. Graceful, flowing, free. . . . He said, 'I'd hoped to avoid bloodshed.'

God save us, the sergeant thought. The lad should have been a parson. Aloud, he said, 'We might do that, sir—if we can find the ring-leaders.' Not that there was much chance of that, since these renegades clung close together and kept as mum as bugs in a blanket.

'And, of course,' said the ensign judicially, 'the evidence to convict them.' For a moment he could hear his Colonel's voice: 'Well done, my boy! A clear-cut case against these villains and all without the loss of a single life! I shall certainly commend you to . . . .'

'Oh, I shouldn't bother with that, sir.' No, not a parson, the sergeant was thinking. A bloody lawyer, that's what we have here. Evidence! 'Not over here, sir. Just flog them until they confess. Then hang them.'

The officer's china-blue eyes widened. He had the uncomfortable feeling, as he stared down at the pock-marked, pitiless face, that he was back in the school-room he'd left two years ago. 'But what if the man's innocent?'

'Well . . .' the broken teeth showed again in a grin, 'a good flogging'll help him stay that way, sir.'

There was a guffaw from the men. By Jesus, but he was a droll dog, the sergeant! The ensign's pink cheeks flushed with vexation. 'Sergeant!' The damned fellow was over-familiar. Time to assert oneself, eh? 'A proclamation!' He stared about. There was a tumbledown shrine on posts beside the track. 'Put one up there!' He pointed.

'Yessah! Sapper!' A private doubled forward, fumbling in his haversack. From it he took a rolled-up notice, a hammer and nails. The statue of the Virgin in the shrine vibrated to the hammer-blows; a jar of flowers fell to the ground with a smash. The private stood back to admire his handiwork. The words A DISTURBED COUNTY stood out dramatically from the text in heavy black letters.

The ensign nodded curtly, still nettled by the laughter. 'Very good, Sergeant.' He touched his mount with his heels. 'Forward!' The girl with the dancing walk was no longer visible on the slope of the hill. Pity. He'd have liked to see what the wench's face looked like . . . .

* * * * *

And he would have been well-rewarded, for Mary Mulvane at eighteen was well worth a glance from any man. Her face was perhaps a little more square than was fashionable; her tall, slim body not voluptuous enough;

4

her hazel eyes too intelligent, her full lips too firm to compete with the languid, vacuous beauties of Dublin and London. But she had the creamy skin of an Irish princess—and, to be sure now, wasn't it well-known throughout County Cork that her parents were the offspring of gentry, her great-grandfather being a Mulvane of Shanbally until the iniquitous English Penal Laws drove him off his land? Even barefoot, in her faded gown and with an old shawl slung across her shoulders, she had the proud air of her forebears and a will of her own within her that was, on occasion, the despair of her parents.

Now, Mary was in a hurry. With her quick, swinging walk, she crossed the farmyard of the white stone cottage and burst into the stone-flagged room that was dominated by a vast fireplace where an iron pot hung over a glowing peat fire. She tumbled her creel of potatoes into a basket in a corner, tossed the creel neatly onto a peg and whipped off her apron.

Her fifteen-year-old sister Elly paused in the folding of an apron that she was about to add to a stack of clean linen. Her mother, pumping at a butter-churn, glanced placidly at Mary but the rhythm didn't falter. There was but one thing that could put Mary into such a flutter and she knew perfectly well what it was. But, for form's sake, she said 'You're in a tearing great hurry, my girl.'

The lack of fuss was characteristic. Still an attractive woman in spite of the five children she'd borne, Cathleen Mulvane had the calm strength that can be deceptive in its gentleness, its lack of aggression. It showed only in the steady hazel eyes, etched with fine lines at the corners, and in the firm, unwavering set of her mouth. It was a strength that had enabled her to accept the loss of her first two children in infancy, the nomad existence she'd led as, in turn, the homes she'd made had been levelled and the land enclosed at the whim of some absentee landlord. It was the strength that overcame the poverty, perilously close to starvation level, that had lined her face and roughened her hands with drudgery. And it was the strength to which she clung to keep at bay her present fears—the terror of the musket-butts on the door, the whip and the gallows that awaited her husband Francis for what he was about.

Mary flung her apron behind a screen and grabbed the clean one out of her sister's hands. She said, trying hard to sound offhand and failing miserably, 'Michael Connor's coming.'

Elly, rosy-cheeked and skinny, said, 'Mary! I've scarcely done folding that apron!'

It was already being smoothed across Mary's slim hips. 'It's meant for wearing, not looking at!' She raced to the mirror and fiddled with her hair. 'Oh, my face!' It stared back at her, flushed and bright-eyed with expectancy. Why, in heaven's name, she thought, can't I be cool and uncaring, the way a girl should be? It was downright unbecoming, and so it was, to betray one's feelings so.

'There's nothing wrong with your face', said Cathleen placidly, still churning. 'And if you stop rushing about and working yourself into a state we'd all be happier . . . .' She broke off as Mary hurled herself into a chair and endeavoured to give the impression she'd been sitting there all morning.

From the doorway Michael Connor said, 'God bless the work, Mrs Mulvane.'

Cathleen smiled at him with affection. Even in his working rig of loose shirt and knee-breeches, he was a fine-looking lad—tall enough to be obliged to duck his shock of black hair as he came through the doorway and with a pair of broad shoulders earned in hard work under the open sky. But a wild one when roused and, at twenty, filled with the crusading spirit of youth—his heart so inflamed with hatred of the English oppression that, to him, the white scarf of the Whiteboys was a badge of knight-errantry, the burning of a hayrick the solution to all Ireland's problems. Which, she reflected with resignation, was one of the many reasons why Mary was so taken with him. For she, too, was a crusader. Cathleen returned his greeting. 'And yours, too, Michael Connor—whatever', she added with a feather-touch of irony, 'it may be.'

6

Michael, not sure whether she was hinting at his forays with the Whiteboys or to his apparently having nothing to do but go a-courting, turned to the younger girl and said, 'Good day to you, Elly.'

She, too overcome with admiration for words, blushed furiously, smirked and stared hard at the neckerchief she was folding. She heard him say in a voice that brought her out in goose-pimples, 'Hallo, Mary.'

'Hallo, Michael.' Mary spoke casually—even managing to throw a little surprise into her voice, as if he was the last person in the world she'd expected to see. But then what she saw in his mazarine-blue eyes caught her breath as her gaze locked with his and her casual air fell away like a cloak. Her soul was in her eyes as she spoke to him without words in a silence broken only by the clunk-slosh of the butter-churn. It slowed fractionally while Cathleen watched them, her mouth softening with the beginning of a smile.

Michael was conscious that he was socially obliged to say something but it was as if he was under a spell. 'I was . . .' he cleared his throat, his eyes still fixed on Mary. 'I was on my way to the fields to gather some furze for kindling.' Nobody commented on this weighty observation. With an effort, he turned to Cathleen. 'And I thought you might like some for your own hearth. . . .' He stopped, then said with a rush, '—if you could spare Mary to carry it back.'

Mary stood up, rather pleased with herself for not making it an unladylike leap.

Cathleen stopped her churning. 'That's very kind, Michael.' It was also a very neat way of getting Mary out of the house. Well, she sympathised with that, but there was a great deal to be done and she'd only the one pair of hands, after all. 'But there's the milk to be skimmed and I'd rather Mary see to that.'

'I can fetch the kindling and still have the milk skimmed before dinner.' Mary was already taking the creel down from its peg.

Elly was watching open-mouthed, entranced with shimmering images of romance, true love, kisses behind the furze-bush. And a terrible shame it would be if 'twas all

7

prevented by a pint or so of rotten old milk. She'd never skimmed milk in her life but, 'I can do it, Mother,' she said. She felt like the fairy godmother in the old story-book. Michael glanced at her and smiled gratefully. She all but swooned.

'Mary!' The pair of them were almost through the door before Cathleen could utter. 'You're not traipsing off without your shoes?'

Mary stopped, half in and half out of the house. 'Oh, none of the other girls wear shoes.'

'But you're Mary Mulvane. Yourself.'

'Mother. . . .' She was already edging over the threshold.

'*And* you're lucky to have them.'

'It'll be winter soon enough.' To hunt beneath her bed for her shoes and put them on would mean at least thirty Michael-less seconds. 'Just for now?'

It was, Cathleen realised, a waste of breath to admonish an empty doorway. They'd vanished. She sighed and the clunk-slosh of the churn began again. Elly said defensively, 'I *can* skim the milk.'

'So can Mary. And she will.' There was a pause. Then Cathleen said, more to herself than to her daughter, 'The girl needs curbing. But, with your father away in the hills each day, who's to do it?'

* * * * *

At that particular moment the blessed Saint Patrick himself, expert though he may have been in the banishment of snakes, would have had his work cut out to curb Mary Mulvane. In fact, if he had appeared to her in a thunderclap and backed by choirs of angels, it is doubtful whether she would have even noticed him. She was with Michael and there was nobody else in the world. She was a princess of the High Kings of Ireland riding with Brian Boru; she was the Helen of the Latin legend taught to her by her father, walking in the gardens of Ilium with Paris; she was Mary Mulvane, barefoot in the soft turf that felt like clouds beneath her feet, going to fetch furze with

Michael. She swung along with her dancing walk beside him, covertly admiring his brown, smooth profile, the length of his eyelashes, the way the blue-black hair curled at the nape of his neck—and all the time seeming to study the sky and the hills and a passing bird, the way a well-brought-up girl should when she walks with a young man. She listened to his voice. Sure, and there was nobody else in the world. . . . She seized his arm as they turned a bend in the road.

Redcoats.

Eight of them. A baby-faced officer, smart as paint on his chestnut horse. A ferocious-looking ruffian carrying a pike. Six louts, enormous in their military trappings, standing woodenly while the officer and the sergeant talked. She looked up at Michael, chilled by the hate in his face. 'We'll just keep on our way', he said quietly. Strange how the lightness of his tone contrasted with the tension, like a coiled spring, in the arm she was holding. She released it. She, too, could be unafraid—even with the eyes of every one of the Englishmen on her as she went forward.

It seemed a long way. There was something menacing about their immobility, the watchfulness of the sergeant's eyes. They were almost abreast of him when, suddenly, he swung his pike across his body, blocking the track, squat and formidable in the power of his scarlet coat. 'Hold hard there!' Mary was put in mind of the deep-throated growl of a guard-dog. As the officer swung his horse round to face them Michael moved a step in front of the girl. The redcoat sergeant said, 'How far to the village of Rathcurran?'

Michael smiled coldly inside himself. The bastards were lost. He said politely, 'By what road?'

'By the road we're on', snapped the sergeant. The big, wind-reddened hands gripping the pike-pole were like rocks, the steel-grey eyes as cold as a pair of pistol-muzzles.

'Well, now.' Michael pondered a moment, frowning and staring up and down the track as if he'd never set eyes on it before. 'That'd depend.'

'On what?'

'On whether', Michael said judicially, 'you turned

through the valley yonder or went straight across the hill.'

'Which is the shorter?'

Michael stared at the hills, then ahead along the track. He thought for a moment, considering distances. He nodded as if sure he'd come to the right conclusion. 'The valley road.'

The saddle creaked as the officer shifted impatiently. The sergeant heard it. He wasn't handling this very well, he knew. 'Then how far', he said savagely, 'by the valley road?'

'Upward of two miles.'

The sergeant turned his pock-marked face up to the officer. At least he'd been right there. 'As I thought, sir.'

'But . . .' Michael added helpfully, 'after the rain we've had, you'd never get through.'

The sergeant's grip tightened on the pike. Christ Almighty, he knew that the bloody bog-trotters hadn't the brains of a louse among the lot of them, but this beat all. 'Now listen, you Irish dolt,' he said between his teeth. 'Sharpen whatever you have in the way of wits. How far to Rathcurran?'

'Not above three miles, sir', Michael said. He smiled charmingly into the sparking steel-grey eyes.

'And why couldn't you tell me that in the first place?'

Before Michael could answer, the ensign walked his mount forward. In his clipped, disdainful English voice he said, 'Do you live in the village, boy?' If the fellow was as guileless as he appeared, it might be possible to obtain intelligence of the machinations of the local rebels— perhaps, even of those ringleaders of whom the sergeant had spoken.

Boy! Michael thought as he stared up at the smooth pink face, the china-blue eyes beneath the white wig and cocked hat. He's no older than I am myself. Aloud he said, 'No, sir.'

'Then where?'

'Beyant the next hill, near the Well of Saint Brigid.'

'And what's your name?'

'Michael Connor.'

'And what business are you on?' Apart, the ensign

thought with a touch of envy, from rogering that very desirable baggage who, if I mistake not, is the girl I saw on the hill. A very pretty piece, by God.

'Gathering kindling wood.' Michael didn't like the way the puppy was ogling Mary—nor his men, neither. He felt her move closer to him for protection. His fists clenched involuntarily. The bastards! Stripping the clothes off her in their dirty minds, they were. God, if only. . .!

The hatred hung about him like a red mist in the cool morning air. Even the young officer could feel it. He saw the clenched fists, the set of Michael's jaw. Perhaps, he told himself, this bumpkin isn't quite as innocent as he would appear. He said slowly, 'Would you swear an oath of allegiance to His Sovereign Majesty?'

Michael stared up at him, seeing the clumsy trap. He tried to look as stupid as he could. 'I don't know what you mean.'

The sergeant's gravelly voice broke in. 'He knows well enough.'

'He may not', the officer said, undecided. It was so hard to tell, really, with these peasants. 'I imagine the boy has no education.'

'I'll warrant he's been to a hedge school.' When the ensign stared down at him uncomprehendingly the sergeant explained, 'They're against the law, sir, hidden away behind the hedges and ditches.' He turned his implacable stare back to Michael again. 'Run by Popish rebels disguised as schoolmasters.'

Mary felt a cold shiver run down her back. She—and everyone in Rathcurran—knew very well why her father was seldom at home to run the farm.

'They take the children and fill their heads with all manner of treason and poisonous Irish tales. The hedge schools', he said with loathing. 'That's where your rebels are spawned.'

'Then we'll hunt them out', said the ensign coldly. 'Destroy them. Sapper!' He half-turned in his saddle. The soldier ran forward, pulling out another copy of the proclamation from his bag and handing it up. The officer held it in front of Michael's face. 'Read this. Or find someone who can.'

Michael stared him straight in the eye and didn't budge.

'Take it!' The ensign's voice went up to a bark.

Michael put his hands behind his back. His face livid, the sergeant swung the pike-butt back. Then, with all his weight behind it, he slammed it into Michael's groin.

The sickening shock of pain was worse than Michael could ever have thought possible. He didn't have the breath to scream—it came out of his lungs in a whistling grunt as he jack-knifed, then sagged forward onto his knees in the mud, hugging himself and retching. Mary's hand flew to her mouth, her eyes dilated with shock, then she moved to help him but he shook his head. The ensign tossed the proclamation down at him and wheeled his horse. Mary knelt in the dirt as the sergeant shouldered his pike and turned away. The redcoat privates filed past, grinning.

'Pigs!' Mary hissed at them. 'English pigs!' She turned to Michael who was on his hands and knees breathing deeply, shaking his head like a beaten prizefighter. 'Michael! We've got to warn Father. They're out for the hedge school!' She picked up the proclamation from where it had fallen.

The ensign looked back at them over his shoulder. So much, he reflected, for the velvet glove. Now, by God, we'll try the iron hand. 'A troublesome breed, Sergeant.' He looked down at the stocky figure trudging beside him. 'It seems you were right after all.'

The sergeant nodded. Of course he was right. Prod them, he'd said—and, by God, hadn't he just done that very thing? He stepped out jauntily, his shoulders square, pleased with the blow he'd struck for England.

*　　*　　*　　*　　*

Michael shambled across the fields, wincing with every step, shamed by the realisation that Mary—a mere girl—was forced to slow down for him. He stopped to catch his breath under the pretence of looking back. When she turned to help him, her eyes wide with concern, he said,

'I'm all right', and ran on, feeling as if his guts were afire. Uphill. Then down, over stepping-stones that spanned a stream. Up again, more steeply, with Mary's bare feet flying over the turf ahead of him. Suddenly she stopped. A small boy had darted out from under a leafless tree, to disappear over a ridge as fast as a lizard. 'The lookout', Mary said. 'We're there.'

The hilltop, rimmed with rocks, seemed to stretch up to the grey, scudding clouds, the bare tree on its summit bending to the wind. As they went over the crest a man's voice came to them, borne on the breeze, as strong and clear as a trumpet-call. 'The *Tuatha De Danaan*', said Francis Mulvane. 'The Tribes of the Goddess Dana. A tall and most beautiful people who found magic in the world around them and who made this land their own.'

A group of ragged children sat in a half circle among the rocks, their eyes on the tall grey-haired man who stood before them, listening so intently that they failed to see Mary and Michael as they came over the brow of the hill. Even the carroty-headed look-out, his warning given, stood open-mouthed. The speaker had the long, sensitive face of a scholar—a man who might be expected to use his mind rather than his hands. Yet the hands that were clasped behind his back were square and capable; he was stocky and well-built and stood easily and with square-shouldered dignity in his shabby coat, woollen stockings and old buckled shoes. He was in his early fifties, with deep lines scored from his nose to the corners of his mouth. His eyes, grey as mist and alive with the tale he was telling, were fixed on his class. 'Then, in the procession of the centuries, came the Gaelic people—great hunters, great warriors—' the strong voice with the Irish lilt in it paused and softened, '—and great poets.'

In spite of the ache in his guts, Michael smiled wryly to himself. Sure, and you could trust the poets to get the special place with Francis Eamon Mulvane, and not the warriors. He disapproved of the Whiteboys. He refused to meet fire with fire, violence with violence. Instead, he put his head in a noose on two counts—firstly, for what he was doing here and now, he a Catholic daring to teach Catholic children; and secondly, for what he had done in the past—taken the forbidden oath of the United Irishmen to unite Catholics and Protestants together in the peaceful subversion of English rule in Ireland. His way had no chance of success at all, in Michael's opinion, but he respected the man for his courage and his convictions—and for his vast amount of learning. So did the folk all around who, in return for the education of their children, helped Cathleen run the farm.

'They tried to crush the people of Dana', said Francis Mulvane. 'They made them wear only the colour green, that they would be humble as the grass. That was in the ancient times. Now, the blood of the Gaels and of the people of Dana is mingled in our veins. But we are not truly our own people. Only when. . . .'

Michael, breathing hard from his running, said loudly, 'Mr Mulvane. Redcoats. Coming to the village.' The children's heads swivelled towards him.

Mary said, 'They're looking for the hedge school.' She held out the proclamation.

Francis took it. 'A disturbed county', he said bitterly as he read. He looked up from the notice. 'A curfew to be imposed.'

'Please, sir.' A child raised a hand. 'What's a curfew?'

'A rule set by the English forbidding us to set foot out of doors from dayfallen to daybreak. It's to begin on the first day of the month. Next Tuesday.'

'Oh, Michael!' Mary turned to him, suddenly remembering. 'Your mother's Hallowe'en party! She. . . .'

'We'll make that the end of the day', Francis told his class. 'Go your separate ways to your homes, now. Your parents will be worried for you. We'll meet again on Monday.' The children, still with the spell of the story on them, scrambled slowly to their feet.

Mary said sharply, 'Father! You can't!'

'One moment.' Francis smiled gently at his pupils. 'This is a time for remembering the ancient people. Those who were driven into hiding and forced to wear the humblest colour—the colour of the grass. But they made it the proudest thing in all Ireland. Remember that. And God go with you all.'

The children flitted away like small grey rodents among the rocks, all but one. Seamus Mulvane, thin-faced, wide-eyed and thirteen years old, went to stand with his father who ranked, as far as the boy was concerned, second only to that other Father in heaven—the one his uncle Dominic, priest and fugitive, could (for some peculiar English reason) get into terrible trouble for serving, so they said.

Francis stared for a moment at the empty, wind-swept hillside where crows cawed and wheeled against the leaden sky. Then he said to Michael, 'Thank you for bringing Mary. But you'd best be off with you now.'

She smiled at Michael as he moved away. She watched him until the dark head turned towards her before it disappeared over the hill-crest. Then she turned to her father, her cheeks still flushed with exertion, her hazel eyes alive with concern. 'You'll not be going on with the school now, Father? Surely it's madness?'

Madness to try to dissuade him, she thought as he smiled his gentle smile at her and said, 'Would you really respect me if I gave up what I believe in because I was frightened?' When she didn't answer he went on, 'You heard what I told the children. It is important, at this time, to keep alive the spirit of our people. That is why we call poetry "the seeds of fire". That is why the English fear it.'

She said stubbornly, thinking of Michael riding at night on horseback, the flames lighting up the countryside, 'But they fear the Whiteboys too.'

He shook his head. 'No. They're glad of them.'

She stared. 'Glad of them?'

'Of course. When the Whiteboys throw a stone at a soldier or kill the landlord's cattle, they achieve nothing. They only give the English the excuse to strike another blow at us.' He held up the proclamation. 'The redcoats wouldn't be in Rathcurran today if the Whiteboys hadn't torn down Squire Buchanan's fences and burned his barn. That's not the way. We must strike at the laws themselves.'

Very deliberately, he tore the English ordinance into tiny fragments and let the wind take them. Then he put his arm round his daughter's shoulders and took his son by the hand. 'Come', he said. 'We'll be off home now.'

CHAPTER TWO

The following day being a Saturday, Francis was at home when Michael called at mid-morning. The hedge-school teacher sat in his shirt-sleeves by the wide fireplace where the peat glowed, smoking his short clay pipe composedly but with an inward smile for himself at the thought that the revolutionary firebrand Michael Connor who now stood deferentially before him seemed to have nothing more on his mind this day than the Hallowe'en party next Monday night. And the women seemed to have abandoned all reason, with Cathleen eavesdropping shamelessly on the men's talk as she stirred the pot, Elly peeling potatoes at the rate of one an hour, and Mary pretending to sweep the floor close by so as not to miss a word. He took his pipe out of his mouth, aware that they were all waiting for him to say something. 'But what of the proclamation, Michael? If it takes effect on Tuesday, you can be assured the English will enforce it from midnight on Monday.'

'To be sure', Michael nodded. 'But we'll end the party in time for everyone to be home by midnight.'

'Oh, Father!' Her eyes shining, Mary propped her broom against the wall. 'Can we go? Please, Da?' Not for the first time, Francis wondered as he looked at her how he could have had a part in the creation of anything as lovely as this girl of his.

Michael said, bringing male logic to support female

blandishment, 'We may not have another chance for a long time.'

It was at that moment that the door slammed open and Seamus rushed into the room like a small hurricane. 'Da!' he said in alarm. 'The landlord's coming!'

Nobody moved. Francis Mulvane's eyes went bleak. He stood up, put down his pipe and said quietly, 'Cathleen. My coat, if you please.' He settled the collar to his satisfaction, adjusted the worn cuffs. Then, unhurriedly, he went to the door, Seamus scampering ahead of him.

Landlord Buchanan was a Wexford man who had made his money out of rack-renting, acting as middle-man or 'forestaller' for an English earl who took a flat rate of rent and let Buchanan make his profit by pocketing the difference between what he charged and what he actually handed over. The difference had been very great indeed, it having been Buchanan's practice to push the rent up slowly to two or three hundred per cent, taking furniture, household effects and housewives' favours in lieu of cash until eviction point was reached. Then, with a fresh tenant to pluck, the same highly-rewarding process could begin all over again. In this way he had been able to purchase his own land and, since it was his ambition to be taken for an English squire, to have his clothes made in Dublin by an English tailor, to ride a mare brought over from England, and to drink a great deal of port with his roast beef. This gave him the fashionable English tendency to obesity and a complexion like an underdone steak. His porcine eyes, however, he owed entirely to nature. Now he was astride his mare in Mulvane's yard, wearing a beaver hat, an elegant riding-cape of Yorkshire wool and a pair of highly-polished boots by Maxwell of Bond Street. 'Here, boy!' he said in the highly-pitched voice possessed by so many fat men. He threw the reins at Seamus and dismounted heavily into a puddle.

Francis stood beside his doorway, his face expressionless. Buchanan looked down at his right boot that was plastered with mud. 'By God, Mulvane,' he said peevishly, 'you keep a damned filthy yard!' He strode past Francis and straight into the house. Francis followed him.

The landlord paused to stare disparagingly at the smoke-mellowed room where the tang of peat hung in the air, at the gleaming pots and pans, at the scrubbed table, at the functional simplicity of it all. He sniffed. To him, functional simplicity·was to be found in abundance in pig-pens. He dropped into the chair by the fire where Francis had been sitting and stared liverishly at Michael, Elly and Cathleen in turn. His eyes slid past Mary, then back again. 'You!' He stuck out his right boot. 'Clean this!'

As Michael stiffened with anger, Francis put a hand on his shoulder. Mary's face went pink and she opened her mouth. Then, catching her father's eye, she went to fetch a cloth. Francis moved to the other side of the fireplace. 'You're three days early for the rent, Mr Buchanan.' The landlord liked to be called 'Squire'—which was exactly why Francis had avoided that form of address.

'I haven't come to collect the rent, Mulvane. Not today.' Buchanan's thick lips curled in a sneer. 'Just to tell you it's been raised. By two shillings a month.'

There was an intake of breath from Cathleen. Francis said disbelievingly, 'You want eight shillings a month? Why, the farm will scarcely pay six. I can't . . . .' He broke off as Michael, his fists clenched, took a step forward. Mary had knelt in front of Buchanan who had stared at her, then shoved his filthy boot on to her apron.

'Then', Buchanan's piggy eyes were still fixed on Mary, 'you'll have to work harder, won't you?' He took in the bowed, shining head of chestnut hair as she wiped the boot, the creamy skin of her neck, the swell of her breasts at the top of her gown. His voice thickened slightly as he said, 'Or find some other way to make up the difference.' For a moment, he played with the idea of striking a bargain on the spot. Half an hour with this molly in return for . . . . Then he remembered Mulvane's reputation—and, besides, money was money and he could buy any number of trollops in Cork for eight shillings. Little knowing how close he'd come to strangulation at the hands of Michael Connor, he looked up at Mulvane. 'If you can't find the money, you'll have to get out.' His voice lost a little of its English veneer as it took on the threatening edge he'd used so often before. 'I'll tumble this pigsty to the ground and graze cattle here. Just be asking your friends the O'Hullans what I can do if I choose.'

Cathleen said, appalled, 'You haven't evicted Mrs O'Hullan? And her with a babe on the way?'

'The bloody Whiteboys pulled down my fences and burnt my barn last week.' At the memory of past injuries suffered, Buchanan whipped himself up into a rage, his voice squeakier and less English with every word. 'I had to find somewhere to store the fodder for me cattle. So, by the saints, it's the O'Hullan cottage I'm using.' He glowered round at them. 'But there'll be no more talk of the brave Whiteboys, I'm thinking, now that the military's here. We've law and order in the county now.'

Mary, her work done, backed off so that Buchanan's boot slammed down onto the stone floor. He glared at her, then levered himself to his feet. 'I'll be back for the money on Tuesday.' Francis followed him to the door in time to see him scramble on to his horse and ride off, showering Seamus with mud.

From behind Francis's shoulder, Michael said, 'Will ye look at your daughter, Mr Mulvane?' His face was taut with fury and a small vein throbbed in his brown throat. 'How much longer can we let them wipe their boots on us?'

Francis walked past him to the fireplace. He stood, feet apart, his hands behind his back. 'Michael,' he said quietly, 'Ireland's full of men like Buchanan. Strike at one, and you strengthen the hand of all the others.'

'Then', Michael hissed, 'strike at them all!'

As in France seven years ago, Francis thought. The attack on the Bastille on that July day had been an inspiration to every young rebel in Europe. The French peasants, however, had been united in a common aim; their masters had been fops and ruffians playing at soldiers.

Here in Ireland it was different, for this was an island with the Royal Navy controlling every Irish port and the Irish people themselves split by religious discord. He sighed. 'One day it may come to that. But only when the people of Ireland are united.'

'And when will that be?' Michael raised his voice, venting his frustration on this calm man who stood before him. 'By the time it happens, there won't be one of us with a roof over our heads. We'll be skulking away in ditches. Like', he said, wanting to hurt, 'childer in a hedge school having their heads stuffed with dreams and poetry.'

Francis bowed his head. Am I getting old? he wondered. Like the old men who sit in the sun talking of what they're going to do and knowing full well they'll never see the fulfilment of it? Is that, perhaps, what Cathleen thinks of me? He looked at his wife, at the careworn face that had supported him unflinchingly in every single thing he'd done over the years. She spoke to him with her eyes and his head came up. 'You may be right', he said, a new strength in his voice. 'Perhaps Buchanan will take the roof from over our heads. But nobody can destroy our dreams. Only we can do that.'

'Dreams?' Michael shook his head incredulously. 'You talk of dreams, with the redcoats tramping over our land? It's guns and pikes we want, not dreams!'

Francis said levelly, 'I don't want this kind of talk in my house, Michael.'

'Very well.' Michael went to the door. 'Then I'll be leaving, sir.' Mary put out a hand but he didn't even see it. He went through the doorway and was gone.

She turned on her father, her eyes blazing. 'Father, how could you talk to Michael like that? It's for you he's angry, don't you see?'

'I've enough anger of my own.' Suddenly, Francis had had enough. His eyes snapping, he stared at her. 'How do you think I feel,' he said savagely, 'standing by while that damned Buchanan sullies you with the mud of his boots?'

She stood looking at him, her anger slipping away from

her and being replaced by an immense sadness. 'It's only cloth,' she said, her voice choking. She jerked off the dirty apron and ran outside.

'Mary!' Cathleen ran to the door. Then she turned back to her husband, her face anguished.

'Let her be.' Francis moved to his wife and put an arm round her. She buried her head on his shoulder as he said, almost inaudibly, 'The boy may be right.'

Michael strode uphill, his legs pumping, trying to drain off the anger that boiled within him, his shoes slashing into the grass as if each tuft was the head of a Buchanan. Behind him somebody called his name; he strode on, unheeding. Then he stopped and turned.

She ran up the slope to him, her face streaked with tears, and when he held out his arms she came into them as if that was where she had always belonged. Slowly, as she clung to him, the sobbing ceased. He felt her stir against him as she raised her face, staring up at him, and he kissed her very gently, the salt of her tears on his lips. As the need for solace, for forgiveness, for forgetfulness, took hold of him he kissed her again, more fiercely. And it was as if all the anger, all the hatred, vanished like mist before the morning sun and there was nothing but peace and Mary and the love they had for each other. For a long moment, they clung together while the wind sang in the grass and the world dwindled into a small and petty thing, a pebble that rolled through time and space unheeded. He released her and they held each other tightly by the hands, looking at one another.

Then hand in hand, they walked uphill beneath the leaden sky.

*   *   *   *   *

The Connors were not ones to stint when it came to a party, whether it was a wedding or a wake or Hallowe'en. Furthermore, with the coming of the curfew, it seemed that this would be the last festivity held in Rathcurran for many a long day, so the locals were determined to take full advantage of the Connors' hospitality. They came not only from Rathcurran but from neighbouring villages as well at the Connors' invitation and one couple rode all the way from Corcaigh itself—Cork, as the English called it. There was a fiddler hired—Blind Daniel, the finest in the county—and a man to play the tin whistle and another for the *bodhran* whose beat was enough to set the feet of a stone statue tapping. And there was food and drink for all, with each guest contributing his gift. Within an hour, the cottage near Saint Brigid's well was bursting at the seams and lit up like a beacon, the tobacco-smoke hazing the room within and the roar of the talk and the laughter competing with the thunder of boots as the dancers beat out the fast Irish dancing-rhythms that got into the blood with their magic.

For Mary, it was a night she would always remember—a time of warmth and friendship and happiness, with the Buchanans and the redcoats forgotten. Years afterwards, she could recall the thump-thump of the *bodhran*, the squeal of the tin whistle and the very tune that Blind Daniel played as she danced the first dance with Michael, so tall and handsome in his best clothes, his eyes seldom leaving hers. It seemed to her as if she was floating on the crest of a wave of pure happiness that was carrying her effortlessly into the even happier future that was waiting for her.

It was later that she realised how merciful a thing it is for the future to be hidden from sight.

And yet the portents had been there on that night of Hallowe'en in that happy, noisy room. Later, she remembered how, when the evening was well advanced, Michael's eyes had fixed briefly on the thin, pale-faced young man who had come in to stand by the door as if waiting for someone. How, when the dance was ended, Michael had excused himself and gone to talk with him. And how, after being drawn into talk with a group of neighbours, she had turned to look for Michael and found him gone.

It puzzled her, made her vaguely uneasy. She wasn't a girl to tie a man to her apron-strings all evening, but none

23

the less she felt neglected. The evening wore on. The pipe-smoke became thicker, the voices louder, the dancers began to flag and sweat with the effort of keeping pace with Blind Daniel's flying fiddle-bow. It wasn't until the curfew was remembered with shouts of indignation and the party was breaking up that she saw the familiar shock of black hair above the heads of the crowd round the door. It seemed, she thought as she saw him slapping backs and waving a mug, as if he was trying to give the impression he'd never left at all. She was about to push through the crowd of red-faced, singing men when her mother took her arm, Elly handed her her shawl, and she found herself in the group of departing guests, some of them slightly the worse for wear. And then she forgot Michael's odd behaviour.

For, after Cathleen had taken her leave and been thanked in her turn for the dish of oat-cakes she'd provided, Mrs Connor turned to Francis. With a touch of embarrassment, she took a small bag out of the pocket of her dress. 'Mr Mulvane,' she said, 'this is for you.'

The slightly-tipsy singing stopped. The voices died, and they all watched Francis with the air of deference that had been apparent in their approach to him all evening. He weighed the bag in his hand, surprised. From where he stood with Blind Daniel, Mr Connor said quietly, 'It's twenty-four pence, Mr Mulvane.' There was a small murmur of approval from the crowd.

Mrs Connor said, 'Michael told us about Buchanan raising your rent. It's a shameful thing, and all of us here have put in.'

Francis looked at his wife. There were tears in her eyes. He felt close to tears himself. 'But, Mrs Connor . . . .'

'Two shillings, Mr Mulvane.' She put a hand on the one with which he held the bag. 'It's little enough for all you've given up for us over the years.'

For a moment, Francis couldn't speak. He held the bag up mutely in his hand as if in salute. Then he said, 'I thank you.' There was a warm, if awkward acknowledgement from those standing around. 'God bless you all', he said softly. For a moment no-one spoke. Then feet began to shuffle towards the door. The party was over. They went out into the cold November darkness, back to the world of curfews and landlords and redcoats. And when Mary went out with her family, looking back over her shoulder, Michael Connor made no move to speak to her.

They came for him next morning, the squat sergeant in the faded coat and a patrol of two men, their bayonets fixed, their faces like stone as they marched into the Connor yard. They beat on the door with their musket-butts and dragged him away, leaving Mrs Connor weeping over the cold ashes of the fire that had warmed the room the night before.

Mary heard of it later that day when Landlord Buchanan came for the rent. His fat hand scooped the coins into his leather pouch with the rapacity of a corpse-robber as he said to Cathleen, 'Tis as well your husband found the money or you'd be out today. I'm in no humour to be lenient after the Whiteboys burnt down the O'Hullans' cottage and all my grain last night.'

Mary felt herself go cold. In her mind's eye she saw the pale-faced youth talking to Michael, their furtive air, Michael's absence from the dancing . . . . She heard the landlord say, 'After the soldiers have done their work today there'll be justice in the county and let the rabble get what they deserve.' When he'd gone, she ran like a hare to the Connor cottage and found Mrs Connor, the tears pouring down her cheeks, lying with her head pillowed on the table.

'They've taken boys from all over', she sobbed. 'Some of them Whiteboys, some not. They say a cabin of Mr Buchanan's was burnt down . . . .'

'But they can't prove anything.' Mary knelt by her side. 'Michael was at the party and all the village can swear to it . . . .' She jumped up in alarm as the door crashed open. Michael staggered in, to collapse face down on a bench near the door.

Mrs Connor screamed, her knuckles pressed to her mouth. The entire back of Michael's shirt, from shoulder to waist, was soaked in blood. 'Oh, Mother of Mercy!' she sobbed as, helped by Mary, she half-carried, half-led her son across to a chair by the table. 'What's been done to you?'

He spoke as if even the movement of his lips was agony. 'I don't want Mary to see it.' As she caught the older woman's eye, Mary moved to face him, holding his hand across the table while Mrs Connor peeled away the hideously stained shirt, her eyes widening in shock when she saw the bloody weals, like the claw-marks of a tiger, across the brown skin. 'I told them nothing', Michael said. 'No-one did.'

'Then let that be an end to it', his mother said, her voice shaking. 'God's spared you this day. But you must give up this madness.'

He shook his head slowly, staring into Mary's eyes as she clutched his hand. 'If I give up now', he said, 'I might as well be dead anyway. They'll never stop driving us. If you kissed the ground in front of them, they'd only tread your face in the mud.' Mrs Connor had fetched a basin of warm water and a cloth. With infinite gentleness, she began to bathe his back. Mary could feel the agony of it herself as the grip on her hand tightened convulsively. Through his teeth, Michael said, 'No man who calls himself an Irishman could live as a slave.' His pain-filled eyes locked with Mary's. 'And no true Irishwoman should want him to.'

For the next week, however, they lived as slaves to the kind of law and order that Buchanan had invoked and the Whiteboys could do nothing but lick their wounds, for the military had Rathcurran in a grip of steel. They patrolled at night during the hours of curfew; they swaggered about the village by day, helping themselves from the shops and insulting the women; they appeared at the most remote cabins as unexpectedly as demons in a pantomime as they escorted the Tithe Proctor on his rounds.

He was, if possible, detested even more than Landlord Buchanan. Under the Penal Laws passed by the Episcopalian majority of the Irish Parliament, all Irishmen were compelled to contribute to the support of their local Anglican incumbent. Landowners were exempt; the cultivators of the soil, who were mainly Catholic, were not. So the Catholics were compelled to support a Church to which they did not subscribe and to provide for a clergyman whom they did not want while their own priests were hunted down like vermin. It was the task of the Tithe Proctor to assess each family's contribution, taking a quarter of the payment for himself.

It was a task the Tithe Proctor of the Parish of Rathcurran carried out diligently. A ferret-faced, mealy-mouthed runt of a man in rusty black, he kept his accounts in a flowing copper-plate that, to him, was a work of calligraphy far more beautiful than anything that had come out of a medieval monastery. With the redcoats on guard at the door, he would run his dirty finger down his columns, smiling and showing his yellow teeth, and name an amount in his soft, polite voice. When the outrageous sum asked for was not forthcoming, he would open chests and cupboards with an utter disregard for the most elementary privacies and impound whatever he took a fancy to.

He impounded the Mulvanes' cow. There was not, as he pointed out, very much else worth the taking. And so, when the procession of four redcoats laden with loot from other farms and preceded by the Tithe Proctor carrying his staff and satchel left the Mulvane cabin, it was augmented by a bony old cow called Biddy, led by one of the soldiers. Michael saw them go as he was on his way to pay his first call on Mary in over a week.

He found Cathleen, her strength broken for once, in tears. 'Praties and oatmeal', she was sobbing as he came to the door. 'Is that all we're to have now? Where's it to end?'

'I saw the Tithe Proctor', Michael said. 'On God's business—stealing your cow.'

Mary said furiously, 'They'd take the pennies out of a dead man's eyes!'

'Mary Mulvane!' Cathleen regained some of her composure. 'That's no talk for a lady!'

'But it's true enough.' Michael's back was still sore. He held himself stiffly as he walked to the fireplace. 'They'll take the pot off this fire, the clothes off your back. And

27

you'll have redcoats billeted in your house while Mr Mulvane's up in the hills teaching poetry. And it's not poetry or dreams that'll bring your cow back.'

Cathleen said listlessly, 'What can?'

'The Whiteboys can.'

'Mr Mulvane would never have that', Cathleen said, the strength back in her voice again. 'And neither will I.' She took some potatoes from a basket in a corner and began to peel them. 'What's it to be—more floggings? We want no part of that.' As Mary picked up a knife to help, her mother said, 'I'll do them. You can build up the fire.'

Michael knelt beside her as she began to break up furze and pile it onto the glowing peat. He said softly, 'I'm going to get your cow out of the pound.'

She glanced at him, startled, then at her mother to see if she'd heard. She whispered, 'You heard what Mother said. She and Father want no part of the Whiteboys.'

'I'll not be asking the Whiteboys to help. I'll do it myself.'

The fire flared suddenly as he spoke and she stared at it, her eyes reflecting the flames. She drew a deep breath. 'Not on your own. I'll come with you.'

Michael glanced at Cathleen but she was lost in her own sombre thoughts as she sliced the peel off the potatoes. He hissed, 'You'll do no such thing.'

'I will. It's our cow and I'm going with you. She's a cranky old devil, that Biddy. But she knows me. She'll come easy for me.' As he opened his mouth she said, 'I'm coming, Michael, so don't argue.'

'How would you get out of the house? There's the curfew.'

'That's for me to worry about.'

He looked at her profile, lit by the fire, and he was astonished as so many young men are astonished when they find that loveliness and stubborn determination can go hand in hand. A woman to be proud of, he thought as he watched the strong, beautiful curve of her lips, the directness of the wide hazel eyes that turned to meet his. He nodded. 'All right. I'll be at the bridge at moonrise. Meet me there.' To compensate for his capitulation he added, 'I'll not wait about all night for you, mind.'

But, of course, he waited, as young men always do. He had a coil of rope, a hammer, a cloth to muffle it with and a cold chisel to break the padlock on the village pound, and he strode up and down on the bridge while the moon came up out of the damp November mist like a huge golden guinea. It turned to silver as it rose, flooding the hillside with a soft luminescence in which the water ran like liquid metal as it gurgled under the bridge. And still he waited while, in the Mulvane cottage, Mary washed dishes with Elly and racked her brain to think of a way of going out into the night without parental opposition. Her father puffed his pipe unconcernedly as he read in the lamplight. Her mother was darning. Seamus had been sent to fetch the very creel of turf that Mary had hoped to use as a means of escape.

'Will you take it slower, Mary?' Elly said in alarm as her sister soused, wiped and rinsed dishes as if doing it for a wager. 'You'll break something, for sure.'

Mary glanced at her parents over her shoulder. 'I want to get the dishes over and done with', she hissed into Elly's ear.

Elly's eyes popped. 'You're not meeting Michael?' Och, the daring of it, she thought excitedly. A lovers' tryst! Holding hands in the moonlight and . . . .

'Hold your tongue, you little *sleveen*!' Mary whispered in anguish. Elly's voice had sounded as if it could have been audible all over Rathcurran. But Francis and his wife read and darned on, oblivious. As Seamus came in with the turf she said brightly, 'I'll just empty the pail.' And if that brother of mine offers to do it, I'll empty it over his head, and so I will, she thought. Seamus, however, had no intention whatever of going out into the cold again. She put on her shawl, her eyes riveted on her parents. Francis and Cathleen didn't even look up. She picked up the pail and opened the door. For a moment, before she closed it very gently, she looked back at the familiar, homely room.

Outside, when she saw the moon riding the treetops, she

was seized with an almost unbearable anxiety in case Michael had kept his word and not waited. She put down the pail, picked up her skirts and ran.

He had almost decided she wasn't coming. 'I'd hoped', he said when she materialised out of the mist, panting and aglow, 'that you might have come to your senses and stayed at home.' He looked at her for a moment as she shook her head, too breathless and excited for words. Then he took her hand and they set off towards the village.

It was unnaturally quiet, Mary thought. The stone-walled pound looked like a fortress in the silver light, the movement of the few animals inside it like the stirring of an alarmed garrison. And the night was full of shadows—menacing shadows that stood about in dark corners with swords and bayonets drawn, muskets and pikes levelled . . . . She almost sprang out of her skin at the first stroke of the hammer against the head of the chisel. Muffled though it was, it seemed dangerously loud. And the next stroke, a harder blow, seemed to echo and reverberate all over the village. Michael paused. He too, was somewhat disturbed at the racket he was making. He'd forgotten how silent the village would be under the curfew. He grunted as he slammed the hammer down again, the ringing like the clang of an alarm bell in the brooding hush. But then, thank God, there was a clatter as the chain fell free. He pulled the gate open. Mary went into the pound like a ghost, the coil of rope in her hands. 'Biddy', she breathed. 'Biddy! Here, girl.'

Michael whispered, 'If you can't get the rope round her, drive her this way.'

And, from the corner of the pound, a voice shattered the silence. 'You there!'

Michael spun round, his heart leaping with fright. Only one voice could challenge the night like that in Rathcurran. As he saw the four-man patrol begin to move towards him, their bayonets striking sparks in the moonlight, he hissed, 'Get down!' Whatever happens, he thought wildly, she mustn't be taken. If I can lead them away from her . . . . He started to run.

Afterwards, it stayed in her memory like a nightmare in which the dreamer stands by, helpless, and watches someone running from a dreadful danger but moving as if his feet were encased in lead. She heard the soldier bawl, 'Halt!' She saw the long barrel of the musket gleam dully as it swung up. She knew Michael was running for his life but his feet seemed to reach out slowly in front of him as if he was struggling through a swamp. 'Michael!' She screamed his name with all the strength of her lungs as she stood in the gateway, willing him to run faster, to surrender—it didn't matter which, if only he was safe. Above all, please, oh, please God, let him be safe and not in the power of that terrible thing that was aimed, rock-steady, at him as he struggled on with his arms flailing and . . . .

The red-and-orange tongue of fire licked out into the night like a flame from hell and the flat report of the Brown Bess musket crashed and echoed off the stone walls. Still in her nightmare, she saw him stumble and fall. But it's only a stumble, she thought insanely as she ran to him. He's only tripped, and then he'll get up again and they'll take him away and beat him and that'll be terrible but not as terrible as that other thing that might have happened. Nothing could be as terrible as that.

But he didn't get up. She fell on her knees beside him in the mud and he looked up at her, his face ashen in the light of the full and silver moon.

And, even as she took him in her arms and his head lolled tiredly against her shoulder, she knew that the nightmare had become the here and now of reality.

CHAPTER THREE

It was very difficult, she had discovered, to think; her mind seemed to have become stiff and numb, like a wounded limb. And none of her thoughts made sense anyway, so she'd given up trying. For example, there had been some sort of punishment called a trial, although all the world knew that a proper trial had witnesses and evidence and a jury—not just two magistrates, one with a wart on his nose, who'd told her she must go away for seven years to 'some part beyond the seas', whatever that might mean. And how could she be punished for 'feloniously stealing, taking away and removing' poor old Biddy, who belonged to her own family, for heaven's sake? Why, there hadn't been time to take or remove the silly creature at all before. . . .

No, it was much better not to think. There had once been a girl called Mary Mulvane who'd danced with a boy called Michael Connor, a girl who had laughed and been happy to think of the future. But that was like a fairy story she'd read. Now there was only a succession of images—of being pushed in and out of unpleasant places, of people who shouted at her for no reason or who stared at her coldly. There were other people, too, who lay like the dead on piles of stinking straw in the most unpleasant place of all, where water oozed down the stone walls and everything was cold and malodorous and filthy. The Gaol at Cork.

That had been where her parents had appeared—and that made no sense, either, with her having to talk to her own father and mother through a barred grating and a gaoler searching through the little bag her mother had brought, even after she'd explained that it contained nothing but clothing and a comb and a bit of oatcake. It had been a dreadful thing for her family to be so distressed. But they'd tried not to show it, although Elly had cried quietly to herself and poor little Seamus had looked as bewildered as she herself had felt. And her dear, dear father had reminded her of the time when some of Ireland's proudest children had been sent into exile. . . .

'Our fathers called them *na Geana Fiadhaine*.' He'd savoured the Gaelic phrase on his tongue. 'The Wild Geese. As though they'd searched all nature for the most beautiful and lonely of her creatures to sing of their grief— and of their hope. Because, when the seasons have turned again and winter is across the land, the wild geese will return again. As you will.' He'd repeated the phrase again when he'd gripped her hand through the bars and kissed her after the warder had told them, roughly, that they must be off. '*Na Geana Fiadhaine*', her father had said. And then there had been the footsteps of her parents and her brother and sister on the stone flags and they'd gone, leaving her alone and too numb and cold even to weep. She remembered wondering how long it would be before some one realised that a stupid mistake had been made, and they came to let her out.

Now, of course, it was too late. She shivered in the biting December wind as the waggon ground to a halt on the cobbled quayside and she looked up at the masts and rigging that appeared to be in motion if one stared at them and forgot that it was the scudding leaden clouds that moved. Already conditioned to the harsh, hectoring voices, she climbed out of the cart with five other women, clutching her small bag of possessions, and joined the line that was shuffling up the gangway. There were two military officers standing at the top among the leering seamen and private soldiers. She had a brief impression of scarlet-and-yellow uniforms and cold, arrogant eyes that seemed to strip the clothes from her back. Then one of the sailors shouted, 'Five of them for'ard! And one to the after prison. You!' Mary, the last in line, was grabbed by a soldier, separated from the other women and shoved aft.

'That's the last of 'em, then.' With a stubby forefinger John Ricketts, First Mate, pointed to the entry in the convict register that bore the heading in ornate copper-plate: '*Britannia*. Captain Thomas Dennott, Master'. 'One hundred and forty-four male convicts. And forty-four women.'

Lieutenant William Burne, New South Wales Corps, nodded. As Ricketts walked away, he turned to his fellow-officer. 'I believe the female convicts improve vastly in appearance as the voyage wears on.' He smiled a man-to-man smile.

The other inclined his head politely but no more. Ensign Maurice Greville did not, evidently, feel particularly man-to-man on the subject of female convicts. A cold fish, Burne thought as he covertly studied the pale blue eyes in the long, over-handsome face, the thin unsmiling mouth, the carefully-barbered blonde hair tied at the nape of the neck with a black ribbon. Everything immaculate, from the black bicorne hat with the silver piping and red-and-white plume to the mirror-polished half-boots with the gilt tops and tassels. Too damned immaculate, Burne thought. Something deuced fishy about Ensign Greville. His sea-chest was too damned ornate, with its beautifully-enamelled decorative work above his name; his scarlet coat, faced and piped with canary-yellow and with its silver epaulettes, silver buttons and silver inserts at the cuffs, was too perfectly tailored; the buff waistcoat and breeches, worn with the maroon sash, looked as if he'd been poured into them. None the less, Burne was determined to be affable. He said, 'Perhaps you might care to join me for a drink in the cuddy?'

Again Greville merely inclined his head. Burne felt a twinge of regret that the Ensign Partridge whom he had been expecting had decided at the last minute to sell his commission to this tailor's dummy. Burne himself was hail-fellow-well-met, anxious only to lead a peaceful,

34

amiable existence and not at all worried by the thought that there were those who might say he was a little late in attaining his captaincy at the age of thirty-two. And it seemed damned odd, he thought as he led the way below, that this young Greville, in his twenties and apparently reeking of money, should have purchased a commission almost on the quayside, so to speak, in order to join a—well, to be frank, an unfashionable regiment like the New South Wales Corps, formed but seven years previously by Major, later Lieutenant-Governor, Francis Grose. On the other hand, it couldn't be denied that there were lucrative pickings to be had in the New South Wales colony. There were advantages, too, in being on the other side of the world where a six-month delay in communications meant that a fellow couldn't be too closely supervised, especially at the present time when the British Government had its hands full with the French War. This Greville must be escaping from his creditors, depend on it, or else he'd got into a scrape with some dolly or other. But a cold fish, decidedly, and not likely to be a convivial companion on this voyage.

Burne sighed as he poured wine and endeavoured to strike up a conversation with the taciturn Mr Greville. The ship's officers weren't going to be of much help as travelling-companions, either. Captain Dennott was, in fact, vaguely frightening with his strangely-compelling eyes, his disdainful manner, his coldly-savage attitude towards the convicts whom he considered to be simply a cargo and not a particularly valuable one at that. Ricketts, the mate, seemed a decent enough chap, but one could scarcely spend one's time carousing with a seaman, eh? And Augustus Beyer, the surgeon—well, there'd be carousing there, certainly, but not of Burne's style. Beyer was a flabby, incompetent weakling with the wine-stains on his greasy coat that betrayed the habitual drunkard. He'd be insensible for most of the voyage. Burne sighed again, bored already with the monosyllabic replies that came his way from the fishy Mr Greville. Yes, this was going to be a deuced long voyage, he could see that.

In the women's prison, aft, Mary was also dismayed by her travelling-companions. She had been shoved down a steep companionway, through an iron grille opened with a clash of keys by a sentry and into a tiny space that stank even worse than the cell in Cork Gaol. It was lit only by a grating in the deck above that was set among massive curving timbers that made her duck her head as she stumbled inside. Two-tiered berths took up most of the space and an iron stove gave off a trickle of wood-smoke that stung her eyes. Eleven women, ragged, filthy and with matted hair, sat or sprawled on the bunks or about the stove. There was a dead silence as the grille was re-locked clangingly behind her and she stood blinking and bewildered in the half-light, hugging her pathetic bundle of belongings.

A voice, husky and with a Dublin lilt to it, said sharply, 'Who are you?'

'Mary Mulvane.' She saw a slim, auburn-haired woman in her early thirties climb to her feet and move forward. She was wearing the tattered ruins of a gown that had once been fashionable, and the gamine face with its large eyes and wide, sensual mouth would have made her extremely attractive to men as she'd gone about the streets of Dublin. But now she was as frowsy as any other incarcerated felon and her face was hard and unsmiling as she studied Mary.

'I'm Polly McNamara. I've been put in charge here and I don't want any trouble. That's your place. There, at the end.' Mary moved obediently to the lower end berth. It had a flabby palliasse and a smelly, paper-thin blanket. She put down her bundle and sat on the bunk. The woman called Polly said curtly, 'Where are you from?'

'Rathcurran.' Suddenly, the hot tears came to her eyes as she said the name. In Cork Gaol, there had been some small hope of mistakes rectified, of some kind of justice, of a month or so in that prison, perhaps, before being sent home. But now she was on a ship, locked up in the bowels of it with these frightening women. No more Rathcurran. No father and mother—not for many years. And no Michael Connor, not ever again.

'What prison, you donkey?' Polly was lounging against the upper berth, staring down at her disparagingly. Another harpy with a foolish, empty stare and a mouth that dribbled saliva down her chin had edged across to sit beside Mary. She smelt horribly of stale sweat and urine.

'Cork', Mary said, swallowing a sob. 'Cork Prison.' Abruptly, the dribbling female snatched Mary's bundle and fumbled with the string. Mary flared up. 'Give that back!' She grabbed and missed. The woman ran off into a corner clutching her booty and began wailing as if Mary had struck her.

Polly strode across and tore the bundle out of the creature's hands. 'Damn you, Jenny Blake, give it here! It's your sticky fingers that got you in here. Now leave off, will you?' She turned to Mary. 'Jenny's simple-minded. Any fool can see that.'

Mary said furiously, 'I'll trouble you to give me my things back!'

'Will you, now?' Polly smiled coldly. 'We've got a right proper lady here, and so we have. Don't try your airs and conceits in here, my girl.'

Slowly, Mary's flare of temper died. She said quietly, 'I meant no offence. Those things. My mother gave them to. . . .' The tears welled in her eyes again.

'You milksop!' Polly tossed the bundle down onto the bunk. 'It's of no use crying for your mother here. And don't expect us to put up with your snivelling for the next six months. Nor yours, either, Jenny.'

The ragged bundle-snatcher shook her head violently. 'No, Polly. Oh, no.'

And, from the deck above, there came a hoarse shout. 'Stand by to cast off! Stand by the heads'l sheets! Hands aloft to loose the tops'ls!' There was a thud-thud of bare feet on the planking above.

The women froze, staring up at the grating. Polly said quietly, 'That's it, then. We've seen the last of Ireland.' She raised her voice as she looked round the prison. 'And you might as well get it into your heads we won't be coming back.'

Mary's eyes were shut tight. She shook her head. 'No!' She opened her eyes to meet Polly's stare. 'You speak for yourself', she said fiercely. 'I'm coming back!'

And so the *Britannia*, with her cargo of human suffering, slipped smoothly into her daily routine under the coldly competent eyes of Captain Thomas Dennott. In the women's prison they began to notice sunlight that sharpened the chequerboard pattern of the grating as it swung to and fro across the floor; mealtimes came and went with a monotony of diet to which hunger soon accustomed them; bells marked the passing of the nights, each one a little warmer as they ploughed towards the Azores; bedding was aired.

It had been on one of these airing excursions on deck, only two days out of Cork, that Mary had seen a convict in a neck-yoke for the first time. She'd looked away quickly from the filthy, tattered figure that stood with his neck and wrists held in the frame, unable to look up and with his weight on his feet for hour after hour, staggering as the vessel pitched and rolled. And it had been on a similar outing that the officer with the cold blue eyes and blonde hair had called her across and asked her her name. She couldn't think why.

She found out that same night. Some of the women were already asleep when the boots thundered on the companionway and the key rattled in the lock. A voice bawled, 'Mary Mulvane!' She sat up in alarm. 'Upstairs!' snapped the redcoat. 'Come on!'

Her first thought was that, somehow, she had committed some offence and was being sent for by the captain, whose dark Mephistophelian figure had filled her with dread every time she'd gone on deck. 'What is it?' She reached for her shawl and tried to arrange her dress. The soldier merely beckoned impatiently. She went out into the yellow light of the swinging lantern and up the swaying ladder, too apprehensive to hear Polly, who came up on one elbow and said as she passed, 'Well! Didn't take you long, did it, Your Ladyship?' Nor did she notice that two of her cell-mates were already parcelling out her possessions. She was taken

38

on deck, down another companionway, this one with varnished woodwork and polished brass handrails. The soldier knocked on a door, opened it and shoved her inside.

Ensign Greville said calmly, 'That'll be all, Sugden.'

The private glanced at Mary, then at the ensign. He said meaningly, 'Good night, sir.' And closed the door.

Greville was wearing an elegant velvet gown in place of his uniform coat. He sat in a chair, smoking a long-stemmed pipe, his gleaming boots resting comfortably on his cot. He said soothingly, 'There's nothing to be frightened of, Mary.'

'I'm—not frightened.' It was a lie. She was so scared her knees felt like india-rubber.

He took the pipe out of his mouth. 'Sit down.' He took his boots off the bunk and pointed. Mary shook her head. He smiled thinly and crossed a boot over his knee. 'Of course you're frightened,' he said gently. He had a good voice. A persuasive voice—one that had persuaded a good many women in its time. 'Caged like an animal. Surrounded by enemies.' He shrugged, sharing her situation with her. 'Who could blame you?' He puffed on his pipe, watching her. 'But I'm not an enemy.' The voice was all honey now. 'You have no reason to fear me. Have you?'

Sure, and I've every reason, she thought. She opened her mouth, swallowed, then said, 'Why was I brought here, Mr Greville?'

He raised his yellow eyebrows. He took the pipe out of his mouth, surprised. 'How did you know my name?'

'Why—' Mary pointed to the decorated sea-chest, '—it's there.'

'It never occurred to me that you might be able to read.' Greville smiled his thin smile. 'You promise to be a more accomplished companion than I dared hope for.'

She said stiffly, 'Please, sir. I want to go now.'

'That', Greville said reprovingly, 'would be very foolish. Don't you understand, Mary? I'm offering you friendship. Comfort. And protection.'

'Please. Let me go.'

He sat very still. It was like watching a clockwork toy run

down, she thought, as she saw the false warmth fade from the pale eyes, the smiling mouth relax into its normal expression of cold arrogance. He put his pipe down and stood up abruptly. 'You want to go back to that cattle-pen—to share your days and nights with a pack of malodorous trollops? Is that what you want?'

She avoided his eyes and said almost inaudibly, 'Yes.'

He stood for a moment, his face like stone. Then he reached past her, opened the door and said savagely, 'Sentry!' There was a pause which gave time for the thought to form in her mind that she had just made a dangerous enemy. Then, when the sentry appeared, he said in a voice like ice, 'Take her below!'

The knowing grin the soldier gave to Greville didn't help much, either.

But it was while she was searching for her stolen belongings down in the prison that she discovered that, if she had made an enemy, she had also made a friend. Polly had asked sarcastically if she had returned for something she'd forgotten. As Mary rummaged about in the dark, the older woman said, 'Now what would you be wanting with a few scraps when you've an officer to look after you? Get back upstairs and leave us be!'

'I'm not going upstairs!' Close to tears again, Mary turned on the woman who lay sneering in the bunk. 'I never asked to! I never wanted to!'

Polly climbed out and stood up. 'What happened, then?'

'He—he wanted me to stay with him.' At the memory of those frightening blue eyes, Mary clutched the bunk for support.

'Did he hurt you?'

'No. But he frightened me.'

Polly studied her for a long moment. The hardness in her face faded. An innocent, that's all this one was. A babe in arms. I'll wager she didn't even know why she was being sent for.

Mary said beseechingly, 'Please, Polly. What happened to my things?'

Polly smiled, a warm and lovely smile, and her voice was

like a mother's when she said, 'We'll find them in the morning.' She put an arm round Mary. 'Have no fear.'

But warm and lovely moments were a rarity aboard the *Britannia*. It was when they were five weeks out of Cork that the first of the floggings took place.

How Dennott's brooding eyes had been able to pick out the scratch-marks on the leg-irons from where he stood gripping the rail of the quarter-deck, it was hard to say. It gave Lieutenant Burne the eerie feeling that the man's eyes had the supernatural abilities of Argus. But see them the captain did, and the voice that could make itself heard all over the ship without seeming to be raised above conversational level said, 'Mr Ricketts. That man's irons!'

Ricketts was airing the male convicts. He hurried to look at the leg-irons of the wretch Dennott was indicating. The voice from the quarter-deck said, 'Well? What is it, Mr Ricketts?'

Ricketts, stooping, looked up at the convict, his face a strange blend of anger and pity. 'Deep scratch marks, sir.'

'What is the penalty for attempting to remove irons, Mr Ricketts?'

Ricketts stood up, staring into the convict's face. 'Six dozen lashes with a right and left cat, if able to bear so much, sir!'

'And can he, Mr Ricketts?'

You poor, bloody, misguided fool, Ricketts thought as he looked at the man's terrified face. There's nothing I can do for you. Aloud he said, 'He's got a hide on him like a bullock.'

There was a silence from the quarter-deck. Then Dennott said softly, 'Very well, Mr Ricketts. Proceed with punishment.'

Ricketts snapped his fingers at two seamen who ran forward and ripped the man's jacket off. Burne shouted, 'Gua-ard! Fix bayonets!' Then, 'At the stairhead—on the double!'

The convict had been too frightened to speak but, as the seamen seized him, he shouted, 'No, please, I never did it! I didn't! For pity's sake, won't you hear me?' The shouts

41

changed to screams when he saw where they were dragging him—to a pair of ring-bolts set in the quarter-deck bulkhead. The military guard clattered up to the quarter-deck and stood with their muskets at the ready. Ricketts opened a canvas bag and produced the two leather-handled whips. He tossed them to the two men he'd chosen as flagellators for their arm-muscles and breadth of shoulder. The captain stood with his hands behind his back, balancing himself to the roll of the ship. There was a silence while the timbers creaked and the warm wind harped softly in the rigging. The man to be flogged hung with his wrists lashed to the bolts, his back bare, his screaming stopped as he strengthened himself for what was to come. Ricketts said crisply, 'All ready, sir.'

'Commence punishment!'

The left-hand flogger stood with his feet apart, the cat in his right hand and lying across the palm of his left. He measured the distance with his eye, shuffled back half a pace. He settled himself. Then he swung the whip up in a high arc, raising himself on to the balls of his feet, his shoulder muscles bunching. He struck with a crack like a pistol shot. His grunt of effort was drowned in the dreadful scream that was a compound of agony, outrage and shock. The convict bucked, straining against the ropes as the right-hand cat struck, whistling, from the other side. The victim choked on his scream, biting into his own left arm in his torment. Ricketts marked the strokes on a slate, his voice chanting unemotionally. 'Three . . . four . . . five . . .'

Burne looked about for the surgeon who, according to the terrible formalities of flogging, should have been standing by. Greville, he noticed, was surveying the scene with an air of bored detachment. But where the devil was Beyer? Burne went below.

The surgeon was half drunk. He jumped guiltily, caught in the act of pouring a glass of brandy as his cabin door opened. With the bottle in his hand, he said unsteadily, 'How dare you bursh—burst into my cabin like this?'

'I advise you', Burne said with contempt, 'to get on deck

directly. A man is being given seventy-two lashes.'

Beyer, his neckband undone, his pallid face unshaven, said, 'I was not informed. I. . . .'

'And I think I should tell you that Ricketts has informed me that he has in his possession written instructions from the Captain to the effect that he and not you will decide whether or not a man can stand punishment. So, if this man should die . . . .'

Beyer lurched to his feet. 'He won't get away with this', he said thickly. He reached for his hat and pushed past Burne to the passageway.

But, as he came out on deck, Captain Dennott forestalled him. 'Doctor Beyer,' he said above the bubbling shrieks and the rhythmic thwack-thwack of the cats, 'would you be so good as to take over your duty of recording the lashes?'

Beyer peered up at him, blinking in the strong light, his prepared speech of protest fumbling through his mind. The chant went on. 'Thirty-eight . . . thirty-nine . . . forty . . . .' As he counted, the mate thrust the slate and chalk into Beyer's shaking hands. Beyer opened his mouth.

Then, as his bleary gaze met the eyes of Captain Dennott, he took up the count himself. 'Forty-four . . . forty-five . . . .' He began scribbling on the slate to catch up with the tally. 'Forty-six . . .'

Down in their prison, the women heard it all, Mary numb with the horror of it, Polly McNamara trying to comfort the simple-minded Jenny Blake who sat rocking herself and moaning, her hands over her ears. And, later, when it was the women's turn to go on deck, it was Jenny who stepped out first and saw the great splash of blood on the planking where the horror had taken place. She screamed shrilly, her hands going to her mouth. Then, still screaming, she ran to the starboard rail and tried to scramble over it.

Captain Dennott, who had just come down from the quarter-deck, happened to be the nearest man. He seized her round the waist and dragged her back. Howling hysterically, Jenny swung a wild blow at his face.

It was as if the sound of the slap had brought the whole

ship to a standstill. The look on Dennott's face silenced Jenny's shrieks as if she had been gagged. In the awful hush Polly whispered, 'Oh, my God!' and moved forward, Mary behind her. A redcoat blocked their path. Jenny, still staring into the Captain's face, began to whimper. She tried to pull away but he had her by the arm. 'You thought to leave us, madam,' he said in his soft voice, 'and without my permission. Mr Ricketts!'

'Sir?'

'Fetch me the bosun's cane.'

In the cuddy, Burne said, 'The man's demented! Greville, do you realise we are in the hands of a madman?'

The ensign, who was composedly making up the guard roster, put his head on one side inquiringly. 'I don't believe I follow you, sir.'

'Dennott. Do you realise that, at this very moment, he's laying into one of the women prisoners with the bosun's cane?'

'Really?' Greville made another entry on his roster.

'That simple-minded Blake girl tried to jump overboard. He's thrashing her for "attempting to leave the ship without permission"! As if seventy-two lashes for some scratched leg-irons wasn't enough for him. I tell you, the man's a sadist!'

'Shocking, sir.' Greville looked up. 'But are we really in a position to do anything about it?'

Burne hesitated. Dammit, why couldn't life be easy and comfortable, the way he liked it? He didn't want trouble—and that, he knew, was what he'd be saddled with if he tried to oppose Captain Dennott. Better let things lie until we reach the Colony . . . . He said, 'Doctor Beyer's in a better position than we are. But look at him . . . .'

Beyer's position just then was quite simple—he was lying on his bunk, stupefied with brandy. 'And very nasty', the sentry told Polly when she'd asked him to fetch the surgeon to Jenny Blake. 'Damned me, damned her. Properly in his cups, he is. I tell you, I'd be near to death before I wanted him near me and I wouldn't be too sure then.'

'I wouldn't trust him with the choking of a rat!' Mary said after the sentry had gone.

'Oh,' said Polly, 'is that the way they talk in County Cork? You wouldn't hear language like that in Tiernan's Lane.'

Mary smiled in spite of herself. 'Is that where you lived?'

'For a while. Before', Polly said steadily, 'my husband died. We lived behind a wig-maker. No room to put a crumb between us, but we didn't care.' No regrets, she reminded herself, no tears for him—or for the daughter she'd left behind in Dublin. The present was bad enough, without thinking of the past. And the future was going to be a lot worse.

It did get worse—far worse. And, as the *Britannia* spread her sails against the blue skies of the South Atlantic, so beautiful to outward appearance but so ugly within, Mary Mulvane, too, was drawn into the web of terror that was being spun by Captain Dennott. She had been sent for, once again, by Greville, this time to be offered a position as his servant. 'I imagine', he said, 'you and the other women were quite upset by the Blake girl being caned.'

'Yes, sir.' Commanded to sit, she was bolt upright on the edge of the cot.

'It would be pleasant to think that nothing like that will happen again. But probably it will.' She said nothing. 'When I offered you protection, perhaps the gesture had no great meaning for you. But I fancy that, now, you may see its value.' He gestured with the slice of cheese he was eating. 'I am in a position to employ your time fully. Cleaning. Perhaps washing. Some mending. You will be spared the cruelties which, I fear, lie ahead. I ask only for a little companionship. What say you?'

Her chin went up defiantly. 'I'm not too proud to be a servant girl,' she said, 'but I won't be a whore.'

The frankness of the word hit him like a blow. For a moment she thought that, in his turn, he was going to strike her. Instead, he picked up his hat and sword belt. 'No-one asked you to be', he said, his voice thick with anger. 'When you've finished cleaning the cabin, you may get back where you belong.' He went out. In the passageway, he said to the sentry, 'I want you to keep an eye on the girl who is cleaning out my cabin.' He slipped the sword belt over his shoulder, his eyes on the soldier. He said meaningly, 'Don't take any nonsense from her. And—' he paused, '—just make sure the cabin's in good order when you leave.'

The man stared after him, unable to believe his good fortune. Then he grinned, licked his lips and went into the cabin. Mary said, 'What do you want?'

He propped his musket in the corner, grinning. She said, 'I'm to clean the cabin . . . .'

'Plenty o' time for that.' He moved forward. She tried to dodge but there was no room and he cupped her face in his hand, gripping until it hurt. He leaned forward to kiss her, his foetid breath in her face, and she broke away, struggling as he grabbed for her. 'What's the harm in a bit o' sport, eh?' Blindly, she picked up the knife Greville had used to cut his piece of cheese. As the man came at her, she jabbed at his groping hand with it.

At the Captain's table that night, Greville said with elaborate casualness, 'I meant to ask you earlier, Doctor: how is the victim of the stabbing?'

Dennott shot him a look and went very still. 'Stabbing, sir? What are you talking about?'

Lieutenant Burne, too, gave Greville a look—of anger. He said, 'I think Ensign Greville is joking, Captain.'

'A stabbing on my ship is hardly a matter for jest, Mr Burne.'

'It wasn't a stabbing, sir. A soldier's hand was slightly cut . . . .'

'A scratch.' Doctor Beyer drank some wine. 'Nothing more than a . . . .'

'Who did this?'

'One of the women prisoners, sir. The girl concerned is of good character and I completely believe her version of what happened. She was molested by one of my men and picked up a knife in her own defence. Any woman of decency would have acted in the same manner.'

'Lieutenant, it seems I must remind you that I am

46

captain of this ship. Tomorrow she goes in the neck-yoke.'

'Captain Dennott.' Burne came as close as he ever would to taking a strong line. 'I am compelled to record this exchange in my journal.'

'Do so and be damned to you, sir! Say to the Government what you will. I am agent for this ship and I will act as I think proper. She will suffer the neck-yoke for two hours!'

And it was while Mary was enduring the full glare of the sun, her head aching, her mouth parched and her body crying out for rest, that James Brannon, a deep compassion in his voice, spoke to her. Unable to lift her head, she was aware only of a pair of leg-ironed feet that moved into her limited line of vision on the sun-drenched deck and of a soft Irish voice that said, 'Take heart, girl. They won't get away with this.' Then he was gone, shuffling away as he saw Ensign Greville stroll out from under the shade of a sail, dabbing delicately at his forehead with a cambric handkerchief.

She heard from Brannon again. It was in the sweltering heat of Rio de Janeiro while Captain Dennott was ashore completing his arrangements for the shipping of his own personal cargo of rum which he planned to sell at enormous profit in New South Wales. To stow the rum, however, a dozen hundred-gallon water-casks would have to be sacrificed. 'Break them up, Mr Ricketts', he had said, overriding the mate's mild protest that it would mean cutting the water-ration. 'This ship is not a water-hoy and I need the space for profitable goods.' While the Captain's cargo was being taken on, Brannon talked to the women who, their faces running with sweat and ingrained with dirt, had been allowed on deck and, at Lieutenant Burne's suggestion, were feasting on the bounty of an orange apiece. Brannon had brought the oranges over to them. 'We plan to take the ship after we leave port', he said, his eyes on the redcoats.

Polly said scornfully, 'You're out of your mind.'

'It was one of your number who gave me the idea. A woman is to fall overboard—a bundle of blankets, ye understand? In the confusion, we take the vessel and throw the bloody redcoats over the side. All we ask of you is some clothing for—' he smiled, '—Our Lady of the blanket.'

'We've no clothing to spare', Polly said.

'It's madness.' To Mary, it brought back all the horror of the night at the Rathcurran pound. 'You'll only bring disaster on yourselves.'

'The morning we're ready,' Brannon said softly, 'I'll drop a farthing through the grating of your prison.' He grinned, his teeth gleaming in his filthy, bearded face. 'A poor price for your fine clothes, to be sure. But your liberty should make up the balance.' A redcoat yelled at him and he shuffled away.

'What'll we do?' Mary asked helplessly.

'Nothing', Polly said shortly. 'If we've any sense, that is.'

'But they're counting on us.'

Polly looked at her. 'Aye', she said bitterly. 'And so they are.'

They sailed from Rio with a two months' voyage ahead of them and the water-ration cut to two-thirds of a gallon a day, so that any kind of attempt at cleanliness became a thing of the past. The heat increased; the wind died to light airs that barely filled the sails and Dennott, furious, calculated that they were making barely thirty-six miles a day with very little chance of a fair wind until they reached the Forties. The water-ration was cut again, this time to two quarts a day. 'What I'd give', Mary said, 'to feel a misty rain cold on my face now.' The rain of Ireland, she thought with a stab of anguish. The soft, sweet rain drifting off the rolling hills, with the clouds grey and sailing in from the west, and the grass green and lush with the tiny raindrops hanging like diamonds on every blade . . . .

'Och, spare a thought for the dribbly noses', said Polly the pragmatist. 'After half a day, you'd be longing for the sun . . . .' Something fell, glittering in the light, to tinkle on the floor.

One of the women picked it up. 'It's a farthing', she said in astonishment. 'Glory be! I'm rich!'

'What'll we do?' Mary asked.

Polly shrugged as she pulled off her petticoat, rolled it up and stuffed it into her bedding. 'We'll do what we must', she said resignedly. 'They haven't much of a chance anyway, so we'll give them what help we can.'

In fact, Brannon and his men had no chance whatever, for the fatal disunity that always bedevils Ireland was at work even on the *Britannia*. Convict Egan's motives were obscure; he may have acted out of jealousy of Brannon, out of fear of reprisal should the mutiny fail, or merely out of a desire for his thirty pieces of silver. At all events, he asked to be taken before Captain Dennott and he blabbed everything—the oath they'd taken, the whereabouts of the crude weapons they'd secreted, the plot to throw a dummy overboard, the names of the ringleaders. Before he was halfway through his betrayal, Captain Dennott had already called the military to arms, lashed tarpaulins over the prison gratings and stopped the water-ration completely.

And then the floggings began.

It was an orgy of retribution that made seventy-two strokes for scratched leg-irons seem like a gentle rebuke. James Brannon to receive eight hundred lashes . . . . Richard Stapleton, eight hundred lashes . . . . John Burke, six hundred . . . . John Cahill, three hundred . . . . Thomas Brady, three hundred . . . .

Eight thousand four hundred and sixty-four lashes were awarded in three days. The men died in torment, howling like animals, shredded of every last vestige of human dignity as first the skin then gobbets of bloody flesh were flayed from their backs until the vertebrae showed through, white and gleaming. Those who somehow survived on deck died later of shock, of loss of blood, of internal haemorrhage. They died writhing in their own excreta without any kind of medical aid whatever; Doctor Augustus Beyer, terrified of entering the convicts' quarters, clutched his bottle and said they could die and be damned.

Then, from intense heat and dryness, they came to the Roaring Forties and gale-force winds, driving rain and a bitter, biting cold. The women's prison became yet another kind of hell, for now the bulkheads ran with water that poured through the tarpaulin that kept them in darkness by day and by night. As the *Britannia's* stern rose and fell wildly, the small space stank disgustingly of vomit and, unable to go on deck to empty their bucket, the women lived in their own filth. Their meals became a revolting mess of rotting pork, a soup made from mouldering peas and biscuit that was as hard as wood and black with weevils. When, after an eternity, the tarpaulin was dragged clear of the grating, they stared at one another in horror, hardly recognising the skeletal creatures who squinted about their prison with hollow, red-rimmed eyes, their paper-white skins blotched with scurvy and encrusted with the dirt of months. On the first day when the women were allowed on deck, Mary was so weak that she could scarcely stand. Ensign Greville was in charge of their airing.

They had come to loathe him even more than Captain Dennott. The shipmaster, brutal and sadistic though he was, performed his cruelties in the open; Greville was cunning, devious and snake-like in his malice. Now, as Mary stumbled and fell in her eagerness to obey, her longing for clean air, he looked down at her with contempt, a handkerchief held to his nose. 'On your feet, you lazy baggage', he snapped. He prodded her with his boot.

Polly flew at him like a tigress defending her cub, scratching and spitting with fury. She had the satisfaction of leaving the bloody marks of her fingernails down his smoothly-shaven cheek before she was seized by a soldier, but the final satisfaction was, once again, to be Greville's. When Polly came back from her interview with Captain Dennott she bore the marks of the last punishment to be awarded on the hell-ship *Britannia*. Her face was bruised and swollen where she had been beaten until she was almost senseless. And her auburn hair had been raggedly cropped to the skull.

And so the *Britannia* sailed up the coast of New South Wales in bright autumn sunshine, fouling the warm air with the stench of her passing. On that voyage, fifteen male and one female convict had died, six of the men having been flogged to death. Others would be crippled for life. Some would carry the seeds of illness that would kill them slowly within a few years. The prisons were running with ordure, the water-casks almost empty and swimming with algae, the stores of salt pork and biscuit crawling with maggots.

It began to occur to Captain Dennott, Surgeon Beyer and the officer in charge of the military guard, Lieutenant Burne, that some kind of reckoning might be at hand. Each, in his own way, began to prepare his line of retreat.

Ensign Greville, naturally, had prepared his already.

CHAPTER FOUR

Lieutenant Burne was worried. Although he knew that the New South Wales colony was run, to all intents and purposes, by the Corps and that as an officer of that regiment he was reasonably safe from punishment or even reprimand, it was none the less an undoubted fact that, when those wretched Irish convicts had been—well, yes, murdered, dammit, by that madman Dennott, he had been in charge of the military guard. Even in the Corps there were internal politics and machinations. It was quite on the cards that, if the reputation of the regiment were to be questioned, he might be saddled with the blame. He was, after all, only a lieutenant and expendable.

But ensigns, he reflected, were even more expendable. It was, after all, only fair that if there was to be any hand-to-hand fighting, the smooth Mr Greville should bear the brunt of some of it. He eased his black neck-cloth in the unaccustomed morning warmth as he stood outside Greville's cabin, the deck now blissfully still as the *Britannia* rode at anchor in Sydney Cove. He tapped and entered. The ensign was piling clothes into his sea-chest. Burne said heartily, 'Can't wait to set foot ashore, eh, Greville?' Strange, he thought, that even after six months' close association, he never used the fellow's Christian name.

In his usual cool, damnably non-committal manner, Greville said, 'At least it will be a change, sir.'

Burne prowled about the tiny cabin, picking things up and putting them down again and wondering why it was that, with seniority both in rank and age, he should feel so blasted inferior with this chap. 'Greville. . . .' He cleared his throat. 'I gather our medical bigwig from the town wasn't at all pleased with the condition of the convicts.'

Greville went on packing. 'Oh, I imagine they like to beat the drum a bit. Put on a bit of a show to keep the reformers happy.' He gestured languidly in the general direction of the little cluster of brick buildings and pipe-clayed houses he'd seen on the hill-slope surrounded by bush. 'And it's hardly a town anyway, sir. Merely a military camp. I think the Corps can take care of any local trouble-makers.'

'You're right, of course. But this Balmain fellow—the Colonial Surgeon—seems to wield a good deal of influence. Bit of a fire-eater—keen on bettering the convicts' conditions. That sort of thing.' He sat on Greville's cot, wishing the man would stop his blasted packing and show some interest. 'Apparently, the sentry outside the Captain's cabin overheard what went on when Balmain came aboard. Bit of a skirmish, he said, between him and Dennott and Beyer. This chap intends to take the whole affair to Governor Hunter and ask for an inquiry.'

Greville closed his chest and sat on it, his legs crossed elegantly, his face showing nothing except polite attention. Burne stared him in the eye. 'It could touch all of us', he said meaningly.

Greville almost yawned. 'Oh, I don't think you have anything to fear, sir', he said calmly. 'After all, you were only doing your duty.'

I was doing my duty? Burne thought. And what the devil were you doing? He opened his mouth to point out that Greville had an equal share of responsibility but the ensign got in first. 'I mean to say, you were under Captain Dennott's orders.' Greville smiled his thin, cold smile. 'As I', he added gently, 'was under yours.'

Suddenly, Burne felt more worried than ever.

And, if he had known what was in the mind of William Balmain, Chief Colonial Surgeon to His Britannic

Majesty's Colony at New South Wales, he would have had good reason for concern. For that forthright Scottish naval officer had spent the last eight years, both at the Norfolk Island penal settlement and here in Sydney Town, in trying to put a stop to this kind of villainy, and he was in a state of barely-suppressed fury at what he had found on board the *Britannia*—the decks reeking of vinegar in an attempt to disguise the stench, the appalling state of the stores, the even more appalling condition of those wretched specimens of humanity who had—God alone knew how—managed to survive the voyage. And yon devil Dennott and that other villainous sot Beyer—not a skerrick of remorse at all! Instead, they were fully occupied in trying to shuffle the blame on to each other's shoulders and showing their teeth at one another like a pair of cornered rats. Aye, well, they'd be made to pay if there was any justice in the world. There'd be witnesses enough—the female convict McNamara who'd had her hair cut off and yon poor bewildered lass Mulvane who'd look bonny enough if she was washed and given a wee while in the hospital. In the meantime, he'd away to Government House and set things in motion. Not even the New South Wales Corps would be able to interfere in this.

But one of the officers of that Corps was already entrenching himself in his carefully-prepared position. After the boring Burne had left him, Ensign Greville went down to the women's prison. The stink of vinegar, he reflected as he descended the companion, was unpleasant but a damned sight more palatable than the odour of felons. He looked through the grille. Feeding time, he thought, at the zoo. The sluts were all guzzling some unmentionable horror out of wooden bowls, wiping the residue up with lumps of bread. How utterly revolting! As he eyed the two from whom he might expect the greatest amount of mischief to arise he heard the Mulvane woman say, 'Is it really true, Polly? That we're to be picked over by the men of the town and just used as they think fit?'

Polly said, 'Let's worry about that when it happens. We. . . .' She broke off when she saw Greville.

He said, looking at the women in general but with special reference to Polly and Mary, 'I gather the Colonial Surgeon has visited you.' Nobody answered. They stared at him, their bowls unheeded. 'I imagine you have given him suitably colourful accounts of your—ah—misadventures.' He lifted a hand and let it fall. 'You must, of course, speak as your conscience dictates. But I offer this caution. When you leave this ship, the captain and the surgeon will have no further influence on your lives. But your guards—the men of the New South Wales Corps—will remain here in the colony. So, should you be tempted to utter petty slanders against us, bear in mind that anything you may say about us can have little effect.' He paused. 'What *we* have to say about *you*, however, will greatly affect your chances in this colony through all the long years to come.' He stood watching Polly and Mary for a moment. Then he turned and they heard his boots on the companion.

Polly looked at the expression on Mary's face. 'Don't let him frighten you.' She put an arm round her shoulders. 'Who knows but we'll never see the hide of him again.'

'I *am* frightened.' Mary looked round the prison which, all of a sudden, seemed a familiar and safe place. 'Frightened of leaving here, now.' Like a caged bird that keeps to its perch even when the door is opened, she was clinging to the security of her cell with its known, if hated, routine rather than face the outside world. The fear of the unknown, she thought. The fear that we all have, all our lives, until we face the last unknown of all.

But, the very next day, they were taken to Sydney Hospital and placed in the capable hands of the plump Matron Purdy who cleansed them, gave them fresh-smelling nightgowns to wear and put them to bed to be stuffed with the plain but nourishing hospital food until they thought they would burst. 'Got to fatten you up a bit,' she said in her homely Cockney voice as she sat comfortably by the fire that had become necessary as the autumn nights took on a chill edge. 'Like a yard of pump water stretched, you look. And what sort of gentleman's going to pick you when you look like that?'

Mary and Polly looked at one another. 'We've no say in it?' Polly asked. 'We're just—picked over, like so many remnants on a stall?'

'This', the Matron said, 'is your chance to better yourselves.' She took down a clay pipe from the mantelpiece and lit it with a twig from the fire. 'You might end up with an officer. Ho yes, you girls can do very nicely here if you play your cards right.'

Polly was listening carefully. It paid to listen, because then you could form your plans to make the best of whatever came along. It was this attitude of acceptance that had brought her through the voyage—and helped Mary to survive. It was the same fatalism that had kept her sane when they'd sentenced her and taken her little daughter from her. If it's to be, she thought, then we must do the best we can with the situation. A woman had weapons that men knew nothing about, and if there was any picking over to be done then, by the saints, she'd be the one to do it and not some gawking farmer who'd come to Sydney Town to find a female slave.

Mary said, 'But what happens if nobody wants us?'

'Not likely in your case, love.' Purdy chuckled fatly. 'But, for some unfortunates, it becomes a matter of doing for a hut full of convicts. Ugh!' She puffed on her pipe. 'You're to make statements for Chief Surgeon Balmain, aren't you? So you'll be kept here until the inquiry's over. Then you'll be assigned.'

*   *   *   *   *

The Court of Inquiry was held three weeks later and, after the first half hour, Balmain knew it was going to be a farce. It took place before the acting Judge-Advocate, Richard Atkins, whom William Bligh later was to describe as 'weak, a blabber, a drunkard, ridiculous and in legal matters subservient to private interest'; he was, moreover, far too friendly with Captain Dennott for Balmain's liking. With Atkins was the Reverend Richard Johnson, a wispy little man with the air of one who is more intent on planning

56

next Sunday's sermon than on a governmental inquiry. On the last day of the hearing, a man of less determination than Balmain would have left the Judge-Advocate's chambers instantly when he saw how they came into the room— Atkins joking with Captain Dennott and the clergyman looking as if he was in a trance. Apart from Balmain himself, only Augustus Beyer, the wine-stains carefully sponged from his coat, seemed to be taking it seriously.

To Balmain's utter astonishment, Atkins began the day's proceedings by terminating the case for the prosecution and calling upon Dennott to read a prepared statement. The Chief Surgeon was on his feet in a flash. 'With respect, Judge-Advocate!' In his crisp Perthshire voice, Balmain said, 'We have a statement here from several more witnesses who, I believe, should be called.' He held up the papers signed by Mary, Polly and some of the other women.

Atkins said coldly, '*More* convicts, Doctor?' He looked bored. 'I think this court has tolerated more than enough mud-slinging from convicted felons. It is high time we granted Captain Dennott the opportunity he has requested.'

'Sir!' Balmain's voice had an edge like a claymore. 'We are investigating a voyage in which sixteen convicts died— six of them flogged to death. In the interests of. . . .'

'Doctor, I admire your diligence. But I think we are already in possession of the facts.' Atkins smiled graciously at Dennott. 'Captain?'

At the back of the room, Burne nudged Greville. 'This fellow Balmain. Told you he was a trouble-maker, eh? Looks as if old Atkins knows what's what, though.' And thank God for it, he said to himself. Granted, Dennott and Beyer richly deserved a hanging apiece. But, if they got their fingers burnt, then so might he. Much better keep quiet about the whole thing, eh?

Captain Dennott swept the room with those dark, strangely hypnotic eyes of his. He stood, spare and trim and deferential, before the court and gave a little bow before he began to read. Balmain listened incredulously as Dennott told them that it had never been his wish to punish the convicts at all, that very few had been punished, and those but slightly. Everybody else, the Captain pointed out, staring straight at Augustus Beyer, had been as earnest in their punishment as he had been himself. '*Humanum est errare*,' he said solemnly, 'and, whether I am condemned or acquitted, I shall ever feel myself under the greatest obligation to this court for the manner in which they have conducted this inquiry.' He bowed and sat down.

A series of horrid naval oaths volleyed through Balmain's mind as he saw the court rise, disappear and return again in the time it would take to drink a glass of wine. Atkins tapped with his gavel, giving the impression of a Solomon who has, after many sleepless nights, arrived at a decision. 'Gentlemen,' he said pompously, 'after maturely considering the evidence on both sides, we are unanimously of the opinion the Captain Dennott's conduct in punishing the convicts was imprudent and ill-judged and, in this instance, may be regarded as bordering on too great a degree of severity.'

Beyer gave an audible sigh of relief and mopped his forehead with a grubby handkerchief.

'But', Atkins went on, 'we are also of the opinion that the Surgeon, Doctor Beyer, was inexcusably negligent and indifferent in the performance of his duty.'

Beyer went as white as a sheet.

'Such is our opinion. In conclusion, we here beg leave to offer His Excellency our suggestion that all ships coming to this colony with transported felons should have on board an officer of the Crown who should be invested with the proper power and authority for the conducting of the ship as well as the management of the convicts on board.'

Nobody would meet Balmain's eye as Atkins rapped again and closed the proceedings. Leaving the chambers, Greville said to Burne, 'I'm delighted to see that, in New South Wales, justice is tempered with mercy.'

Burne said, remembering the screams and the whistle of the lash, 'That depends on who's being judged, I suppose.'

Greville was looking up and down the street. 'I must

leave you now, sir. I'm having dinner with Captain Wiltshire and I've one or two matters to attend to first.'

Burne acknowledged his casual salute. Hasn't taken him long to achieve dining status with his commanding officer, he thought. As he walked away, Burne wondered just how long it would take Greville to overtake him on the promotion ladder. . . .

*　*　*　*　*

SYDNEY GENERAL HOSPITAL
Assignment of Female Convicts
The Chief Colonial Surgeon announces that
no Applications for the Assignment of
female Servants from the above Institution
will be received prior to 9 in the
Forenoon of Thursday, 22nd June 1797.

The queue of townsmen, dressed in their best, had begun to form before eight o'clock. By nine, the women felt as if they'd been sitting by their beds in their clean white dresses, white caps and aprons since the day they'd left the *Britannia*. Polly primped in a mirror, trying to tweak a few tiny curls from under her cap before she returned to her stool. 'Well, I've looked better in my time', she said resignedly. 'But this is the best I'll manage this morning.' She glaced critically at Mary. 'Pinch your cheeks. Ye look pale.'

Mary shook her head tightly. 'I don't care.'

Polly said gently, 'Mary, love! Some things you can change and some you can't. This—assignment business is going to happen whether we care or not. So I'm going to be the one who does the picking. When I walk out of that door with—whoever it is, things are going to go the way *I* want. Sooner or later.'

'And that'll be goodbye.' Partings, always partings, she thought. She'd read somewhere that every parting was a little death. She hadn't understood, then, what it meant.

'I suppose it has to be. Another of the things we can't

change.' Polly looked up sharply as the door opened. Matron Purdy sailed in, a mob of men peering over her shoulder. Mary dropped her eyes to her sewing, trying to tell herself this wasn't happening.

A red-faced, big-bellied townsman stared about the ward with the air of a cock let loose in a hen-roost. He saw Polly, grinned predatorily and swaggered towards her. Instantly, she was seized with a cough that would have drawn attention even in a lazar-house. Her eyes bulged, her face went puce and she gasped for breath, making a noise not unlike a death-rattle. The suitor's grin vanished. He hastened on up the ward and Polly, recovering miraculously, smiled secretly to herself.

Mary, who had stopped sewing to stare at her friend in alarm, almost stabbed herself with her needle as she caught the eager smile of a portly, prosperously-dressed man old enough to be her grandfather. She began sewing frantically but, out of the corner of her eye, saw the man accost Surgeon Balmain, who had come into the ward, and point to her. With a sense of inexpressible relief, she saw Balmain shake his head, talking quietly. In his turn, the man nodded regretfully and moved away.

Suddenly, Polly dropped her reel of cotton. It rolled across the floor into the path of a small stocky man in his late thirties who was clutching his hat to his stomach as he wandered hesitantly down the ward without daring to look at any of the women. He picked up the spool and glanced bashfully at Polly. She said, 'Oh, thank you kindly, sir. I'm in such a state, you see—my hand's trembling like a leaf.'

Mary, surprised, could not but observe that her friend's hand was as steady as a rock as it took the reel and that it was the man's hand that was dithering. 'This', Polly said with an air of pathos, 'is a trying time for me. I'm not used to talking to strange gentlemen. Of course, for a man of the world like yourself. . . .' She looked up at him helplessly.

His chubby pink face attempted unsuccessfully to assume the devil-may-care, man-of-the-world expression appropriate to one accustomed to accosting strangers at any time and place. 'Of course.' He cleared his throat. 'Yes, of course. Why, yes.'

Polly smiled appreciatively at this conversational gem. 'My name', she said shyly, 'is Polly McNamara.'

'Er—Wilberforce Price.' He ducked his head.

He was, Polly thought, rather sweet in his embarrassment. She cast a flicker of a glance at his clothes. Good but worn. The darning that needed to be done to his stocking showed he had no other woman about him. 'I'm ever so glad to meet you, Mr Price', she said with a brilliant smile. But he certainly hadn't kissed the Blarney stone, this one. Yet another point in his favour. 'What is your calling, Mr Price?' she asked casually, sewing with dainty little dabs of her needle.

'Oh, er—I'm an inn-keeper.'

Blessed Saint Patrick! Couldn't be better. 'Oh? I was once in a situation in a tavern myself. In Dublin.'

'Did—er—did you like the work?'

'Indeed I did, Mr Price. My employer was very satisfied.' She let that sink in. 'And I have the happiest recollections of my time there.'

'Would you like to work in a tavern again—er, Polly?'

She smiled up at him meltingly. 'Oh, indeed I would, sir.'

He was already edging away, his hat rotating violently. 'In my tavern?'

'Of course, Mr Price.'

'I'll just—I think I'll have a word with the Surgeon.' He hurried down the ward.

She turned to Mary. 'Well, wish me luck.' Mary nodded quickly. Polly picked up the bundle that was rolled and ready on her bed. 'I hope you find someone nice.' She saw the tears standing in Mary's eyes. 'This is the way of it, Mary', she said very gently. 'Things come to an end—so quick. It only hurts if you try to hang on to them.' But she could feel the hot prickling in her own eyes, too.

'Oh, Polly!' Abruptly, Mary jumped up and threw her arms round the only friend she had in the world.

'Goodbye. And good luck to. . . .' Polly found that it was difficult to speak for the huge lump that had risen in her throat. 'Good luck to you. And my thousand blessings on you, Mary.' Gently, she disengaged herself. At the door she turned back to wave but Mary was already sewing again with the tears pouring down her cheeks.

Gradually the ward emptied and, slowly, another fear came into her aching mind: *For some unfortunates, it becomes a matter of doing for a hut full of convicts.* She glanced about her now as she sewed on doggedly. An officer of the New South Wales Corps, middle-aged and distinguished in his captain's uniform, was looking at her thoughtfully as he spoke to Surgeon Balmain. She looked away hurriedly.

A rough voice said, 'You're to come with me.'

She looked up. The others had gone. She was alone in the ward with the young man who'd just spoken—a broad-shouldered, dark-haired fellow in a none-too-clean shirt and torn knee-breeches who was staring at her broodingly. 'With you?' There was a vague menace in the big hands that hung by his sides, in the deep-set eyes that seemed to look straight through her.

'Yes, Mary.' Balmain came into the ward. 'You have been assigned to Captain Wiltshire. I believe it will be a good situation for you.' He nodded the young man. 'The Captain's servant will take you to his farm outside Parramatta.' He smiled at her. 'I wish you well.'

She nodded, thanked him, and picked up her bundle. So this is it, she thought. *You might end up with an officer. Ho yes.* . . . Her refusal to be Greville's whore had been in vain; in the long run, it had all come to the same thing. With a flare of temper, she walked out ahead of the dark, silent young man. At least *he* wasn't going to see her cry.

*   *   *   *   *

Polly was beginning to wonder whether, after all, she'd chosen wisely. Instead of escorting her to some cosy local hostelry, Wilberforce Price had stuck her up behind him on what looked like a cart-horse and she'd made the horrifying discovery that his inn was a wayside tavern, with not a living soul for miles around. But he was a kind man, and so proud of the inn he'd built himself that she hadn't the heart to tell him she wouldn't be found dead in such a God-forsaken spot as the one he described. He came from Surrey, she'd discovered; she began to wonder, as the day wore on and she eased her aching bottom from side to side, whether he intended to ride his wretched horse there. . . .

* * * * *

Mary sat beside the captain's servant on the cart that was laden with boxes, barrels and sacks covered with a tarpaulin. Her anger had gone, leaving her cold and empty. Her fear of the young man had gone, too, after he'd offered her a slice of pie and they'd exchanged names. He was Jonathan Garrett, from Essex, and an assigned convict like herself. She'd expressed surprise when he'd told her he was allowed to travel, even with the pass he had in his pocket, and she'd asked him why he didn't try to escape. He'd laughed at that, a laugh that lit up his dark face with warmth, and pointed at the grey-green of the bush. 'That's all there is. It just goes on and on. Don't you see? That's why they brought us here. You can't escape.' It was a chilling thought. He'd sensed that and told her she was safe, that the worst was over, that things would start getting better.

She realised there was a warmth and sensitivity about him that she hadn't expected. 'This officer', she said after a long silence. 'Captain Wiltshire. What's he like?'

'Oh, all right. Seeing he's one of them.'

'Them?'

'The New South Wales Corps. Think they're God Almighty. It's . . .' he shrugged, holding the reins, '. . . it's as if this whole place and everybody in it is just for them. But the Captain isn't so bad. Anyway, you'll have more to do with Mrs Wiltshire.'

Mrs Wiltshire! Mary breathed a prayer of thanks. 'What's *she* like?'

Jonathan didn't answer for a moment. 'I expect', he said carefully, 'she'll be nice to you.' He seemed to be about to add something else when he checked and turned his head at the sound of hoofbeats coming up fast behind him.

Mary turned too. It was an officer, his blue-black stallion at full gallop and as handsome as he was himself in his scarlet and yellow and silver, his blonde hair flying in the wind, his pale blue eyes fixed on hers as he drew alongside.

Greville.

She turned away sharply and looked ahead. He eyed Jonathan, then wheeled his mount in front of the waggon, holding up his hand. Jonathan, forced to halt on a hill, cursed under his breath. 'Get something behind the wheels', he said to Mary.

Greville said, as if speaking to a dog, 'Are you a convict?'

'Yes.'

'Yes what?'

'Yes, I'm a convict.'

Greville walked his stallion forward a pace. 'Sir!'

'Sir!' Jonathan spat out the word like an obscenity.

Greville looked down at Mary who was on her knees wedging rocks behind the rear wheels, her hands and apron dirtied. 'As I thought. A pair of grubby felons. What have you got in that cart?'

'Supplies.' Jonathan stared at him with smouldering hatred in his dark eyes.

'Of what kind?'

'You can look for yourself.'

'I will.' The ensign gave his thin smile. 'After you've unloaded them.' Jonathan's big hands clenched on the reins but he didn't move. Greville said harshly, 'Unload the cart.'

Still Jonathan didn't move. Then, very slowly, he climbed down, untied the tarpaulin and threw it back. He took a grip on a crate that had 'Capt. Wiltshire, Westbury' chalked on it.

Greville went very still. He sat in his saddle for a

moment, horrified at the thought that he had been about to search his commanding officer's belongings. He said, 'Wait! Did your master give you a pass?'

Wordlessly, Jonathan took the paper from his pocket and handed it up. Greville read it. He looked up. 'The girl. Is she assigned to Captain Wiltshire?' When Jonathan nodded, he threw the pass down into the dirt, swung his horse round and spurred away.

As Jonathan picked it up, Mary came from the rear of the cart. 'Could I see it?'

He shrugged and handed the paper to her. When he saw her eyes following the handwriting he said, almost in a whisper, 'You can read.' She looked up at him. Then, roughly, he snatched the pass from her, strode to the horse's head and urged the animal up the hill.

Greville trotted the stallion into the stable-yard at Westbury, Captain Wiltshire's hundred-and-fifty-acre farm, and threw the reins at a passing convict. He strode along the wide verandah of the spacious homestead that was set among lawns and trees, and was received with warmth by the Captain's wife. Although Greville was some ten years her junior, they were surprisingly similar in appearance and might have been taken for brother and sister. Louisa Wiltshire, too, had the same cold good looks, the same brittle, dispassionate voice, the air of arrogant boredom. She was gowned, coiffeured and delicately perfumed in a manner that might have seemed more appropriate to an afternoon tea-party at Carlton House than to the day-room of a property in New South Wales. 'How nice to see you, Mr Greville', she said, smiling as he was ushered in. 'Such a pleasant surprise.' He had come as a light in the Antipodean darkness with his good looks, his flattery and his reminders of a society she badly missed, and it gave her a delicious thrill to realise that, from the moment of their first meeting when her husband had invited him to dinner, he was obviously mad for her.

Greville bowed, smiling inwardly at the note of intimacy in her voice. He recognised it from long experience and it was apparent that the silly woman thought he wanted nothing more than to hop into her bed. The bed, for God's sake, of his commanding officer! Well, let her think it. The wives of influential men could be very useful if they could be made to pant a little. 'I have often wished to avail myself of your kind invitation, ma'am. Alas, my duties have prevented me. Your husband, the Captain, keeps my nose well and truly to the grindstone.'

'Then I shall scold him severely, Mr Greville. There are so few people in this colony with any art of conversation.' She settled gracefully on a sofa and waved him to a chair. 'He should be home presently with our latest acquisition. A maidservant from the *Britannia*.'

Greville raised his eyebrows. 'From the . . .? You surprise me, ma'am.'

'How so?'

He appeared slightly confused. 'As you know, I myself came out on the *Britannia*. . . .' He let his voice tail off as if regretting he'd spoken in the first place.

'Yes?' Louisa was intrigued.

'Well, I. . . .' He made a deprecatory gesture. 'The fact is, I hesitate to offend your sense of delicacy, ma'am. But I feel duty bound to tell you that the convict women on that vessel were highly immoral in their conduct. Without exception, they behaved throughout the voyage in a way that was repugnant to any man of decency.' He saw her eyes widen, her hand go to her throat. 'Forgive me, ma'am. I have distressed you.' He stood up. 'But my conscience forbade me to hold my peace. There are your children to. . . .'

'Please, Mr Greville.' She rose and put a slim hand on his arm. 'You must not apologise. I know you have our welfare at heart.'

'True, ma'am.' Greville was a noble figure, his face full of concern, his back ramrod-straight against the forces of evil. 'When I think of you sheltering such a woman in your family, I cannot remain silent.' He patted her hand. She deserved that much, at least.

*   *   *   *   *

It hadn't been at all what she'd expected, Polly reflected as, full of a really satisfying stew, she sat in the firelight in the tiny back room of 'The Bird in the Barley'. The inn was so far from civilisation that only a simpleton would have thought of building there, ten miles beyond Parramatta where a track ran through a hollow under the tall trees. It wasn't much bigger than a large dog-kennel, really, and it was painfully obvious that it needed what Mr Price had called a woman's touch. That was rather endearing; it was nice to be needed. And Mr Price himself was rather a dear, with his high hopes of bringing all the world to his inn-door, his ambition to set up as a brewer one day, and his child-like honesty, his consideration. It had occurred to Polly that she hadn't been all that honest with him herself in the matter of her cropped head, but when she'd pulled her cap off at last to show him all he'd said had been, 'Oh, lass, what have they done to you?' He'd been a convict, too—transported for stealing a pheasant net and sent out with the First Fleet. Now he had his liberty, but he had no desire to return to Surrey and his poacher's life. He was, Polly reflected in the warm, cosy glow of the fire, a man you could become rather fond of, in a motherly kind of way. But hardly. . . . She looked up at him. 'Where', she asked conversationally, 'will I be sleeping, Mr Price?'

'The. . . .' He avoided her eye. 'The bed's up there.' He pointed to a kind of large shelf that ran back under the ceiling. A ladder was fixed to the wattle-and-daub wall in a tangle of empty sacks, bags of onions, ropes and pieces of harness.

'Is it all right if I have a look?'

'Of course, Polly.' He rubbed his hands in front of the fire without looking at her. He adjusted a glowing log with great care and precision.

'It's so cosy up here.' She stood on the ladder, looking at the possum rugs and blankets.

'Er, yes. It catches the warm air from the fire.' He hummed a little tune under his breath.

'It'll be very nice.'

He turned his head and looked up at her. His chubby face

broke into the smile of a small boy promised a toffee apple. Why, yes, he thought, it'll be very nice, to be sure. It had been very lonely here at 'The Bird'.

'Where do you sleep, Mr Price?'

'Up there, Polly.'

'And you've given it to me!' Polly said gratefully. 'You're a very kind man. But where will you sleep now, Mr Price?'

The smile faded like that of a small boy whose toffee-apple has been rudely snatched away. 'There's—well, there's the guest accommodation off the tap-room. I'll bed down there.' He sighed and picked up a candle. 'Well, goodnight, Polly.' He raised it to her in salute and went out to the front room of the inn.

'Goodnight, Mr Price.' Polly stood on the ladder, smiling gently as the rough-timbered door closed. Yes, he *was* rather a dear, was Wilberforce Price.

* * * * *

It was quite inexplicable, Mary thought as she sat with a dish of cold meat in front of her in the vast Wiltshire kitchen where the golden light of the candles reflected off the gleaming copper pans, the rows of spotless china, the polished glass of the cupboards. Inexplicable—and frightening, too, the hostility that had been shown to her by the middle-aged cook. The woman had almost pushed Jonathan out of the kitchen after he'd carried Mary's bundle in. Then she'd slammed the food down on the table and eyed Mary as if she'd had the plague before she'd gone to fetch Mrs Wiltshire. And Mary had heard her say under her breath as she went, 'Well! You wouldn't think it to look at her!'

She sat with little appetite for the food, miserably wondering what it would be like here and feeling desperately tired after the journey on the jolting cart. Then she heard quick footsteps on the stone floor. She stood up as a slim, fair-haired woman with an oval face and a small, compressed mouth walked into the kitchen and said, without any preamble at all, 'I'm afraid you are not the sort of servant we require. It is quite impossible for you to remain here with us.'

Mary stared at her, wondering if, perhaps, she was dreaming. But Louisa Wiltshire's cold, clipped voice went on, 'When you have finished eating, Mrs Kemp will show you to bed. You will be going back to Sydney Town in the morning.' She turned and went out.

CHAPTER FIVE

'I must confess,' Captain Wiltshire said, 'I'm surprised.'
He had come home later than he had anticipated, tired after
his long ride through the dark, and domestic fusses were
the last things he desired. He stood with his back to the fire
in the elegant, lamplit day-room, a handsome, slightly
florid man in his mid-forties, frowning a little as he
watched his wife who was seated on the brocade sofa with
her embroidery frame. 'What has she done?'

'It isn't a matter of what she has done, Charles.' Louisa
had that slight edge to her voice, he observed, that always
meant a long, involved argument. He sighed mentally,
went to a side-table and poured himself a glass of brandy.
She said, her needle jabbing precisely, 'It's a matter of what
she is. A girl of poor moral character.' The needle stabbed.
'A drab.'

He put the stopper back in the decanter. There had been
drabs in that hospital ward, certainly, but the girl who'd
been pointed out to him hadn't been of that description.
Pale and scared-looking, her eyes luminous with tears, but
with character in her face. Pretty little thing, too, in a
healthy, honest sort of fashion. That had been Balmain's
view, at all events . . . . 'And what led you to form this
opinion?'

'Mr Greville was here this afternoon.'

'Oh.' He went back to the fire with his drink. Bit of a
devil with the ladies, Ensign Greville, he wouldn't be

surprised. Type Louisa would take to—suave, polished, debonair, what? But far too ambitious to try any nonsense with the wife of his commanding officer. Poor Louisa. He sipped his brandy.

'He told me.' Louisa raised her china-blue eyes to her husband. 'The females on the *Britannia* were of a particularly dissolute character. Without exception.' He raised his eyebrows, wondering if Greville had obtained his information from first-hand experience. 'It's a disgrace', Louisa said firmly, 'that they should even consider assigning such a girl to us.'

If it came to a choice between Greville's opinion and that of William Balmain, the captain reflected, he knew which he'd plump for. The Chief Surgeon's ability to assess men, women and horses was a byword in the colony. 'I'm sure they haven't', he said. 'The girl was singled out by Surgeon Balmain as being of good character and intelligence. He was anxious that she should be assigned to a suitable home.'

'Well,' the cutting edge in Louisa's voice was a little sharper, he noticed, 'she seems to have ingratiated herself with Doctor Balmain, but are we to ignore Mr Greville?'

'Not at all.' Wiltshire never ignored anybody's advice. But he never failed to weigh it carefully, either. 'I think, however, we are obliged to give the girl a chance to prove herself. Particularly since there seems to be no-one else remotely suitable.'

Louisa said sharply, 'But I've already told her she won't be staying.'

The Captain's level stare met her cool blue eyes. There were times when dear Louisa had to be reminded that she was not his Corps commander. He said in a voice that his junior officers would have recognised very well, 'Then we must simply tell her that we have reconsidered and that she will be given a fair trial.' She dropped her eyes to her embroidery. 'Well? Are you going to speak to her?'

'Since you insist,' she said bleakly, 'I shall. But not now, Charles.' This absurd sympathy he had for the lower orders was most vexing at times. She had been compelled to surrender to it but she could still fight a brief delaying

71

action and obtain a little of her own way in this matter. 'Let her wait until morning. It will do her no harm to pass the night in thinking of her—possible future.'

And so, in the morning, Mary was even more confused than ever when she discovered, after a wretched night, that Mrs Wiltshire had reversed her decision. It was done with obvious reluctance, with the threat of instant ejection from the household being thrown in as the penalty for pilfering or slovenliness. Mrs Kemp, the cook, followed up with a list of daily duties that sounded like the Labours of Hercules, offering a box on the ear if they weren't performed to her satisfaction. But, at least, the uncertainties were over for Mary and she knew where she was to lay her head that night.

Louisa Wiltshire, however, did not forget what the fascinating Mr Greville had said. She kept a cold blue eye on Mary and it was on that same morning that she was able to vent her feelings a little by giving the girl the edge of her tongue.

The newly-appointed scullery-maid had gone out to the pump with a pail. Jonathan Garrett, in a leather apron, had been paring a horse's hoof with a rasp. He'd hailed her, then walked across to help her at the pump. It was at that moment that Jonas Pike, the overseer, rode into the yard, followed by three convicts.

He was a curiously frog-like man, thick-set and with a flat head, an abnormally wide mouth and bulbous eyes; he had been a former prisoner of the Crown, but it was more than a man's hide was worth even to hint at it. He turned his protruding green eyes on Mary and demanded the water in her bucket for his horse.

She said apologetically, 'This water's for the house, sir.' Mrs Kemp was waiting for it, her red, work-toughened hand ready with the promised box on the ear if the water wasn't instantly forthcoming.

Pike's pallid face reddened at being crossed. 'Then you'll needs draw another bucket, won't you?'

'I don't have the time, sir. I'm needed inside.' She was edging towards the kitchen door.

'But you've time for idle chatter with Garrett there. Mooning about and gossiping!'

A tall, black-haired convict with a blue-stubbled, weather-beaten face said, 'Sure and it beats scrub-bashing in this brutal desolation, and that's no lie.' He waved a dirty hand airily. 'Morning, miss.' The other convicts sniggered at his impudence.

Pike began to swell with rage. Jonathan moved forward and took his horse. 'It was my fault, Mr Pike. I started her talking. I'll see the horse gets water.'

Pike glowered as Mary went indoors with her pail and Jonathan led the horse away. Then, his face still flushed with fury, the overseer waddled into the house. It was only a few minutes later that Louisa stormed into the kitchen. 'Just now,' she snapped at Mary, 'you were seen idling in the yard with Garrett. That is precisely the type of behaviour that will not be tolerated here. You may regard this as your first and final warning.'

Angry and bewildered, Mary was sent out for more water by the smugly hectoring cook and it was when she went into the yard that she saw the other half of Jonas Pike's small revenge.

Jonathan and the other three men, jeered on by Pike, were in the shafts of a loaded cart, being used as draught animals.

*   *   *   *   *

In 'The Bird in the Barley', however, all was peace and quiet. So much peace, in fact, and so much quiet that Polly was bored almost to distraction. Will said defensively, 'It's a slow trade this early in the week.'

'I just thought, as it's getting on to midday . . . .' She went to stare out of the window at the trees. There wasn't much else to do, after sweeping up and tidying everything in sight.

Will Price was racking up mugs. 'Oh, there'll be customers by and by. But Saturday nights are the busy times. Why, I counted fourteen heads in here Saturday

73

before last. Near run me off my feet, they did, all singing and laughing fit to bust. So there's nothing amiss with a little peace and quiet among all the jollity.'

She said carefully, not wanting to hurt his feelings, 'True, Mr Price. But I was thinking that, while we were waiting for the trade to build up, I could employ meself making a few improvement here and there.'

He nearly dropped a mug. 'Improvements?'

She said quickly, 'Oh, it's a grand place that ye have, to be sure, Mr Price, but—well, I was thinking how nice it'd be to see some curtains on the window. Some nice gingham curtains, perhaps.'

'Curtains?'

'Aye, such a simple thing to set the place off to perfection. To go with the sawdust on the floor.'

'Sawdust?' What was the woman thinking of? All these fripperies would cost a fortune . . . .

'And the elegant spittoons we'd be providing, to show the customers they're among gentlefolk.'

He drew a deep breath. 'Now look, Polly . . . .'

'Gentlefolk', she said meaningly, 'who are not above paying a little extra for the comforts of respectability out here in the virgin wilderness.' She paused. 'D'ye see what I'm driving at, Mr Price?'

'I do.' His round face took on a touch of awe. 'Oh, yes, Polly. I do indeed.'

* * * * *

There were others in the colony also who, like Polly McNamara, had an eye for the main chance. The New South Wales Corps, in fact, thought of little else. Captain Charles Wiltshire, although a man of kindness and humanity, had come to the colony to achieve a station in life that he could not have attained in England. Now, he informed his wife, he was being hamstrung by Governor Hunter who begged the pastoralists to increase their herds but who was extraordinarily niggardly in the provision of felons to do the work. There was, however, a certain Captain John Macarthur who opposed the Governor not only in the matter of convict labour but also concerning the officers' trading privileges with which the Governor wished to meddle. Macarthur had offered to sell to Wiltshire one of the strongest of the merino rams that he had lately imported from the Cape of Good Hope. Now that Spain had joined with Bonaparte and ceased to export wool to England, it was quite possible that a far-sighted producer of the raw fibre could corner the market in the wool trade. 'Think of it, my dear', Wiltshire said enthusiastically. 'This struggling infant colony supplanting the might of Spain to become one of England's most important trading partners!'

If it came to a choice between Governor Hunter and Captain Macarthur, it was obvious where his loyalty would lie.

Greville's loyalty lay only with himself. Piqued that his scheme for Mary's dismissal had failed, he derived much satisfaction, when he was next invited to dine with the Wiltshires, from baiting her obliquely while she was placing dishes before him. 'Rumour has it', he said, 'that Corporal Bonaparte will look to the Irish to assist him against England.'

Louisa had been listening to him with rapt attention. 'Pudding, Mr Greville?' she asked.

'Thank you, ma'am.' He watched Mary place a jug of cream on the table. 'But the Corsican would need to be in dire straits before calling on assistance from the Irish—although it is stated as fact that they can charge in several different directions at once when the mood takes them. Even backwards.' He watched her leave the room, her face pink with anger. 'I see', he said casually, 'that you have kept the *Britannia* girl on.'

Louisa glanced briefly at her husband. 'Charles and I are yet in some disagreement over her future, Mr Greville. She is on a period of probation.'

'In view of the war,' Greville said, coming as close to

expressing his disapproval as he dared, 'I believe we shall have trouble with the Irish convicts and it will take more than probation to restrain them.'

Captain Wiltshire frowned. 'Then it must be the gibbet and the lash for the trouble-makers. The easiest way to put down a rebellion is to stop it before it begins.'

That, Greville thought, was Captain Dennott's philosophy exactly. Strange to hear it from the good-natured Captain. It showed what these reformers and humanitarians and the like were capable of when their self-interest was threatened. He ate his pudding, pleased with his little triumph over Mary.

She, with the resilience of youth, was beginning to settle down at Westbury into a pattern of daily drudgery—a routine that was broken only by the arrival of a visitor, some domestic crisis or, on one momentous occasion, a convict being brought into the kitchen by Jonathan with snake-bite.

He was the tough, tall, blue-jowled fellow who had bidden her good morning in the yard on the occasion of her encounter with Jonas Pike. He was a 'Government stroker', she'd heard, on loan to Captain Wiltshire from the prison farm at Toongabbie. He came limping into the kitchen, groaning piteously. Mary said, 'Mother of God!' Snake-bite, she knew, could be fatal and, very often, there was little that could be done about it. 'Are you in pain?'

Jonathan supported the casualty to a seat at the kitchen table. The convict with the black hair said, 'A noggin of rum'd go a long way to ease me suffering.' A pair of bright, bird-like eyes stared into hers. One of them, to her surprise, closed in a wink.

Jonathan said, 'Where's cook?'

'Lying down.' Mary moved away. 'I'd best fetch her to dress that wound.'

He raised a hand. 'Ah, don't trouble yourself. Truth to tell, it was no snake. Didn't I make the marks meself with a twig?'

'Why, in heaven's name?' Mary went back to the table.

'Oh, I just felt like a change of scenery and a chance to

76

talk with a fine upstanding cut of a girl like yourself.' She smiled at his cheerful impudence. 'And a smile like that', he said, grinning at her, 'would cure anything from snakebite to starvation, and so says Dinny O'Byrne from County Wicklow.'

She laughed. You couldn't help it, with his eyes twinkling like that. 'I'm Mary Mulvane.'

'So Jonathan told me. Over on the *Britannia*, I hear.'

'Aye. For seven years. And yourself?'

'Ah,' he said vaguely, 'about the same.'

Jonathan, who had been peering nervously out of the window, turned his head. 'I heard you was a lifer.'

'Well, maybe I am and maybe I'm not. Life's a thing of elasticity, I always say. But I'll tell you one thing.' The banter went out of his voice and the twinkling black eyes hardened. 'I'll survive. Because I can face up to the realities of the situation, Miss Mulvane. And if you can conform to the system, devilish and brutal as it might seem, then there's a chance you'll survive it, too. It's far better to bend like grass before the wind than be shattered like the tall oak.' He turned to Jonathan. 'And the same applies to you, boyo!'

Jonathan came away from the window. 'But it's not easy to bend to Pike. I don't know how you keep your temper, Dinny.'

Mary saw the smouldering rebellion in his eyes. She said quickly, 'Mr O'Byrne's right. There's nothing to be gained by a show of defiance. It only gives them the excuse to strike another blow at us . . . .' She stopped. With a sudden chill she realised she was using the very same words her father had used on an Irish hillside on that day, so long ago now it seemed, when Michael Connor had shown him the English proclamation. She said quietly, 'I've learnt that from my own bitter experience.'

She thought a great deal about Dinny O'Byrne's philosophy during the next few weeks while she watched Jonas Pike goad him and Jonathan, jeering at them while he worked them like slaves. She herself worked like a slave in the kitchen from dawn until the final scrubbing of the kitchen floor after everyone else was in bed. One day in July, when she was fetching wood for the fire in the day-room, she overheard Louisa Wiltshire conducting a lesson for her children. Edward, a thin-faced, fair-haired six-year-old, was reading aloud, half his attention on the window for a glimpse of the waggon that was due to arrive with his father's merino ram at any moment. 'A dormouse', he read, his voice flat and bored, 'is a sleepy mouse but this is not a . . . .'

'Why', asked Elizabeth, a pretty child of seven, 'is it called a dormouse, mama?'

'Gracious heaven,' said Louisa fretfully, 'am I to be expected to know everything?'

'Begging your pardon, ma'am,' Mary said, 'but they're called dormice because they sleep through the winter months.'

Edward eyed her scornfully. 'It's because they have doors on their houses.'

'It's because they sleep, Master Edward,' Mary said gently, 'all winter long. Their name comes from *dormire*, the Latin word meaning "to sleep".'

To Louisa Wiltshire, it was as if the bookcase had suddenly addressed her in fluent French. 'How', she asked, astounded, 'do you know that?'

'Why, I learnt it at school, ma'am.'

'School?' said Louisa blankly. Schools were for those who could afford them. How could an Irish peasant girl go to school?

'My father was schoolmaster at Rathcurran, where I lived.' She found she could say it now, and proudly, without the tears filling her eyes.

'You mean—you can read and write?' Somehow, Louisa felt as if she'd harboured an impostor in her house. 'Why was I not informed of this?'

'No-one ever asked me, ma'am.'

Edward, sensing his mother's preoccupation, ran to the window. 'It's papa! And he has the merino. Come on, everyone, it's the sheep from Spain!'

And it was while they were admiring the ram that Captain Wiltshire gave her a note to take to Jonas Pike who was supervising the removal of the stump of a tree, his method being to have his men dig around the roots then put on harness like horses and pull it out of the ground. He made sure that, of the six convicts in the gang, Dinny and Jonathan were singled out for the heavier share of the labour. Mary stood appalled at the bleeding weals across their shoulders where the harness cut into them, the state of complete exhaustion of one of the older men called Stokes. The overseer tore the note out of her hand, read it, then told her to take herself off. 'Travers,' he said, 'I'm leaving you in charge while I'm gone. I want that stump out by the time I return, or it'll be the worse for you.' He climbed onto his horse and rode off.

Dinny O'Byrne went to the white-faced, gasping Stokes who had collapsed in a heap. 'Get me some water', he said to Jonathan.

Travers, proud of his temporary authority, said, 'All right! Take the strain! You heard what Mr Pike said.'

Jonathan gave his canteen to Dinny O'Byrne, who held it to Stokes's blue lips. Travers shouted, 'I'm in charge, O'Byrne! Pick up the harness!'

'Now is that any way to talk to a fellow-convict, Travers?'

'You're a bloody fool, O'Byrne', Travers said furiously. 'There's nothing to be gained by mutiny.'

Dinny put back his head and laughed. 'Mutiny, is it? By all the saints, Travers, if I had a mind to mutiny I'd pick a more formidable opponent than a broken-down whore-master from Leicester Square. I reckon the break'll do none of us any harm. It might even save poor Stokes's life.'

And so it was that, when Pike returned after half an hour, the work was very far from being completed. As he rode up he yelled, 'Travers, you bastard! I told you I wanted that stump out of the ground!'

Travers said cringingly, 'They refused to work, sir. O'Byrne and Garrett and Stokes.'

Pike glared at them. 'Your handiwork, I'll warrant, O'Byrne. You're nothing but a trouble-maker. I picked it the first time I set eyes on you.'

'He does the work of three,' Jonathan snapped, 'and you know it, Pike!'

A vein in the overseer's thick neck swelled as he bawled, 'Hold your tongue, you young lout!'

Dinny said quickly, 'Steady, lad. I can handle me own problems.'

But Jonathan's big hands were clenching and unclenching as all the fury and frustration came pouring out. 'It's a miracle we can lift a hoe on the rations you hand out, let alone strain like bullocks. You cheat us out of our food so you can sell it . . . .'

Pike, his face contorted with rage, kicked his horse towards Jonathan. 'If you can't learn to hold your tongue, Garrett, then by God I'll teach you!' He lifted the quirt that hung from his wrist. Jonathan side-stepped, grabbed him by the leg and pulled him off the horse.

The overseer, mouthing incoherently, scrambled to his feet. And, with the hatred and loathing of months behind it, Jonathan's work-hardened fist slammed into his mouth and felled him like a tree.

'No!' Much too late, Dinny managed to get a grip on his friend. 'For the love of God, man!'

Pike came up on one elbow, wiping blood from his mouth. 'You'll pay for this!' he said thickly. 'Striking an overseer. You all witnessed it. You'll go to the magistrate for this, Garrett.'

He was interviewed first by Captain Wiltshire. Mary tried to comfort him while he was waiting in the kitchen. The Captain, she said, was a kindly man. Everyone knew that. But Jonathan had been with Wiltshire longer than she had. He knew that Wiltshire was also an Army officer, a disciplinarian who could never let a blow struck at a superior go unpunished. He knew, before he went into the day-room where Wiltshire sat as if at a court-martial, how it would go. Next morning, Mary saw him dragged out of the stable, where he had been locked up all night, by Pike and his toady Travers. They tied his hands; Pike mounted his horse. Then Travers handed the end of the rope to the overseer and the horse moved off, Jonathan stumbling behind it.

Even as she watched, she too was sent for by Captain Wiltshire. Filled with apprehension, she went into the room where he stood at the window, a military, erect figure with the light catching the dark, greying hair that was tied back with the regulation black ribbon. Louisa sat in a chair, her eyes on her embroidery as she worked. Wiltshire said, 'Mary, I am told you know how to read and write.'

'Yes, sir.' Her mind filled with the picture of Jonathan stumbling as he tried to keep up with Pike's horse, she said, 'Am I to be punished for it?'

'Of course not, girl.' Why in heaven's name should she think a thing like that? Wiltshire wondered. Does she think me an ogre? 'Far from it. I have suggested to mistress, and she has agreed to the proposal, that you be given a trial as temporary governess until someone more qualified can be found. Would you like the position?'

Mary stared at him, taken aback by the suddenness of it. Governess! Why, that would mean children to teach, and books, instead of pans to scour and the bullying Mrs Kemp. 'Yes', she said at last. 'Yes, sir, I would.'

*　　*　　*　　*　　*

Wilberforce Price had noticed with misgiving that Polly was becoming 'moony', as he put it. While still cheerful and industrious, there were times, increasingly frequent, when she would go to the window and stare out through the smart new red-and-white gingham curtains, or merely stand still wherever she was, lost in thought. One evening, after he'd counted the takings, he said, 'Polly girl, if I had a hat I'd take it off to you. That's the best Tuesday I've had since I can remember. What d'you say to a nip of brandy to celebrate our success?'

She said quietly, 'I think I'd prefer to turn in, if it's all the same to you.'

He straightened up from where he was scooping money into a bag. 'Not feeling poorly, are you?' he said with concern.

'I've felt better.'

'It's the long hours, girl. You've been pushing yourself too hard.'

She shrugged. 'Oh, it's not the hours I mind. Or the work. I think it's the talk that wearies me. Men talking all day about cattle prices and who runs the colony and . . . .'

He said, with more perception that she had imagined him to possess, 'You're missing the company of your own kind. A little female chat . . . .'

She nodded. 'Aye.' She was silent for a moment. 'There was a girl that sailed with me on the *Britannia*. Mary Mulvane. We were good friends.'

'I'll ask about', he said instantly. 'See if anyone's heard of her.'

Some of her dullness seemed to vanish. 'Would you do that for me, Mr Price?'

'I'll do it . . .' he grinned his chubby grin at her, '. . . on the condition that we drop all this Mr Price business and you start calling me Will.'

'Why, I'll be more than happy to,' Polly smiled her warm, lovely smile back at him, 'Will.'

* * * * *

The Reverend Samuel Marsden was over-weight for his thirty-three years but his stocky frame was still that of the man who, at one time, had worked with his father as apprentice blacksmith in the village of Farsley in Yorkshire. Red-faced and choleric, he prided himself on being a simple man of simple faith. And indeed he was, for selfishness, avarice and brutality are basic simple qualities, and Marsden had them all. While having all the hypocrisies of the period on his tongue, he was guided by one simple precept, the old Yorkshire dictum that said: 'If ever tha does owt for nowt, allus do it for thysen'. A magistrate and man of the cloth, he was known professionally as The Flogging Parson.

Jonathan was taken before him at a bad time, when a cargo of particularly choice trade goods had arrived on the *Reliance*, and Marsden wished to investigate their possibilities as soon as possible. He and his two fellow-magistrates had disposed of the previous case with celerity and he saw no reason why there should be any delay in dealing with the surly ruffian who now stood before him. 'Proceed, Mr Fitchley', he said impatiently.

The clerk read, 'Jonathan Edward Garrett, convict labourer assigned to Captain Wiltshire of Westbury. Charged with insolence, refusing to perform his allotted work, and striking the overseer, Mr Jonas Pike.'

Marsden scowled. 'And is Mr Pike present in this court?'

Pike, swollen-mouthed and a picture of injured innocence, stood up. 'I am, Your Honour.'

'And are there witnesses to the aforesaid action?'

'There are, Your Honour. George Travers.' The clerk passed up a paper to the magistrates. 'And, further, a signed deposition by John Hopgood. Both convict labourers from Westbury.'

Marsden blew his nose resoundingly, then rustled through some papers on his bench. He looked up, his eyes like flints as he stared at Jonathan. 'So you're an insolent fellow, Garrett?'

'No, Your Honour.' Jonathan looked about the courtroom like a bull in a pen, and with about as much understanding of what was going on. All this writing things down and reading them out—what was it for? If only he could read and write, perhaps it would make sense. And what was a 'deposition'?

'Mr Pike swears you are.' Marsden tapped a paper in front of him. 'He has a witness to prove it, what's more. Why do you refuse to work?'

'I—I don't refuse, Your Honour.'

'But I have it before me in black and white.' Another document. '"Refused to do his work", again with a witness. And when Mr Pike attempted to chastise you for your sinful idleness, you struck him. Well?'

Whatever you said didn't matter, not if it wasn't written

83

down in black and white. Why had he never realised before how important it was to be able to read? Mary could read . . . . Now, Marsden was taking up yet another paper and the clerk's quill was scratching, scratching . . . . 'Transported to the colony for seven years per *Indispensable* for highway robbery.' All that had happened on the other side of the world, all down on a small piece of paper for Marsden to read. So what could he say? It was all true—well, in one way, but not in the way it sounded, and he had no pieces of paper to prove otherwise . . . .

'Have you nothing to say in your defence?' As incorrigible a rogue as any I've set eyes on, Marsden said to himself. Big. Powerful. Malevolent. The very personification of the forces of darkness. 'Come, sir, we are not here at your disposal. If you have anything to say, then say it, man!' The scratch-scratch of the quill sounded like a sputtering fuse as the clerk wrote *The prisoner remains silent*. Marsden turned to his colleagues. 'I take the silence to be an obvious admission of guilt.' The others nodded. Marden cleared his throat. 'Jonathan Edward Garrett,' he said solemnly, the flat Yorkshire vowels echoing round the court-room, 'I find you guilty of the charges and tainted with the canker of rebellion. It is the Lord's will that such canker be rooted out before it corrupts and destroys beyond all redemption, and it is in accord with His will that I sentence you to a punishment of seventy-five lashes. Next!'

It took two burly redcoats to drag Jonathan out, shouting and fighting. Pike and Travers smirked at one another. 'Seventy-five lashes!' Pike said. He chuckled. 'And I'd only hoped for fifty!'

CHAPTER SIX

Gestures of defiance, Jonathan realised, were futile. In dealing with the Jonas Pikes of this world brains would beat brawn any time and, even while he was lying bloody and gasping in the stable after they'd brought him back to Westbury in a cart, he'd asked Mary to teach him to read and write. She had agreed with enthusiasm and, while he was recovering, she'd sat at his side with a slate, patiently teaching him to draw letters. But he was not a good student. All his life he had dealt in practicalities and he wanted to be literate within the hour, as one would accomplish the shoeing of a horse. As the lessons dragged on, he fidgeted and allowed his attention to stray, leaping up to attend to the bay mare that needed liniment for the gall on her withers and leaving Mary hurt and exasperated. Finally, after she had chided him for whittling a stick when he should have been attending and he had told her he would do as he pleased, she had flung out of the stable in a temper and the lessons had come to an end.

That had been on a Sunday in the August of 1797 when Mary had been in the New South Wales colony for two months. It was on that same Sunday that Will Price and Polly had decided to close the inn at midday to make their journey to Westbury, for Will's efforts to find her had been successful and with typical good nature he had insisted on accompanying Polly on her visit. Polly's efforts at improvement at the inn had also been successful—too successful for her liking on this particular occasion, for the tap-room was full and the customers grumbled when they were told to drink up and leave its cosy conviviality to return to their wives.

The middle-aged man in the shabby knee-breeches and rusty brown coat, however, finished off his pickled pork and corn willingly enough, tossed back the remains of his drink and complimented Will on his victuals as he paid his account. He was Isaac Nichols, a shrewd, blunt-spoken north-countryman who, in spite of his down-at-heel appearance, held a post of considerable importance in the colony—that of Chief Government Overseer for convict labour. He smiled civilly at Will and he was on his way to the door when the New South Wales Corps sergeant came in.

'Sorry, sir', Will called cheerfully. Polly was in the back room, her shawl and bonnet already on and the basket of cakes and savoury pies packed for a picnic with Mary. 'We're closing for the day.'

The sergeant, ruddy-faced and heavily-built, stared at him expressionlessly. On his back he carried a squared-off knapsack in black leather with the royal monogram in yellow. His scarlet and yellow coat, buff breeches and black leggings were dusty and travel-stained; his white gloves were soiled and there was mud on the haft of the pike he carried. He said with a Lancashire accent, 'Good. Then we're just in time.' He turned and shouted, 'Bid the men step inside, Corporal!'

Will leaned on the bar, pleasant but firm. 'I said we're closed.'

The sergeant nodded at Nichols who stood watching. 'He doesn't seem to think so.'

'What I think', Nichols said levelly, 'is none of your concern, Sergeant. I happen to be just leaving.' A corporal and four privates, all with knapsacks and carrying Brown Bess muskets, pushed through the door, ducking their heads; in the tiny tap-room with its low ceiling they seemed like a regiment.

The sergeant eyed Nichols's craggy face, the slightly

hunched stance, the pewter buttons on the sleeve of the worn woollen coat. Nobody of consequence, he thought. 'We won't detain you, then. On your way.'

Nichols's eyes glinted. 'Here! Mind your manners!'

'Out, I said!'

Will rapped on the bar. 'Now just a minute!'

Nichols said angrily, 'You'll not talk to me like that and get away with it.'

'Oh, won't I?' The sergeant turned to the watching, grinning redcoats. 'Corporal! Show His Lordship to the door and be quick about it!' The corporal made a mock bow and held the door open.

Nichols, his eyes hard, his mouth set like a trap, clamped his old hat on his head. 'You'll hear more of this', he said grimly. He went out.

The sergeant placed his bicorne hat on the bar and moved to face Will. 'Now,' he said softly, 'you were saying summat about closing?'

They took off their packs and their shoulder-belts, their cartridge pouches, their bayonet-scabbards, and set to. In half an hour they were drunk; in another half-hour they'd lit a fire with the hessian mats Polly had made for the tables, pulled down her gingham curtains, overturned a table and smashed a chair in a fight. Polly had to take off her smart bonnet and cook for them, smearing herself with soot and flour; Will served the liquor. In return, their guests threw their unwanted scraps onto the floor and spilt rum and wine into the mess. There was no question of payment. 'Being but poor honest soldiers,' the sergeant said, grinning at Will, 'we're a bit short on hard cash. But I'm sure we can come to some arrangement. Seeing', he said meaningly, 'as how we're going to pass this way every two weeks.'

When they'd finally gone, the tap-room looked as if it had been sacked by enemy troops, then used as a cattle-pen. Polly looked at it and tears trickled down her cheeks at the cruelty, the stupidity of it. She said hopelessly, 'I suppose it's too late to go, now?'

Will slipped an arm round her shoulders. 'We'll leave all this', he said firmly. 'Put on that new bonnet of yours and we'll go and see your Mary.' When she turned to look at him they both knew that, out of this hurt and anger, a new stage had been reached in their life together.

*   *   *   *   *

Isaac Nichols was not a man to tolerate easily the insolence of office. He had business, in any case, with Captain Wiltshire that afternoon and so would be able to kill two birds with one stone. 'It concerns', he said after he had been shown into the Wiltshire day-room, 'the assignment of convict labour to your property.'

He had the Captain's fullest attention. It was that same unpaid labour, together with his grant of land, that enabled him to live as he did. And it was that life-style that had given his wife most of her *nouveau riche* pretensions and had, only a few minutes ago, led her into an argument with her husband about whether Nichols should be shown into her house at all. Wiltshire had explained why it was essential that Nichols, unprepossessing though he might be, former convict though he undoubtedly was, should be well received. The profits from their land, the upkeep of their household, the very food they ate, depended on the goodwill of this dour-faced man in the shabby coat who sat, now, perched on the edge of the sofa. 'Then', Wiltshire said hopefully, 'I am to receive the additional men for whom I applied?' He stood in front of the fire, the buttoned-back tails of his coat drawn aside to receive the welcome warmth.

'No, sir', Nichols said without any emotion whatsoever. 'His Excellency has instructed me that the Government'— he pronounced it 'Gumment'—'can no longer meet these constant demands for extra convict labour.'

'Surely,' Wiltshire frowned, 'His Excellency must realise . . . .'

'And, further,' said the flat, inexorable voice, 'that the Gumment can no longer afford to feed and clothe the three thousand men working gratis for the civil and military officers of this colony.'

'Come, come, Mr Nichols!' There was always a way round these difficulties, Wiltshire reminded himself. A gratuity, an honorarium, call it what you liked. 'Let us be realistic . . . .'

'By all means, Captain.' Nichols grubbed about in the flapped pockets of his rusty brown coat and tugged out a notebook. 'Here at Westbury,' he flicked through the pages with a none-too-well-washed thumb, 'you have thirteen male and female convicts employed on various duties. Fed and clothed by the Gumment at a cost of two hundred and sixty pounds per annum.'

'Well?' Fellow with a coat as old as that shouldn't be too difficult to persuade. How much, though?

'The Gumment can afford no more. In fact,' Nichols stared directly at the Captain, 'before long you will be required to support these men and women yourself.'

Good God! Wiltshire walked to the window and looked out to conceal his shock. He'd be ruined! After all his dreams of the Yorkshire mills competing to buy his wool. 'That is absolutely out of the question.' But all would yet be well. He remained at the window, his back straight, his shoulders square, waiting for his cue: *Of course, Captain, I could stretch a point in your case if* . . . . But Nichols said nothing. Wiltshire turned and met the Chief Overseer's level stare. Something in it told him there'd be no points stretched, no hints at a bribe. Very well, he thought grimly. If we can't outflank the enemy, we'll try a frontal attack. He said quietly, 'It would be foolhardy, Mr Nichols, to set yourself against the entire New South Wales Corps.'

'Maybe so.' The fellow didn't sound as if he cared a rap for the New South Wales Corps. 'Though I've already had one skirmish with your troops today. Even your rank and file have an exaggerated sense of their power.'

Louisa was right, Wiltshire thought. We should never have allowed the man into the house—his insolence knows no bounds. 'I must ask you', he said bleakly, 'to explain that, sir.'

'Aye,' Nichols said, 'I shall.'

*   *   *   *   *

To Mary, sitting lonely and unhappy by the creek after her quarrel with Jonathan, the totally unexpected appearance of Polly had been like a childhood Christmas. The two had flung themselves into each other's arms with Will Price grinning delightedly by, and then there'd been the picnic with the food as an actual impediment to the amount of talking they wanted to do. They talked of 'The Bird in the Barley', of Louisa Wiltshire, of Mary's promotion to governess, of the bad times and the good. They also talked of Jonathan Garrett. Mary became astonishingly reticent on this topic. 'And is he a nice lad?' Polly asked while Will was fetching water for the kettle.

'Who?'

'Why, the one you're teaching.'

'Nice enough. But', Mary added with a touch of fire, 'as stubborn as Paddy's mule.'

Polly was grinning for no apparent reason. 'That's a good sign in a man, I always say. A sign of determination. Is he nice-looking?'

Mary shrugged. Polly said dryly, 'You're a regular fountain of information.'

But, incredibly soon, it was time for Polly and Will to leave, with promises of further meetings and much waving from the cart as it lumbered off leaving Mary standing by the track, a forlorn figure dwarfed by the creek gums. When she returned to the house, Jonathan called to her from where he was filling the horse trough, but she went straight across the yard and indoors. She looked rather unhappy, he thought.

But not as unhappy as he felt himself.

And when, on the following day, Dinny O'Byrne asked him how the lessons were progressing, Jonathan gave him a short answer. They were beyond him, he said. Dinny snorted and moved on with the sack he was carrying, muttering to himself about people who gave in too easily. Jonathan stood glaring after him in none too good a temper; the exertion of unloading the waggon had opened up the weals on his back and they hurt like hell. He was definitely in no mood for the Wiltshire children who came playing round him. But Edward had been brought up to believe that convicts had been placed on this earth solely for his service and entertainment. He pointed imperiously at the cart with his toy sword. 'Where are those goods from?'

Jonathan said briefly, 'They're off a ship.'

'But where did the ship come from?'

'You'd better ask your father.' Jonathan reached for a tea-chest.

'I don't have to', the boy said triumphantly. 'It's written there. See?' He jabbed at the tea-chest with his sword. 'They're from Calcutta, in India.'

Jonathan said through his teeth, 'You're a very bright lad.'

Edward smirked. 'Elizabeth can't read yet. That's why she's my prisoner.' He led his captive off, she protesting that she could read perfectly well. Jonathan leaned with both hands on the tea-chest, staring at the stencilled letters.

Later, when Dinny brought him some tarts he'd stolen from under the cook's nose, he was still withdrawn and silent. 'I've been talking to Mary Mulvane', Dinny said, through a mouthful of tart. 'She said she might have been a little impatient.' He hoped God would forgive him for the terrible lie he'd just told; Mary had, in fact, merely informed him that Jonathan was too stubborn for his own good. Still, in for a penny, in for a pound. 'She hopes you'll overlook it, just this once.' He peered with his bright eyes at Jonathan but the lad just went on munching his tart as if he hadn't even heard. 'Well?' Dinny said, exasperated. 'What more can a girl do?'

Jonathan growled, 'She can make the first move.' He went off with a sack, wincing as it dug into his back.

'Oho!' Dinny called after him. 'So that's the way of it? Hurt your pride, has she? Bruised yer sense of importance . . . .' Instead of taking a sack on his own back, he jumped down from the tailboard of the cart. 'Here,' he said as a thought struck him, 'you've not taken to the girl, have you?'

Jonathan dumped his sack and returned. Dinny said, serious for once, 'Jonathan, you're thinking it's none of my business and maybe it's not. But I'm asking anyway.'

Jonathan reached up for a crate. Then he stopped. 'And why the devil should I give you an answer?'

'Because, if you told me you were getting keen on the girl, I'd have to tell you two things. First, she's not the sort of girl you can dance a jig with and then leave when you're sick of the tune.'

Jonathan was standing sulkily at the tail of the waggon, removing fragments of straw one by one from its floor. 'I know that.'

'And, second, ye can't think of marrying her. She's the one dream in her heart—to go back to Ireland. It's what she lives for.' Jonathan looked at him for a moment, then dropped his eyes. 'On top of all that,' Dinny said reasonably, 'I'd have to ask: what does a poor convict slave like you—or me—have to offer a girl like that?'

That evening, Jonathan sat on the dirt floor of his hut off the stable. In the light of a lantern, he was studying the tea-chest that stood against the wall. Into a piece of wood, he was laboriously carving the words CALCUTTA, INDIA. That was how Mary found him. 'I just came so see how you are, that's all', she said with a fine show of indifference. She looked away when she saw the dried blood on the back of Jonathan's shirt. *Like Michael Connor, when they beat him . . . holding his hands across the table . . . .*

He said, 'I'm fine.' He looked up from his carving. 'If you came to say you're sorry . . . .'

'Me?' She stared at him disbelievingly. 'I'm the one to be sorry?'

'Aye. Dinny told me . . . .'

'I came to ask', she said hotly, 'whether or not you wanted to continue lessons. I didn't come to be insulted.'

'Insulted? How have I insulted you?'

'A question foolish as that has no need of an answer. Do you want the lessons or not?'

Jonathan climbed to his feet stiffly. He looked at the carving he'd done. He turned to Mary and saw her looking at it, too. 'It's hopeless, isn't it?' he said miserably.

She said softly, 'It's very good, Jonathan.'

He kicked a bit of dirt. 'I—I want the lessons, Mary. If you'll give them to me.'

She looked at him for a moment. 'I'll just get the slate', she said.

*   *   *   *   *

The Officers' Mess at Parramatta Barracks was reminiscent of a London club—comfortably furnished, elegant in the proportions of its doors and windows, their dark wood contrasting with the white plaster of the walls, and snug on this wintry day with a log fire blazing for the comfort of the dozen or so officers who sat about drinking or playing cards in a haze of tobacco-smoke. Ensign Greville stood warming himself and studying a crude caricature of Governor John Hunter who was depicted in naval uniform with an arm slung round the shoulders of a villainous-looking convict in leg-irons. The caption read 'Comrades in Arms'. He passed the sketch across as Wiltshire came up to the fire. 'What d'you think, sir?'

Wiltshire looked at it. 'Frankly, I think it's seditious.' Damned childish, too, and in devilish poor taste, he thought. But he had other matters to discuss with Greville. He passed the sketch back to the ensign. 'Mr Nichols, the Chief Government Overseer, has complained of offensive behaviour by some of our men in a public house. A detail *en route* to the Hawkesbury. I've placed the sergeant concerned on report.'

Greville shrugged. 'We've met our obligations, then.'

'Not quite. Mr Nichols is already opposed to the military on the matter of free convict labour. I don't want this incident to cloud the issue.' He paused. 'Perhaps you should go and see the inn-keeper concerned. Make sure he's happy.'

'Apologise, sir?' The devil I will, Greville thought. To an inn-keeper?

'Of course not. Just be your usual—er, urbane self. Charm him, Greville. And', Wiltshire said pointedly, 'the sooner it's done, the better, eh?'

93

'I'll do my best, sir.' As Greville moved away he inclined his head deferentially to a tall man with a slightly prominent nose whose dark hair was cut shorter than most and whose eyes seemed to dominate the room as he entered. 'Captain Macarthur', Greville murmured as he passed.

The other nodded briefly and strode to the hearth. 'Charles! All is well, I trust?' he said, still with a touch of his native Devon in his deep voice. At the age of thirty, he had already held the posts of Inspector of Public Works and Paymaster to the New South Wales Corps and he was one of the most substantial farmers in the colony. He was also one of the most aggressive, having fought a duel with the captain of the *Neptune* transport before he'd even left England with the Second Fleet, then transferring his wife and infant son to the *Scarborough* in mid-ocean because of a quarrel with his senior officer, Captain Nepean.

'Hardly, John.' Wiltshire picked up the caricature that Greville had left on the mantelpiece. 'Not with things like this turning the Governor against us.'

Macarthur snorted. 'My dear fellow, Hunter's been against us for the past eighteen months. In that time he's done his utmost to withdraw our trading privileges, to ban the trade in spirits and now to squeeze us from our land by denying us convict labour. His aim is clearly to strip power from the military and place it in the hands of freed convicts—like the intractable Isaac Nichols.'

Wiltshire tapped the sketch. 'But he's the King's representative, when all's said and done. This smacks of treason.'

Macarthur's voice hardened. 'None the less, I don't intend to stand by and see everything I've worked for threatened by the wrong-headedness of a crusty Scottish naval officer. We must close ranks and make a stand. Hunter must buckle under or go.'

*   *   *   *   *

Spring came and went. By January, Jonathan had made considerable progress in his reading. Books had become familiar, if still not fully-understood things and he liked

94

more than anything to lie under one of the tall gums near the creek and be read to by Mary, enjoying the warm, soft air of summer, the gurgle of the water and, most of all, that soft, lilting voice that was like music to him, even when it was reading from a book concerning the geography of New South Wales. She looked at him after she'd read a passage. 'Is that the kind of land you're thinking of?'

Jonathan nodded. 'A place where I can make my own mark when I've served my time. In four more years.'

'Have you no ties at all with England?'

He shook his head. 'My father farmed near Romford, in Essex. He died before I was born, my mother soon after. I've no wish to go back. And land's all taken up there. Here, there's room to move.' He thought of the new factories that were being built, filling the rivers with filth, the sky with smoke. 'Here, everything's fresh.' He plunged his hand into the grass. 'The feel of it. Fresh.' He paused. Without looking at her, he said, 'Dinny tells me you'll not be staying when your time's up.'

'No', she said. 'No, I won't be staying.'

And, from the look of things, Dinny O'Byrne didn't think he'd be staying long, either. He came into the kitchen next day in a state of suppressed excitement, his manner so furtive that Mary thought he'd come to steal more tarts. 'Dinny!' He was opening the store-room door, peering out of the window. 'What is it?'

He came to the table where she was shelling peas, it still being part of her duty to help Mrs Kemp occasionally. He hissed into her ear, 'It's happening! At last! The rebellion of all Ireland!'

She dropped a pod-full of peas all over the floor. 'What are you saying?'

He glanced over his shoulder. 'Some lads fresh from Ireland told me. The news is six months old, but every county is to rise in this year of '98. And the French are to send a great fleet of ships to come to our aid and drive the English from the shores of Ireland for ever!'

She was shocked to see the tears standing in his eyes. Dinny, the one who laughed and joked with her! The philosophical Dinny who preached acceptance and talked of bending like the grass! 'Don't ye see, Mary,' he said, his voice thick with longing, 'we can all go home!'

But nobody went home. Dinny lived with his dream for fifteen months, impervious to argument or reason, until in the March of 1799 the news was brought by the *Rebecca*—that the bloody rising of '98 with its hideous atrocities committed by both sides had indeed taken place. The French General Humbert had, in fact, landed at Killala Bay and overcome the local militia. But Lord Cornwallis, the Lord Lieutenant, had kept the situation in check and Humbert had surrendered his sword at Ballinasloe on 9 September.

Greville was sent to read the governor's proclamation in 'The Bird in the Barley', together with the news of Nelson's victory at the Battle of the Nile. He threw in a bonus: 'A further piece of news to rouse your spirits', he said in the crowded tap-room, looking at Polly McNamara. 'I have just received a grant of forty acres of land, in this district. We are almost to be neighbours!' Both Polly and Will managed to keep their joy well in check at this news.

In the Officers' Mess at Parramatta, Wiltshire and Macarthur were also discussing Nelson's triumph over a game of rummy with two junior officers. 'As usual, they've made a great fuss about a *naval* victory', Wiltshire said disparagingly. 'Even made an anagram of Horatio Nelson's name: *Honor est a Nilo*—"There is fame from the Nile", or some such nonsense.'

Macarthur played a card. 'Let them choose what heroes they will, Charles, as long as their attention is diverted from the colony.' The junior officers chuckled dutifully. 'I have it on good authority that Governor Hunter is to be prised from the ship of state like the old barnacle he is, and not even Nelson's victory can save him.'

Wiltshire nodded absently as he studied his cards. Gubernatorial politics weren't much in his line and there were more pressing problems . . . . 'Touching the matter of convict labour—' he began.

Macarthur smiled. 'To be sure, Charles. We must do

something about Isaac Nichols, must we not?'

They interviewed him a day or so later, although it was more like a trial by ordeal than an interview. Nichols, his hair unkempt, his shoes muddied, sat uncomfortably on the edge of the sofa in the Wiltshire day-room, nervously balancing the cup and saucer Louisa had given him and made even more nervous by her genteel manner, her clipped politenesses, her offers of more tea, milk, sugar, as she hovered about him. Wiltshire, Macarthur and Greville, elegant and formidable in their military pageantry, sat watching him expressionlessly, relaxed and completely at ease. When the Chief Overseer had been made to feel sufficiently loutish and Louisa had retired into a corner with her embroidery, Wiltshire said, as if expressing only mild interest, 'Mr Nichols, are you in complete accord with His Excellency's policies on convict labour?'

Nichols tried to sip his tea without slurping it. 'I try to avoid policies, sir. I simply observe the prescribed regulations.'

'As I see it,' Macarthur said quietly, 'decisions regarding the allocation of convict labour are made almost entirely by you.'

Nichols put down his cup gingerly. 'You could say that, Captain. But all my decisions are dictated by the standing orders.'

'Of course, of course', Wiltshire said impatiently. 'But, Mr Nichols, you must understand our position. We control the largest farms, the largest herds. Surely you can't expect us to be crippled by measures designed for convict settlers and the like?'

Louisa's needle stopped. The three officers sat very still as they waited for Nichols's reply. For this, really, was the key question. To them it seemed perfectly reasonable that the regulations should be bent a little so that the rich might become even richer, the poor left to struggle as they could. To Nichols, it did not. The nervousness went out of his manner as he said, 'If the regulations make no distinction between you gentlemen and the convict settlers, then neither can I.'

The north country voice hung in the room like a challenge. Greville said coldly, 'You mean you choose not to, sir.'

'I have no choice.'

Macarthur nodded. The trial was over, the verdict passed. He pronounced sentence. 'Then, Mr Nichols, neither have we.' He inclined his head. 'Thank you for your time, sir.'

*   *   *   *   *

To Dinny O'Byrne, the failure of the '98 rising was a crushing blow. And, as if fate had wanted to crush his spirit even more completely, it was his arch-enemy Jonas Pike who had brought him the news, sneering at the Irish rout and throwing his hat in the air with glee. Dinny went into the kitchen with a load of wood, feeling as if the world had come to an end. 'If Bonaparte had won,' he said to Mary, his gypsy face contorted with disappointment, 'if only he'd succeeded, we'd be free now. Free to go home and start afresh.'

She stared at him, shocked at the change in his appearance, with the twinkle gone from his eye, the jaunty smile wiped from his lips. 'It's a cruel blow,' she said gently, 'but it's not the end. You must follow the advice you once gave us, Dinny. Bend like the grass, remember? And, one day . . . .' But he'd flung out of the kitchen, slamming the door behind him. She stood biting her lip. We're all changing, she thought, Dinny with the life and the laughter gone out of him and me, of all people, counselling patience.

'He's taking it hard, is Dinny', she said that evening when she sat in the lamplight at the kitchen table with Jonathan, hearing him read aloud. He had changed, too. The surliness that had come from a feeling of inferiority had gone now that he was literate. There was a new eagerness, a sense of purpose, about him when he spoke of the farm he would own one day.

'Of course he's taking it hard', Jonathan said. 'Bonaparte was his last hope of getting back to Ireland, because he's here for life. I can look to my ticket of leave in a year or so—as you can, for that matter. But what's poor Dinny got except for the likes of Napoleon?' He looked up sharply at the whinny that came from the darkness outside. 'There's someone at the horses!' He went to the door, Mary at his shoulder, and out into the yard. Then he pulled her back into the shadows and closed the door to shut in the light.

Greville, leading his horse, had come out of the stable, followed by Jonas Pike. They heard the overseer say, his voice oily, '—and thankee, sir. I'd think it an honour to work for you, sir, on the terms you mention.'

Greville's cool, dispassionate voice said, 'Good. But, before you leave Captain Wiltshire's employment, there is another matter. It touches Isaac Nichols, the Government Overseer. An obstructionist and trouble-maker, wouldn't you say, Pike?'

'I would indeed, sir!' Pike had crossed swords with Nichols more than once on the matter of the disposal of surplus convict rations.

'There are certain gentlemen', Greville said carefully, 'who would consider it in the colony's best interests if Mr Nichols were to be removed from his position.' Pike nodded, a grin beginning to spread across his frog-like face. He knew how these things were done, even before Greville said, 'It will be presented that Nichols has received an amount of stolen tobacco. We would prove doubly grateful to a man of conscience who would swear that he knew of this transaction.' He paused. 'Do you still follow me, Mr Pike?'

Pike gave a croaking chuckle. 'Perfectly, sir.' The two men walked away into the gloom.

In the kitchen, Mary and Jonathan looked at one another. She said, 'What can we do?'

'Nothing', he said bitterly. 'There's nothing we can do. Who'd take our word against Greville's and Pike's?'

'We could warn him.'

'What do we say? That there'll be false witnesses? He knows that. The officers of the New South Wales Corps, they run the courts, same as they run everything else.'

There was nothing they could do—and there was nothing Isaac Nichols could do, either. He was given no time; besides, he had known ever since that interview in the day-room what the outcome of his integrity would be. Too stubborn to bend like the grass, he was shattered like the oak. They sentenced him to fourteen years at the penal settlement on Norfolk Island.

And, as the new century began, an Act of Union tightened England's grip on Ireland and the Peace of Amiens ended the French War—'A peace which all men are glad of but no man can be proud of', as that brilliant Irishman Richard Brinsley Sheridan called it. Governor Hunter was succeeded by Philip Gidley King, and the Grevilles and the Pikes prospered in their partnership of villainy. But there was one small triumph for Jonathan Garrett. On a rather special day in March 1802 he was trudging back from the Commissary's office in Sydney when he saw two horsemen approach. They reined in when they saw him, Pike sneering and Greville with the words, 'You're a long way from home, Garrett. Let me see your pass.'

Jonathan remembered the day five years before when, on that same road, Greville had made the same demand. Again he pulled a paper from his pocket. But this time he said, 'I've got something better than a pass.' He handed it up. 'A certificate of freedom.'

Greville took it. He read it, then he looked at Pike, the familiar loathsome smile on his lips. 'This is no certificate of freedom', he said contemptuously. 'It merely allows you to travel the highways of the colony without first obtaining your master's permission.'

Pike gave his croaking snigger. 'You've made a blunder, haven't you, boy? You'd best scuttle back to Wiltshire's before they report you as a bolter.'

Jonathan stared up at them expressionlessly. Greville, still smiling, gave him back his pass. Jonathan drew a breath, looking down at the paper. He read, 'This is to certify that seven years have elapsed since sentence of transportation for that term was passed on Jonathan

Edward Garrett . . . .' He looked up. Greville's smile had frozen on his pale face. Pike's jaw had dropped. '. . . who was tried at Tottenham Assizes on the twelfth day of March, seventeen ninety-five and who arrived in this colony in the ship *Indispensable* in the year seventeen ninety-six . . . .'

Greville jabbed his spurs viciously into his horse and galloped off. Pike, glowering, followed. Jonathan stood in the middle of the road shouting after them as he read the words, the wonderful, wonderful words: '. . . The said Jonathan Edward Garrett is restored to all rights as a free subject.'

Captain Wiltshire was sorry to lose him and offered him the post of overseer vacated by Pike. When he saw Jonathan's mind was made up, however, he made no objection to recommending him for a grant of land. In the kitchen, Mary said, her manner slightly strained as she folded a tablecloth, 'So you're going.' She should be overjoyed, she thought, that he was free.

'Aye.'

'Captain'll be sorry to lose you.' It was very important that the tablecloth should be folded with great exactitude. 'But then you're bent on your land and your freedom. What's he got to offer against that?'

'I dare say it'll be the same with you when your own time's up.' He watched her but she wouldn't meet his eye. 'You want to go back to Ireland.' She didn't speak. 'Would anything change your mind?'

She looked up at last from her folding. 'No.' But it wasn't as positive as she'd intended so she said it again, more firmly. 'No. I must go home.'

He gave her a wry smile. 'You don't give up easy, Mary.'

'No.' She was thinking about partings. Once, there'd have been tears at this moment instead of this dull feeling of regret and sadness. 'But, then, neither do you, Jonathan Garrett.'

CHAPTER SEVEN

When, in the March of 1803, Mary discovered that Captain Wiltshire intended to visit England, she decided to apply for a ticket of leave—a document that entitled a well-conducted convict to work for wages and choose his own master. Wiltshire had, in fact, already recommended her for this privilege but, knowing that his wife needed Mary, asked her what plans she had. Marriage, perhaps?

'No!' Mary turned away to the window of the day-room where the Captain, in the high-necked coatee that was part of the revised uniform of the New South Wales Corps, stood in his favourite position before the fire. 'No, sir.' It had been a whole year since she had seen Jonathan Garrett. That probably meant he'd found somebody else, and what was it to her if he had? 'I want to go back to Ireland.'

'In that case, you'll need to save.' He gave her his fatherly smile. 'When your ticket's granted we'll pay you a wage.'

She went away with plans buzzing in her head. But Louisa Wiltshire, who had overheard the tail-end of the conversation, also had plans for Mary Mulvane. The girl was a model servant and Louisa had no intention of losing her. So, when her husband told her he had met Jonathan that day near the government farm at Castle Hill and that the young man had asked permission to pay a visit, her mind worked quickly. 'When does he propose to call?' she asked casually.

'Tomorrow.' Wiltshire went back to the article in the

recently-published *Sydney Gazette and New South Wales Advertiser* that he was reading. 'On his way to Sydney for stores.'

Next morning she packed Mary and the children off for the day with a luncheon basket. And when Jonathan arrived Louisa was all charm, commenting how well he looked, how long it had been since he'd left Westbury and, in answer to his request to see Mary, 'Oh, yes . . . .' She pretended to recollect. 'I did mention to her that you intended to call. But she decided to take the children out for the day.' She accompanied him back to the cart he was driving and stood smiling a satisfied smile after he'd gone.

That evening when Dinny, almost back to his old self again, came looking for any odds and ends there might be from the roast lamb, Mary was astonished to hear that Jonathan had been seen on the Sydney road that morning.

'You mean', Dinny said, his mouth full, 'he didn't call in to see you?'

'Well, it's been a year.' How could she be so hurt when she didn't care? She began to feel angry with herself at her foolishness. 'Why should he call in? He'll have forgotten us all by now.'

Dinny, his cheeks bulging with bread and meat, mumbled, 'He's not married.'

Her anger mounted at the sense of relief. 'It's nought to me whether he is or not.'

'He'll be wanting a wife.' Dinny closed one of his black gypsy eyes in a wink.

She flared up. 'Well, it can't be me! I'm getting my ticket of leave and working for wages and going home to Ireland, d'ye hear?'

'I can't help it, the way ye're shouting.' He grinned and tore off some lamb with his teeth.

'I'm not shouting!' Mary shouted. 'And I'm going home to Ireland!'

He said unexpectedly, 'Ye'd be a fool.' When she stared at him he reminded her that, with the Act of Union, things were now worse than ever in Ireland, with priests being transported like common felons. 'Ireland!' he said, no longer grinning. 'Ah, *sean bhean bhocht*!'

'Ireland's not a poor old woman! She's my land and yours and I'm going home. What is there to look forward to here?'

'For myself, I'm being sent to Castle Hill soon and all I've got to look forward to is being flogged to death before I see you next. But you,' he shrugged, 'you've got Jonathan Garrett. Ye could marry him, start a farm and raise a family. Make a new Ireland out here.' He grinned again. 'He's a fine man—for an Englishman.'

'Fine he may be', she said coldly. 'But he didn't travel a mile or wait an hour to see me today.'

* * * * *

There was a good deal of strenuous drinking going on in 'The Bird in the Barley' that night. Polly had been sent for to act as midwife by a neighbour and, on her return, the child had to be suitably pledged. Father Dixon, a transported priest, was to officiate at the christening that would take place at the inn—the wedding, too, now that the Reverend Samuel Marsden wasn't the only man of God in the district. The thought of the Flogging Parson sobered them somewhat. 'There's one sleeping rough tonight that Marsden'd like to get his hands on', Will said. 'Trouble at Castle Hill. Big Mick from Sligo killed an overseer and bolted.'

Polly sighed. 'Poor man. It's a long road he has to travel. And Marsden's waiting at the end of it.'

The reverend gentleman would have agreed with her. He sat next day in the Wiltshire day-room, sipping brandy and dressed more like a country squire than a clergyman. 'This brute who escaped from Castle Hill will be brought to see the error of his ways in the end. The Law and the Church,' he said pontifically, 'we're both schoolmasters, both teachers. And neither can afford to spoil the rod.'

Louisa shuddered slightly in spite of the warm autumn sunshine pouring in at the window where she sat. She remembered the text Marsden was said to have used on his first Sunday sermon in the colony nine years before and that he had never tired of quoting since: 'For the great day of his wrath is come; and who shall be able to stand?' She looked up from her embroidery as Mary came into the room. 'Excuse me, ma'am—Reverend. If I may take a book for the lessons?' She went to the glass-fronted bookcase and took one down.

When she'd gone Marsden said, 'Your governess.' He knew Mrs Wiltshire prided herself on possessing such a prestigious household article and preferred that title for her convict servant. 'I've not seen her with you and the Captain at Matins?'

'She's Papist. Irish.' When her visitor had grunted meaningly she added, 'She wants her ticket of leave.'

'These tickets are a pestilence!' Marsden stood up to give himself more room for oration. 'Tickets straight to Hell itself! Taking the morally weak away from good influences—giving them the illusion of freedom before they're ready. . . .'

This, as Louisa well knew, could go on all afternoon. She cut in smoothly. 'You think it may be against her interests?'

He waved his glass. 'Madam, I know it to be so! Despite any inconvenience to you, the girl's best interests must surely be served by remaining here.' He took a refreshing sip of brandy.

'So even if it meant restraining her, I could count on your help in this matter? If I should need it?'

Marsden smiled expansively. 'But, of course, ma'am! I'm at your service!' He bowed. Louisa smiled sweetly. Her plans for Mary were coming along well.

But they received a setback on the following morning. She was sitting at her writing-desk, dressed to perfection in a cornflower-blue gown with a shawl of Mechlin lace, when she heard a cart enter the yard. She glanced casually through the window. Then she leapt to her feet in a most unladylike manner. 'Jonathan!' she cried as she came out on to the verandah.

'Morning, ma'am.' He climbed down from the seat and tethered the horse.

'What are you doing here?'

'Government stores asked me to bring this out, Ma'am.' He heaved a crate off the waggon. Helplessly, she watched him shoulder it and head for the kitchen.

The cook was preparing a luncheon basket. Edward was pinching his sister. Mary was reproving him and threatening Latin verbs in place of the botanical excursion when the door to the yard swung open.

After what seemed several minutes she was able to say, 'Hallo, Jonathan', in a voice that sounded reasonably normal although her heart was beating so fast she could barely utter.

'Mary!' He stood with the crate on his shoulder, looking at her with a hunger in his eyes that made her head swim. She heard him clear his throat. 'I hope you have been well?'

'Yes. Yes, I have, Jonathan. I hope you have been well?'

'Yes.' There was a profound silence while the cook and the two children stared at them in amazement. 'I was past the other day.'

'Dinny told me.'

'Oh.'

'He's going to Castle Hill.'

'Devil's own place, that.' There was another hiatus. Eventually Jonathan became aware of it. 'Well—I'd better be going.' He turned, the crate still on his shoulder. Then he remembered it. 'Where d'you want it, Mrs Kemp?'

The cook, intrigued, indicated the pantry behind him. Before he turned away, Mary said, 'The children and I were going to the creek. Perhaps we could ride with you?'

A lamp seemed to be lit behind Jonathan's eyes as he grinned. And, from the doorway, Louisa Wiltshire's lips tightened as she saw it.

It was as if, Mary thought as she arranged plates on a cloth on the ground while Jonathan went for wood, everything had become warm, perfumed, crystal-clear. The lacework pattern made by the eucalypts against the blue of the sky had never been so delicate, the wildflowers in the bush had never looked so beautiful, the creek had never sung so sweetly over the stones. Not even with Michael. . . . She paused for a moment with a feeling of treachery. Then she smiled gently. Dear Michael, dead these seven years. There was nothing she could give him now, nothing she could withhold from him. The only treachery would be to forget him completely, and she could never do that. She looked up, aware that the children were missing. 'Elizabeth?' she called. 'Edward?' She went through ferns to the creek. A bush moved. She smiled, moved to it and jerked it back. Elizabeth sat hiding her eyes to make sure she couldn't be seen. She opened them and giggled. 'Caught!' Mary said. She tickled Elizabeth and led the squeaking child back. Another bush moved as she passed. She put a finger to her lips, glanced at Elizabeth who had a hand jammed over her mouth to avoid warning the hidden Edward. Mary pulled back the bush. 'And you're caught, too!' Elizabeth screamed with all the strength of her powerful young lungs.

It was like discovering a wild animal, a feral thing that glared savagely and showed its teeth in a cornered snarl. The bolter leapt out of his hiding-place and went at a shambling trot straight for the food. He crouched, stuffing meat and bread and cake into his mouth, snuffling like a pig. He was a big, hulking man, his trousers slimed with mud, the blood-stains criss-crossing his filthy shirt from the lash-marks on his back. Mary said, 'Oh, you poor man!' He kept his eyes on her, wolfing the food. 'Your back's torn. You need help.' He shook his head.

Edward came from behind a tree like a small explosion, landing on the convict's shoulders and being brushed off like a fly. 'Edward! Stop it!' Mary shouted. Elizabeth shrieked again as her brother went rolling. Then the man scrambled to his feet and limped off into the bush as Jonathan ran up, his arms full of firewood.

Captain Wiltshire questioned them about it when they returned. Louisa wanted to know why they had not taken the man and Edward boasted that he had indeed tried but Mary had said . . . . He was too big, Edward said after a pause. Wiltshire had agreed, expressed his gratitude that the children were safe, and requested Jonathan to remain while he went into Parramatta for a detachment of soldiers.

Mary and Jonathan went to the kitchen while Louisa kept Edward back. 'You were going to tell us what Mary said?' she asked with maternal solicitude. And, as Jonathan sat on guard in the kitchen with the loaded pistols the Captain had given him, he asked Mary to go with him on the following day to see the house he had built in the bush and the land he had been watering with his sweat for the last twelve months.

Nothing, Jonathan thought, could spoil the beauty of that day, the early morning sunlight turning the air itself to gold-dust, the trees hung with the silver filigree spun by spiders, the grass hung with rubies, topaz, sapphires. And Mary, more lovely than he had ever remembered, sitting beside him as they drove off. Not even the troops marching off to search for the bolter, their muskets at the high port, could break the spell. It took most of that golden morning to reach the small farm. But then came the moment when he tied his scarf over her eyes, drove on a little way then removed it and said, 'We're here.' He sat looking at the tiny bark hut at the top of the hill, at the raw earth and the young crops, and seeing a somewhat confused composite of the Palace of St James, Westbury and Hyde Park. 'What d'you think of it?'

'You've done so much!' A girl of the land herself, she knew how much work had gone into this, insignificant though it seemed against the immensity of the bush. 'Out here all year by yourself!'

'Come and see.' There were marigolds in a small bed near the door of the hut. He picked some, quickly and awkwardly, and gave them to her. He opened the door and followed her inside.

'It's very nice, Jonathan.' She stood holding the flowers in both hands, looking at the rough-hewn table and benches, the cleanliness of the whitewashed walls, while he took down the wooden bars from the shutters and swivelled them on their pins to let in the light. Again she said, 'You've done—so much!'

'I . . . .' He stood stockstill staring at her. Then, suddenly, he blurted out, 'It's for you—all of it. For you.'

When she turned her head to look at him, he said, 'Marry me, Mary.'

It was so unexpected. Well, not unexpected, she thought, but she hadn't been prepared for it at that moment. She'd always shut it out of her mind, anyway. 'I can't.'

'Why not?'

'I can't.' She shook her head to try to make him see how impossible it was. 'I'm tied to Ireland. All my people back there—the living and the buried. I can't cut the tie, Jonathan, or my own heart'd bleed to death inside me.'

He said, quietly, 'I love you, Mary. I did this. . . .' He gestured at his twelve months' hard labour.

'They need water.' She wasn't really conscious of what she said as she gave him the flowers. She went outside while he was putting them into a crock with the care he'd have bestowed on as many orchids.

He followed her out and said defensively, 'It's got a kind of beauty, Mary.'

'A grey kind. It isn't Ireland, Jonathan.' She felt a great sadness welling up inside her, a terrible sense of loss as she walked slowly back to the cart. They drove back in silence, Jonathan merely saying he wanted to talk to the man who owned the cart before they returned to Westbury. She hardly noticed that they were pulling up outside a small thatched building that had an inn-sign swinging over its door.

A husky Dublin voice said, 'Well! I never thought she'd get into a cart with a desperate fellow like yourself, Jonathan Garrett!' and Polly came running to meet her.

Mary stared from one to the other of them. 'You never told me you were neighbours!' For her, it was a welcome break in the silent tension with Jonathan. There was to be a christening, with a wedding to follow, conducted by the first priest she'd seen in years. Father James Dixon, from Wexford, had been transported for life after the commuting of his death-sentence for alleged participation in the Rising of '98 and had been conditionally emancipated by Governor King to allow him to exercise his clerical office.

Slim, pale and dark-haired, he looked far younger than his forty-five years as he swung down from the saddle, walked into the tap-room and, with a couple of forthright sentences, put a stop to the drinking until the sacraments were over. They all watched as he slipped into the soutane, the surplice, the purple stole; conditioned as they were to religious repression, it seemed as if he was committing some wild act of defiance. It took some thought to make them realise that this man had brought with him the first official recognition of the Roman faith in Australia. He smiled as he saw their faces, knowing what they were thinking. 'Ye like the surplice, do ye? Made for me by the good ladies of Parramatta out of a set of curtains. Godfather, ye're on the godmother's right! Now. . . .'

'Two godmothers, Father', Polly said quickly. She put the baby into Mary's arms. 'We think she may need them, the way the colony is.'

Mary looked down at the small, helpless, pink-faced scrap of humanity and felt a sudden rush of tenderness. Polly winked at Will. Jonathan had told them what he wanted the cart for when he'd borrowed it, and Polly approved wholeheartedly. Nothing like holding other women's babies, she thought, to make a girl want one herself. And Father Dixon seemed to catch her mood for, when the sacraments were over and the revelry had started up the minute he'd left the tap-room, he said to Mary and Jonathan as he bade them good-bye, 'If there's anything I can ever be doing for you two in the matter of some of the sacraments . . .?'

Mary said stubbornly, 'I'm going back to Ireland, Father', and at that moment a grim procession came along the track. The search-party of soldiers was led by a sergeant; Mick, the bolter, was led by a chain. His eyes met Mary's as he passed.

She said, watching them go, 'That's how it'll always be.'

At her shoulder, Jonathan said quietly, 'And is it any different in Ireland?'

* * * * *

Louisa Wiltshire breathed a sigh of relief when Mary, after close questioning about her outing, told her that she would not be marrying Jonathan Garrett. The evening was chill and Louisa sat by the fire, the screen placed to shield her fair complexion from its heat. Her husband sat at the writing desk. When Mary had gone, he turned to his wife, his smooth ruddy face smiling in the lamplight. 'I was correct, you see, my dear. She intends to return to Ireland. She told me so only a few days ago.'

Louisa nodded and went on with her embroidery, her face shadowed by the screen, her mind busy with plans. It would be inadvisable to pay the girl *too* well when her ticket of leave was granted. It would be most inconvenient for her to return to Ireland before—what? Seven years? Yes, for Elizabeth was now thirteen; in seven years she might be expected to have made a match. Until that time, Mary would be needed; afterwards, it mattered little what happened to her. Unless . . . . Louisa paused, staring unseeingly at her work. Unless Elizabeth might wish to employ the girl as a nanny? In which case, she might be required indefinitely. . . .

It had been the sensible decision to make, Mary kept telling herself—although she hadn't relished being told so by Mrs Wiltshire. But, if it was so sensible, why did she have to keep staring out of the window all the time, mooning about it? Either that, or roaming restlessly about the farm and lying awake at night, staring at the stars. When Dinny O'Byrne came to say good-bye she realised guiltily that she'd hardly given him a thought of late—forgotten, even, that he was being sent to the ill-famed Castle Hill. She went to him and kissed his bristly cheek. 'I'm sorry you're going, Dinny.'

He grinned his devil-may-care grin. 'Ah, it's just the beginning. It's a great place for trouble, is Castle Hill—trouble for the English, that is.'

She said, 'Dinny. . . .'

'It'll come, Mary.' He looked at her, his black eyes sparking. 'Guns and swords and whips and chains—that's what *they* use. Well, we've got hands. And we can get the guns and swords and whips and chains, and then we'll see who's master!'

She looked at him, frightened by the aura of violence that

hung about him like a flame. And frightened for him . . . He said, 'Mick, that they hanged—he was just a big child, Mary, just a big dumb horse of a man. And they put the spurs and they put the spurs again and then he bucked. When they hanged Mick they hanged a child. I knew him.'

She said quietly, 'Dinny, don't run after the guns and swords. Or they'll hang you.'

'What else can we do?'

'There's Jonathan's way. Getting land, working it. You could do that.' But he couldn't, she reflected numbly, even if he wanted to. Someone had told her that it said in his record: *Desperate, and ripe for any scheme from which danger and destruction are likely to ensue.* That was why they'd never assigned him—why he was, and always would be, employed directly by the Government. Nobody was ever going to recommend Dinny O'Byrne for a ticket of leave or a land grant or anything other than a tickle with the cat.

The twinkle came back into his eyes as he looked at her. 'And you'll never know whether his way is the right way, will you?'

'Why not?'

He chuckled. 'Because you're the girl that's going back to Ireland.' He patted her shoulder. 'I'll be seeing ye, no doubt.' And, pausing only to fill his pockets with some potatoes from a sack, he was gone.

Jonathan Garrett had been doing his share of mooning, too. And he worked harder than ever, the earth flying from his spade as he dug, as if every clod was a personal enemy that stood between him and Mary Mulvane. He was slamming wedges into a tree-trunk, the metal ringing like a bell, the wood groaning under the impact when, suddenly, he could stand it no longer. He grabbed his shirt, draping it across his sweating body as he walked towards 'The Bird in the Barley'. Within ten paces he was running. Within half an hour he was thundering towards Westbury on Will Price's horse.

Mary was talking to the cook when the hoofbeats galloped into the yard. Some instinct told her who it was and she made a half-hearted attempt to run, to leave the kitchen by the other door. But Jonathan had already flung the back door open and was standing there, his eyes locked with hers, his male strength calling to her female weakness. Claiming her . . . . Mrs Kemp's jaw dropped as she looked from one to the other. Then he strode across the kitchen and took Mary in his arms. And she, the girl who was going back to Ireland, turned up her face to his with her soul in her eyes, her lips waiting for his kiss.

Louisa Wiltshire, too, had heard the horse and when Mary, her face radiant, came in answer to her mistress's call, it was apparent who the visitor had been. 'Ma'am, I want to marry Jonathan Garrett', Mary said, and all Louisa's schemes fell apart like a house of cards.

She said coldly, 'This is a very sudden change of mind, Mary. Are you sure you *know* your own mind?'

'Yes, ma'am.'

'I'd like you to think again.'

'I've thought, ma'am.'

Louisa went to the window and stared out unseeingly. She didn't really like what she was about to do but, if the wretch persisted in this absurd course, there was no other way. 'You have to realise, Mary,' she said slowly, 'that it's my duty to consider your moral well-being.'

'Ma'am, it's marriage he's offering.'

'You have been sheltered here, both from the common lot of other felons and from your own actions. As your employer, I took a merciful view of some past occurrences. However, if I am not to be your employer, then my clear duty is to the law of the land.'

Mary's eyes clouded. 'I'm not sure what you mean, ma'am.'

'I mean that you and Jonathan Garrett gave aid to an escaped convict who was later hanged.'

It was so bare-faced a lie that it took Mary's breath away. 'Ma'am, I. . . .'

'No, Mary, listen. I am trying to help you to understand the difference between right and wrong. You gave the murderer food, you made no attempt to apprehend him. Indeed, you prevented my son from trying. . . .'

'He would have hurt Master Edward!'

'. . . prevented my son from trying. Now, if you persist in your disloyal attitude to me, then you and Jonathan will find yourselves before Mr Marsden—and we'll see what *he* thinks of your actions.' Louisa paused. 'My husband tells me', she said silkily, 'that Jonathan's farm is looking very well. But', she shrugged, 'if you are both back in chains, then he will have no farm, will he?'

Mary could never have believed, in the next few days, that she could have hated anyone so much. It frightened her when she discovered that she could actually think of ways of ending another person's life. It was all too hideous, too cruel, too wicked, and she felt physically sick with the violence of her own turbulent thoughts. The children went about, silent and scared at the cold anger in her voice; Captain Wiltshire, concerned, told Louisa that the girl looked like a corpse. Louisa shrugged and reminded her husband that the Irish had their moods. It was even worse when Will Price came to offer his congratulations and say how pleased Polly was and what a fine man Mary had in Jonathan. She stared at him hollow-eyed, told him it was all off and that all she wanted was Father Dixon, to make her confession. Will left, worried and shaking his head. When he told Jonathan, the lad didn't believe him. Will could hardly believe it himself. Rejections, confessions—it didn't make sense. None the less, it was Jonathan, in a torment of anxiety, who went off to find the priest.

Father Dixon heard her confession in the stable, his purple stole over his travelling clothes as he listened to the flat, dull voice of the girl with the black smudges of sleepless nights under her eyes. 'Bless me, Father, for I have sinned. I have not made confession for . . . .' The voice tailed off.

He prompted her. 'Yes?'

Suddenly the voice caught alight. 'There's a woman I hate so much, Father.' She began to sob. 'I hate her so much and I pray that I won't but the hate is like a cold stone in me!' She shook her head blindly. 'She won't let me marry Jonathan. She says she'll have us both before the magistrates and Jonathan will lose his farm and . . . .' She choked. Then it came out in anguish and fury. 'I want to kill her!'

The priest stood up. He took off his stole and hung it on the door. 'Now, Mary,' he said calmly, 'd'ye see that? That's what makes the confessor. Without it, I'm just a man, not a priest, and I don't have to keep my mouth shut. So, for the love of God, will ye stop your crying and tell me why you can't marry your Jonathan?'

She told him.

Then, after he'd ridden away, she went back into the house and confronted Louisa Wiltshire. 'I'm going to marry Jonathan Garrett', she said.

There was something in her voice that made Louisa quail for a moment, but then she reminded herself who and what this girl was. 'I thought we'd come to an arrangement on that matter?'

'I'm going to marry him.'

To Louisa, the flat statement of fact was like a slap across the face. She said, her voice like ice, 'Then there's nothing for it but Mr Marsden.'

It would be best, she thought, if Charles arranged it. She announced to him, when he came home from Parramatta, that she had a painful duty to perform and she had her story of convict treachery all ready, with suitable expressions of sorrow and hopes that the magistrate might not be *too* severe. . . . She had, of course, no way of knowing that her husband had met Father Dixon on the road. Or, rather, that Father Dixon had contrived to meet her husband.

And the Captain was enraged. To him, Mary was like a daughter; he respected the sheer determination to succeed shown by Jonathan, and it shocked him to realise the duplicity of which his wife was capable. So he told her, in blunt military sentences, that if she continued in her course of action he would appear in court against her and cause a scandal that would rock the colony. She made the mistake of raising her voice to him and he shouted her down. Then she wept and he remembered that she was only a woman and spoke kindly to her. But he had his way. And, to give

Louisa Wiltshire credit, she was a good loser. She called Mary in and, with a very fair imitation of sincerity, said, 'Mary, the Captain and I are extremely pleased concerning your plans to marry Jonathan Garrett. You go with our greatest goodwill.'

It was only after Mary had left the room that she was able to believe her ears.

They were married under a tree near Jonathan's house, Mary very lovely in a white gown embroidered with tiny flowers, her chestnut hair cascading from under her bonnet, the groom strangely elegant yet blushing at Polly's talk of all the babies they'd have. 'Now because Jonathan's not of the true faith,' said Father Dixon, 'it'll be the short service and I shouldn't even be wearing these vestments, but the nearest bishop's in South America and if you don't tell him then I won't.' He stopped as he saw Mary looking about.

She said, 'Oh, Dinny's not going to be here', and a cloud of dust appeared out of the bush. Dinny fell off the horse he'd borrowed, resoundingly drunk even before the wedding had begun.

'I've come', shouted Dinny, 'to give the bride away!'

Father Dixon sighed. 'If ye showed your face in Church more often, ye'd know we didn't do that. Now behave yourself or I'll lay ye cold in the dust!' He turned to Mary and Jonathan. 'To begin . . . .'

Later, as the celebrations in the tap-room of 'The Bird in the Barley' reached a crescendo of jigs and reels, Dinny reeling with the best, the couple slipped away into the cool May night. At the house, Jonathan lit a candle, looking with a sense of awe at this beautiful stranger who stood looking at him so seriously, her eyes mysterious, her lips slightly parted as she faced him. She put out a hand, very slowly and gently, and touched his face. He took her in his arms. And then she was a stranger no longer but his Mary, and there was only the present with the pain and the sorrow forgotten in this quiet little room with the candle-flame standing still and unwavering and the two shadows on the wall that blended into one.

CHAPTER EIGHT

'If the rain holds off,' Jonathan said, 'we'll have the wheat harvested before the week's gone. As much as ten bushels, there'll be. It'll be a good year.' He watched Mary arrange in an old bottle the vivid little bunch of wildflowers he'd brought in from the fields. He smiled at her. 'Already has been.'

She paused, looking at the dusty, sweat-stained man in the old smock and knee-breeches—the man who'd made it the most wonderful six months she'd ever known—before she turned to serve out the evening meal of salt pork and vegetables from the iron pot that hung over the fire. It had been six months of hard, unremitting toil—a time, some might say, of the starkest poverty in this one-roomed hut with its crude furniture and bare necessities. But at least the hut and the furniture and even the vegetables were their own. What they had, they enjoyed in freedom; on 29th December Mary would attend the muster as a free woman for the first time. Aye, a good year, 1803, with the promise of even better times to look forward to.

Dinny O'Byrne thought so, too. For in his case things could hardly be worse than at the prison farm at Castle Hill, at the mercy of the constables and Robert Duggan the flogger and with convicts, overworked and underfed, dropping dead in the fields. He, too, was looking forward to freedom—but freedom of a different kind from that enjoyed by Mary and Jonathan. 'No man or woman in this colony can ever be free', he said to Polly and Will, 'until the Government's pulled down and the military thrown out altogether.'

Will looked round the tap-room in alarm. 'Have a care, Dinny. Men have been hanged for saying no more than that. You're talking madness.'

Dinny O'Byrne's face, lined and wrinkled beyond his years, had a strange look, almost of exaltation. 'I'm not talking madness,' he said softly, 'I'm talking rebellion.'

Christmas came and went, then January, dry and grillingly hot. In the fields at Castle Hill the convicts toiled in the sun, spurred on by their warders, with thirst and stinging flies adding to their torment. They were given work quotas to fulfil; by devious means Dinny and two fellow-prisoners found it possible to perform their tasks in less than the allotted time so that they might meet at 'The Bird in the Barley' for a purpose of their own. One of these men, a former stone-mason and soldier called Phillip Cunningham, was slightly-built, pink-faced and with thinning fair hair, quietly dressed in a fawn coat, grey waistcoat and buff breeches with a white scarf tied round his neck. Liam Johnston, some ten years his junior, was tall, dark-haired and, in his old royal blue coat with its tattered ruffles and his torn pink knee-breeches, looked something like an unemployed actor. Both were Irish; both were introduced to Will Price with the military title of Captain. He, who had never clapped eyes on either of them before, found them highly mysterious. They sat conspiratorially with their heads together while Dinny was helping Polly with some soup in the kitchen. Will would have been even more intrigued if he had known they'd come to his inn to meet their future commanding officer.

'The man', Dinny was telling Polly in the back room, 'who can beat the English at their own game, whose forces kept fighting in the hills of Wicklow long after the main rebellion was put down in '98. Why, it's even said the English offered him a commission in their own army to fight Napoleon. He's a true hero of all Ireland, is General

Joseph Holt, and our rebellion needs him as a figure-head. But, even more, we need him to turn us into an army.'

In the tap-room, however, Cunningham was ill at ease. He spoke in monosyllables and, when Liam Johnston asked him what was amiss, he shrugged. 'Ah, 'tis nothing. It's just that I can't get it out of me head that General Holt manages the Brush Farm for William Cox. And Cox happens to be Paymaster at this time for the New South Wales Corps.'

The younger man drank from his mug. 'We should allow him to speak on his own behalf, Phillip. It's only British justice that seems to judge a man on the grounds of his station in life.'

'Some say he betrayed other leaders of the '98 in return for being allowed to bring his wife and family with him into exile.'

Johnston frowned. 'The bloody English have always tried to ruin our cause by false rumours and scurrilous attacks on our leaders. They'll say . . . .' He broke off as Dinny and Polly came in with the soup. At the same time, the front door opened and General Holt entered.

He was a man of extraordinary magnetism, one whose every movement seemed to be carried out with an air of authority, so that it was hard to believe that his title of General was self-bestowed. His eyes held a man's and were never the first to shift their gaze; his voice, though soft with its Wicklow speech, seemed to command attention like a bugle call. Yet he looked ordinary enough as he stood just inside the closed door looking them over, a stoutish round-faced man in his late forties, dressed inconspicuously in a caped chocolate-brown coat, fawn knee-breeches and grey stockings with dusty black shoes. He held his bicorne hat in his hand, revealing a head that was balding at the top but with thick grey hair at the back. Dinny, smiling and ducking his head, ushered him to a chair at the end of the table. He nodded to Dinny whom he knew, shook hands with Cunningham and Johnston who had sprung to their feet, and refused soup. Will was joined by Polly at the bar.

The other three sat down and waited for Holt to speak. 'You are aware, gentlemen,' he said quietly, 'of the consequences should your rebellion fail?'

Cunningham said curtly, 'We don't intend to fail, General.'

'D'ye think the free settlers will support you?'

'Some might.' Dinny was not too over-awed by Holt to neglect Polly's soup. He waved his spoon to indicate that, although his mouth was full, he would have more to say directly. Then he went on, 'But they don't have to. Many will supply us with arms,' he inhaled some soup, 'whether they like it or not.'

Holt glanced at Cunningham. 'And the training of your men, Captain?'

'Some fought for Ireland. But, in truth, most have no experience.' Cunningham leaned forward. 'But, like Dinny here, they've a will to freedom, General. And, with several hundred of us, we should greatly outnumber the redcoats.'

'We plan', said Johnston, his eyes burning, 'a rising at Castle Hill and at the Hawkesbury settlement simultaneously. We'll then join forces at Toongabbie and march on Parramatta.'

'And Sydney?'

Cunningham broke in. 'After we've taken Parramatta we'll seize the ships in the harbour, destroy those we don't require and sail for South America.'

Holt said, 'Why not hold the colony?'

They stared at him. Johnston said incredulously, 'Stay *here*?'

'Disarm the military. Release them on ships. Then set up a republic on French lines.'

Johnston shook his head. 'It wouldn't work.'

It was all one to Dinny whether they set up a republic or a skittle-alley afterwards. This politicking was time-consuming. The main thing was to clapperclaw the redcoats. 'At least', he said, steering the topic back, 'you agree with the first part of the plan.'

Holt smiled thinly. 'Gentlemen, the New South Wales Corps are so weakened by their own squabbling that I could take and hold this colony with fifty men, let alone the five hundred you promise.'

'Then you're with us?' Dinny said eagerly.

Holt nodded. He looked, Will thought, not unlike a down-at-heel schoolmaster granting a half-holiday. 'I'll support your rebellion, as I supported the '98. But bear this in mind. Revolution worked in America and France because men were opposed to tyranny and committed to a new social order. They didn't succeed by proposing to run away as soon as they'd achieved their freedom.' He stood up. 'We must be completely prepared. One miscalculation, and we are all of us dead men.'

That was what worried Will Price when, after Holt had gone and the conspirators had toasted Ireland and liberty, Dinny turned to him and asked him if they had his support. It worried Mary even more. Dinny, a flame burning inside him now, had taken the news to her and Jonathan and they were appalled as they listened to his eloquence. 'A just and noble uprising', he called it, 'of convicts and settlers alike. An end to tyranny, to the Grevilles and the Pikes. We mean to rise at Castle Hill and on the Hawkesbury.' He stared at Jonathan. 'Will ye join us?'

'No!' Mary said violently.

In his turn, Dinny was astounded. She was Irish, wasn't she? She and her man had both suffered, hadn't they? So what had they got against a nice quiet little revolution to set matters straight?

'I can't agree', she said, 'with the destruction of life, no matter how you justify it. Violence brings nothing but violence. Look at our own country. Look at France.'

He stared at them, the flame going cold behind his eyes. So this was what happened when convicts got their freedom. They turned into lackeys, people who'd let their friends go to hell as long as they could grub about in their bit of land. 'People like me aren't given their freedom', he said quietly. 'We must take it.' But I'm being harsh, he thought. She's a woman and wants to protect her man. He turned to Jonathan, about to appeal to him.

But Mary said, 'Dinny, back in Ireland I knew a boy who

121

talked like you. And I watched him die with a musket-ball in him. I never want to see that again.'

Jonathan spoke up at last, but his eyes wouldn't meet Dinny's. 'We can't support killing, whatever we think of your cause.'

Dinny stood up and moved to the door. 'Or is it', he said softly, 'that ye've too much to lose?'

Jonathan and Mary took their doubts and fears to Will and Polly, but they were just as doubtful, just as fearful for Dinny. Polly was inclined to think the rebels could succeed. The convicts outnumbered the redcoats many times over and they were led, Dinny had said, by a great general. Will scratched his head and didn't know what the devil to think. Jonathan, as he talked to Will, began to wonder if, perhaps, Dinny was right and he was throwing away a principle for thirty acres of land. 'I'm better off than he is,' Jonathan said, 'but I can't help knowing how he feels. At home, the King's mad and the war with France has broken out again. So who cares what happens here? Things'll only get worse unless we make them better.'

'You're starting to sound like Dinny', Will said. 'You've got a grant of good land and a beautiful girl for a wife. That's a lot to lose.'

Jonathan smiled wryly. 'Now *you're* beginning to sound like Dinny.' When Will frowned uncomprehendingly he said, 'D'you want me to take the easy way out when the time comes?'

'When the time comes,' Will said slowly, 'no way's going to seem easy. I suppose it's something a man can only decide for himself. Some men are happy to risk everything on the thin chance they can win some', he gestured, '—oh, some magic golden prize. Me, I'm not a gambler. But Dinny and his mates at Castle Hill have got nothing to lose, so what have they got to risk?'

Their necks were at risk but, as the fever of rebellion infected them, they didn't care. 'Give me liberty', Patrick Henry had said at the time of the American Revolution, 'or give me death!' Whether they came out of this dead or alive,

Dinny O'Byrne told them, at least they'd be free. And, as February came in, a sudden depletion of government stores began to take place at Castle Hill—mainly objects of a pointed or edged nature. Axes were mysteriously lost while trees were being felled; a constable would wake up after a refreshing snooze under a tree while the men worked in the sun, only to find he'd mislaid his bayonet; pitchforks showed a sudden tendency to tumble down wells.

A date was set for the rising.

General Holt and his three captains—for Dinny had also been elevated to that status—met at the inn after it had closed for the night. Father Dixon, with memories of the '98 still strong in his mind, joined them. 'My mission tonight', he said, looking at the four faces in the candle-light, 'may not be a popular one. I've come to preach moderation and restraint.' Polly moved about quietly, clearing away mugs. Will was dividing his attention between the meeting and the window where he was keeping watch.

Phillip Cunningham shook his head. 'It's too late for that, Father.' The others murmured approval.

'Examine your consciences', Dixon said. 'Can ye guarantee there'll be no bloodshed?'

Dinny put down his mug and wiped his mouth. 'Ye'll have to ask the redcoats that, Father.'

'Ye've much to lose, my son', Dixon said quietly.

Cunningham grunted. 'Sure, and hasn't every man at this table already lost a home, a country, the comfort and support of his family? And hasn't . . .?'

'I was thinking', the priest said, 'of your immortal soul.'

There was a silence. Then Holt's firm voice cut in. 'I share your concern, Father. But I ask you to remember two things: we outnumber the enemy, and we have the element of surprise. God willing, this matter will all be over in a single night, with as little bloodshed as possible.'

Dixon said nothing. He was beginning to wonder whether General Holt was as good as his reputation. Sure, they outnumbered the soldiers, but in the way a flock of sparrows outnumbers a cat. As for the element of surprise, why, the rising seemed to be becoming a topic of conversation as common as that of the weather. He remembered the story that Holt, a Protestant, had been unwilling to join the '98 at all until a neighbour had denounced him as a rebel to satisfy a personal grudge and caused his house to be burnt down.

Holt went on, 'The rising doesn't bother me. What happens afterwards does.'

Johnston said, 'I see no problem, General. Those who wish to sail away should be free to do so. The rest can remain here to set up a republic.'

Holt frowned. 'I don't like the division of our force, Captain, either before or after the rising.'

Dinny was refilling his mug at the tap. 'Some of us are determined to go.' He came back to the table. 'This colony has ever been a gaol to us and we've no desire to rise merely in order to possess that gaol.'

Division already, Dixon noted gloomily. Ireland all over again.

'But', Cunningham said, 'we wish ye well, General. I say we should plant a tree of liberty in Parramatta—a gift from us who leave to those who stay behind. A symbol of the common cause of both our goals. Freedom here in New South Wales and freedom on the high seas.'

Father Dixon, his ear sharpened by years in the confessional box, was probably the only one who picked up the edge of cynicism in Holt's voice when he said, 'I'll watch over your tree of liberty, Captain, with the utmost care and devotion.'

Cunningham bowed, sitting, to him. 'Are we still agreed, then, to hold to the date of the rising? One week from Sunday. The fourth of March.'

'Aye', Dinny said.

Johnston nodded. 'We *must* be ready by then.'

Holt said slowly, 'So we rise on Sunday the fourth of March.'

'At nightfall. The signal will be a fire.' Cunningham looked round the table. 'Gentlemen!' He raised his tankard. 'I give you my pledge. Liberty or Death!'

As the others drank, Dixon said softly, 'God's will be done.'

A common topic of conversation it was becoming, as Dixon had told himself. During the next ten days or so it became the only topic. So it seemed quite logical to the simple-minded convict John Leary, who on the morning of Saturday 3rd March was repairing the thatch on the roof of 'The Bird in the Barley', that he should bring it up while talking to Greville's overseer, Jonas Pike. It was only in the form of the mysterious hints they all used—'things will soon take a turn for the better for poor men like ourselves' and 'soon, a man might have a musket and be able to walk across the Blue Mountains to China and freedom'—but it was enough to terrify Will Price who came out, berated Leary for an idle gossiper whose mind was half gone, and took Pike into the tap-room for a free drink. When Dinny called with another load of thatch Will said, 'That Leary's been blathering to Pike about how great things are in the wind and how he'll be setting off for China soon.'

Dinny stared, then shrugged. 'Is that all?'

'Aye. But it's a good thing events take place tomorrow. Another day, and I'll wager they'll be discussing it over tea at Government House.'

It was, in fact, being discussed at that very moment, not at Government House, but in the office of Captain Edward Abbott, Commandant of Parramatta Barracks and former Town Adjutant and Inspector of Outposts at Norfolk Island where, just ten years previously, he had helped to suppress a mutiny. Jonas Pike, his bulbous green eyes gleaming with loyalty, his wide mouth set in an ingratiating smile, stood before the Captain who sat at his desk, Pike's sworn Information before him. Abbott, late of the 34th and 73rd Regiments and who had gained his lieutenancy in the Corps at the age of seventeen, was a soldier to the backbone, a member of a military caste that did not much care for toad-faced little men who crawled into one's office with intelligence that, it seemed, had been obtained from a half-wit, and an Irish one at that, on the roof of an inn. It was a wickedly hot day; Abbott's uniform felt like a blanket and his office was droning with flies. His eyebrows elevated slowly as he read: 'The said John Leary then indicated to me that he would soon be in possession of arms and that, once so possessed, he intended to march over the Blue Mountains in a bid to walk to China.' *China*? He eyed Pike warily across the desk. He looked at his sergeant, who stared back at him woodenly. 'It's all a little—fantastic, Mr Pike.'

'It's true, sir, that Leary's simple-minded.' Pike bobbed his reptilian head respectfully. 'But I don't think he invented the matter of a rebellion.'

'Hm.' Abbott's eyes went down to the statement again. He turned over in his mind whether perhaps this revolting little man might not have a touch of the sun. Or too many nights alone with a rum-bottle, possibly. They went like that, one knew, out here. He read on: 'With other information gleaned from our conversation and from reports to hand in the area, I believe the said outbreak will take place tomorrow, Sunday 4th March 1804.' Instantly, the wording put him in mind of the chap who'd sauntered into this very office only a month ago and informed him, cool as dammit, that the end of the world would take place at four o'clock on the following afternoon. Good God, Abbott thought. My barracks is becoming a refuge for bedlamites. 'All true and correct, eh?' he said kindly. 'Walking to China—outbreak to take place tomorrow—all gleaned from this lunatic Leary?'

'Aye', said Pike eagerly. To Abbott, the gleam in his eyes bore a strong resemblance to the mad glare of dementia. 'And there's more important fellows than young Leary involved in it, sir, though he didn't name them. You can be sure . . . .'

Oh, I can be sure, depend on it, Abbott said to himself as he struck savagely at a blue-bottle on his desk. His Excellency the Governor's bound to be privy to the plot, and probably the Cham of Tartary and my Lord Addington, the Prime Minister of England . . . . 'Just sign the statement, Mr Pike.'

'Of course, sir. Yes, to be sure.' Pike took the quill from the impassive sergeant and scrawled his name. He bowed, clutching his hat to his chest as he backed to the door. 'I'll pass on any other information, sir, should it come to hand. It's as well that people loyal to His Majesty should . . . .'

'Do that, my dear fellow.'

As the door closed behind him, the sergeant said, 'Hardly a day goes by, sir, when they're not going to break out at Castle Hill.'

The Commandant nodded. 'I doubt if there's any need to advise Sydney.' He exchanged a knowing smile with his NCO. 'Just file it, eh, Sergeant?'

* * * * *

On that Saturday evening Will and Polly closed the inn and drove over to Jonathan's. They spent a quiet time, enjoying the cool air after the heat of the day and listening to Jonathan playing his tin whistle. Polly had talked nostalgically about Saturday night in Dublin, the pubs, the theatres, the dances, the people strolling in the streets like a deep breath of life before Sunday . . . . She broke off. It had been the topic they'd all been trying to avoid.

Mary said, 'You'll be staying home tomorrow?'

'We will.' Polly nodded. 'If things go badly, there's no telling who'll be abroad.'

Will looked at Jonathan for a moment before he said, 'You'll be keeping close to home yourselves?'

Mary watched her husband. He could go either way, she thought. Ever since Dinny had called he'd sat brooding and when, only that morning, she'd tried to extract a promise from him that he wouldn't take part in the rising, he'd refused to give it. She said, 'Aye, we'll be here. Won't we, Jonathan?'

He didn't answer. Suddenly, the evening seemed to turn very chilly. She shivered.

* * * * *

Captain Abbott glanced at the clock above the empty fireplace in his office, stood up and reached for his shako and sword-belt. End of the week's work, thank God. Now he'd have a drink in the Mess—two, possibly—then a cooling bath before dinner. And for dinner there would be . . . . There was a tap at the door and the sergeant came in. 'Begging your pardon, sir.' He offered a letter. 'From the Reverend Marsden, sir. Seems to confirm what Jonas Pike told us about a rebellion.'

'Damnation, sergeant!' Abbott said irritably. 'At this time of night . . . .'

'Sir, he also mentions the date as tomorrow, sir.'

Abbott put down his hat and, breathing hard, glanced at the letter. He handed it back. 'Well, dammit, you can see what's happened, can't you? That bloody little man's been pestering the civil magistrates as well. And Marsden's taken him at his word.' He would, Abbott thought. He probably searched nightly for convicts under his bed. 'I suppose we ought to advise Major Johnston in Sydney. But, for God's sake, don't alarm him.' The Major was an irascible man and would not relish being routed out from the Mess on Saturday night. 'Tell him I feel an outbreak on a large scale is unlikely.'

'The Irish *have* given some cause for concern of late, sir.'

'Sergeant, the Irish have been a cause for concern since King Henry's time. They're an incorrigible, pugnacious lot, but I doubt if they're likely to take on the whole colony, as the reverend gentleman suggests.' He picked up his shako again. 'I confidently predict that tomorrow will be as uneventful as any other Sunday.'

It certainly began so. At Castle Hill, the Reverend Thomas Hassall preached to his convict congregation, choosing as his text St Paul's Epistle to Titus, chapter 3, verses 9 and 10: 'Exhort servants to be obedient to their own masters, and to please them well in all things; not answering again; not purloining, but showing all good fidelity; that they may adorn the doctrine of God our Saviour in all things.' In the ranks, Dinny O'Byrne, Phillip Cunningham and Liam Johnston listened impassively. Who, Dinny wondered, were going to be the servants and who the masters this time tomorrow?

General Holt's face was impassive, too, when he walked down the main street of Parramatta on that hot, sunny Sunday. He turned as a soberly dressed townsman, a friend of his, hailed him. They shook hands. 'This post as overseer of convicts', said the man, 'leaves me little time to spend with old friends.' He paused, looking at Holt oddly. 'Are you riding back to Cox's this evening?'

'Yes.' Holt stared, puzzled by the man's manner.

'I'm glad of that, Joseph. You'd be well advised to be off the roads as soon as you can and stay behind closed doors tonight.'

Holt's self-control prevented him from showing the alarm he felt. 'Why do you say that, Timothy?'

The overseer looked over his shoulder. He lowered his voice. 'The news is not yet about, but it's come to my knowledge that the Irish at Castle Hill are planning a mutiny tonight.' He added meaningly, 'It would go badly against anyone found abroad and not where he should be.'

In the hot afternoon sun, the sweat trickling down the General's back felt like ice. But his voice was as calm as ever when he said, 'For my part, I place no credence in these endless rumours concerning the Irish convicts. But I am grateful for your concern, Timothy, none the less.' The other man bowed and walked off. Holt stood watching him for a moment.

Then he turned and walked rapidly to where he'd left his horse.

It was a spectacular sunset that evening, a great sheet of red and orange that flooded the sky as if the clouds reflected a world on fire, and it seemed to turn everything to the colour of blood. Polly and Will watched it from the tap-room of 'The Bird in the Barley', empty on this Sabbath, both of them tense and expectant. Jonathan watched it from the doorway of his hut while Mary ladled soup into bowls. For the first time, there was something between them that they could not share. Mary was in a state of anguish, terrified for her man but equally terrified of being an obstacle in the path of something he believed he should do; Jonathan was sick with indecision, torn between his loyalty to the oppressed and his love for his wife. They'd hardly spoken all day. As she gave him his soup he said, 'It'll be dark soon. And still no fire.'

She saw that he'd turned away from the blood-red sunset. He was staring to the east, towards Castle Hill. She said gently, 'Eat your soup, Jonathan. There's nothing you can do.'

The sun went down in fading pinks and yellows as the night came out of the east and the candle-stubs were lit in the convict barracks at Castle Hill. Cunningham was speaking in a whisper, urgently, to the circle of filthy, bearded faces whose eyes glowed with excitement in the yellow light. 'What of the constables?'

Dinny said, 'Observing the Sabbath with their usual enthusiasm.' There was a subdued chuckle. 'They've seen nought amiss. Another half hour or so and most of them will be drunk or asleep.'

'Very well.' Cunningham nodded. 'We go ahead as planned. Our watchword is "Saint Peter", for one thing's certain. Whichever way this night goes, the gates of heaven will open for us.' He paused. 'As soon as the guards are overpowered, we'll light the signal fire. Then we'll form into our companies and await the arrival of General Holt to take command of our army.'

The moon rose early. In its light, General Holt was riding at a gallop, lying forward and urging on his horse as he tore along the dusty road. In the same moonlight, the constables were being taken one by one—seized from behind as they patrolled, pulled from their beds with dirty calloused hands clapped over their mouths, lined up and menaced with bayonets fixed to poles, with the muskets seized from the armoury. 'Is the fire ready to be lit?' Cunningham asked.

Dinny, his face sweating and transfigured, shouted, 'It's been ready for months!' The others stared at him. 'For isn't it me own hut I'll be putting the torch to? After this night, I'll have no further use for it.'

Joseph Holt's mind was a turmoil of rage and fear as he lashed at his lathering horse, the thundering hooves seeming to beat into his brain: Too-late, too-late, too-late. The rising at Castle Hill was like a mine that had sputtered to the end of its fuse, impossible to prevent from exploding. Even if he'd been able to warn them they'd never have desisted at this point—he knew his Irishmen too well. It was always the same, he thought bitterly. We're too emotional, too undisciplined, and that's why the cold, precise English will always beat us. We Irish have to talk, to tell the world of our hopes and our dreams and then, even when we know all is lost, to fall back on the mysticism of our race and go blundering on to our own destruction. It was the very reason he'd tried to iron all emotion out of his own nature and substitute an impassivity he'd copied from the English.

And there'd be more talking, he told himself, when the rising failed, as now it must with the authorities fore-warned. The English were good at that— at flogging a man until he broke and screamed of the fine General Holt who'd helped plan the rebellion and would soon return with a new army to sweep the bloody redcoats into the sea.

So, if they'd already doomed themselves by their bragging, what harm would there be if he tried to save himself? He had his family to think of. *He* hadn't betrayed the plot and, with the military doubtless marching from Sydney, he couldn't save them now. He dragged his sweating horse to a plunging halt outside Paymaster Cox's darkened house and, as his employer came out half-dressed and holding up a lantern, Holt shouted, 'Mr Cox, I've come to warn ye. The Irish convicts have risen at Castle Hill!'

Cox wasted only a few minutes in foolish questions. Then he sent for a sergeant and four men, who proceeded to turn the house into a fortress under Holt's direction. 'With your permission, sir,' he said, 'I'd like to send for my wife and children. I fear the rebels may call at my home and try to force me to lead them.'

'Of course.' Cox, stout and unmilitary in spite of his half-buttoned uniform, was in a twitter of alarm. 'They know you as a general and may well try to do so.' As Holt continued to snap orders at the soldiers, the Paymaster added, 'Joseph, it is apparent that your experience in these matters is greater than mine. Will you take command of our defence?'

Holt bowed. He knew that the fortified house of an officer of the New South Wales Corps would be the very last place the rebels would wish to visit. 'I place myself entirely at your service, sir.'

Cox clapped him on the shoulder. 'This will be the best night's work you've ever done in New South Wales, Joseph.'

At the prison farm, the whooping, triumphant convicts had locked the last of the constables into a hut and had gathered, many of them with blazing torches in their hands, outside their quarters. Cunningham mounted a barrel and there was a roar of exultation that died into silence as he raised his arms. 'All right, lads!' he shouted. 'We've struck our first blow for freedom. And we won!' They cheered again, slapping each other on the back, their faces blood-red and black-shadowed in the torchlight. 'Now there's no turning back. The die is cast. We are all brothers here and soon we'll be marching side by side with our brothers from the Hawkesbury—marching to freedom! Now our suffering is our strength. What man among us hasn't felt the lash of the cat and sworn vengeance? What man hasn't been torn from his loved ones, seen his house tumbled, been persecuted for his beliefs, unjustly accused or transported for a trifling crime? They'll say we are rebels, that we turned against the King. But isn't it our duty, in the name of all men, to turn against the tyrant?' They roared again. 'Let us now prepare to march to Parramatta, there to plant a tree of liberty. And let our hope be this: that at last some natural justice *does* emerge to sweep away the years of corruption, cruelty and ignorance. This is the time. Now the hour is right. We are free—or we are dead. Death or Liberty!'

'Death or Liberty!' they bawled. Dinny ran forward and set his torch to the thatch of his hut and the flames leapt up into the night sky.

In the doorway of his cottage Jonathan stood watching

the quiet peace of the moonlit night. And, in the far distance, he saw the tiny spark that bloomed into a red flower of fire. He turned to his wife. 'Mary,' he said, 'it's begun.'

CHAPTER NINE

'Where the devil', Cunningham asked angrily, 'is General Holt?' In the light of the flames that roared up from Dinny's hut, the prison farm looked like a scene from Dante's *Inferno* as the ragged shrieking convicts capered about brandishing pitchforks, their faces lit hellishly by the fire.

'It's five miles from the Brush Farm.' Dinny, too, was worried, but he didn't show it. 'No easy ride at night.'

'He said he'd be waiting nearby.' Johnston peered into the night that was pitch-black in contrast with the burning hut.

Dinny said, with a confidence he prayed would be justified, 'Ah, he's sure to be here soon.'

'We can't wait any longer.' Cunningham watched as the roof of the wattle-and-daub hut collapsed in a great cloud of sparks. 'We have to be in Parramatta by dawn so we'll carry out the first part of the plan. Each of us will take a column to move through the countryside and collect every weapon and every convict servant we can find. Captain O'Byrne, you go to the west, Captain Johnston to the east. I'll push southwards.' Dinny and Johnston nodded. 'Split your companies into platoons under the lieutenants and move fast. We'll marshal on Constitution Hill with the men from the Hawkesbury before we move on Parramatta.' He paused. 'I'll send a man to the General's farm to ask him to meet us on the hill in time to lead the attack. Until then,' he shook hands with them both, 'may God be with us all.'

Dinny held out his home-made pike, pointing west. 'All right, lads', he roared above the clamour. 'Follow me!'

'This way, men!' Johnston waved eastwards with the home-made cutlass he'd picked up.

Cheering, the men broke up into their three groups and went off into the night. Once into the bush, small detachments split off from the main bodies. They burst into the homes of the settlers. From the more prosperous they took the expensive muskets made by Joseph Manton, the silver-mounted powder-flasks, the ornately-cased matched pairs of pistols; they took with them the younger and more adventurous of the assigned servants. From the huts of the less well-to-do they took the edged tools, hoes and axes, that were just as lethal as the firearms in the hands of desperate men. Soon, every man had a weapon as they spread like a bushfire across the countryside.

It was all so silent, Jonathan thought. He didn't know quite what he'd expected—the roar of cannon? Trumpets? But, apart from some distant cheering after the fire had been lit, it had been like any other night. 'Something must have gone wrong', he said, prowling edgily round the hut. 'Perhaps the fire we saw wasn't the signal after all? There's no fire now. Nothing.'

Mary looked up from where she was patching a shirt to give her hands something to do. 'Or perhaps it's all over.' She glanced with distaste at the musket that was propped against the wall. 'Either way, there's no need to keep that thing loaded. You can put it away, you can close the door, then we'll douse the fire and go to bed and let this night pass us by.'

'I couldn't.' Jonathan shook his head stubbornly. 'Not with Dinny and the others out there. You can't expect me just to forget them.'

'And why not?' She looked up at him. 'It's what I have to do, and they're my own countrymen. If I let myself think of them going to fight the redcoats, I see faces . . . .' Her voice faltered for a moment. 'Faces of Michael Connor and

James Brannon of the *Britannia*, and that poor bolter Mick. Faces of dead men. And I see Dinny's face—and yours, Jonathan!'

* * * * *

At the barricade that now surrounded William Cox's house, General Holt rested his musket on the breastwork, the cold self-accusatory thoughts lying heavy on his mind like a dead man's hand. And Cox, with his nervous chatter, was nearly driving him mad. 'A strange turn of fate, Joseph', he was saying. 'Transported for your part in the '98 rebellion and now fighting side by side with the forces of His Majesty.'

The cold hand seemed to grip a little tighter. But hardly *fighting*, he told himself. Merely establishing my *bona fides* so that I may try again at a better time. The French had a phrase for it: *reculer pour mieux sauter*. To move back so as to jump better.

But Dinny O'Byrne would have a phrase for it, too. To mizzle off so as to save your own neck.

He stayed there with his thoughts as the long night passed, his son Joshua appearing at one stage to tell him that the rebels had been to his house, asking for him. And, towards the end of the night that, to him, was like a wake, Cox said, 'It must only be a matter of time before they surrender. Whatever made the deluded fools think they could succeed? I mean—a rabble of convicts against trained soldiers?'

Holt said quietly, 'They could have done it. If they had held the advantage of surprise, they might have carried the field.'

'But they didn't, and they won't, eh?' Cox chuckled—a' smug, Paymaster-like chuckle. 'I shall see that the Governor hears of your loyal conduct, Joseph. You have served His Majesty well.'

And the cold dead hand lay heavily on Joseph Holt as he said, 'I only did, Mr Cox, what I saw to be my duty.'

* * * * *

Mary had fallen asleep across the table, her head in the crook of her arm. Jonathan shivered suddenly. The fire in the hearth had died to a heap of white ash; he took a blanket and draped it round his wife's shoulders. As she lifted her head he said, 'I didn't want to wake you. But, now, why don't you go to bed?'

She pulled the blanket round her more closely. 'Will you come, too?'

'I couldn't sleep.' He kissed her gently. 'But I promise I won't go out of the house and leave you. Not tonight.' He was leading her to the bed when she stopped, listening.

Outside in the summer night a twig had cracked under a boot. A voice muttered hoarsely. Then with a suddenness that made them both jump, a fist beat on the door. Dinny O'Byrne called, 'Jonathan!'

He went to the door, unlatched it and swung it open. Dinny stood with his head up, his pike by his side like a lance, his followers crowding behind him. He said, 'Are ye coming with us, Jonathan?'

Jonathan looked at Mary, then back to Dinny. His voice decisive now, he said, 'No, Dinny. I'm not.'

Dinny nodded tightly. 'It's as I thought.' He jerked his head at the musket that leaned against the wall. 'Ye'll understand if I take it?' He moved inside and picked up the gun, handing his pike to one of the men who came into the hut after him.

Jonathan took down the powder horn and shot pouch from a peg. 'You'll need these as well, Dinny.' Out of the corner of his eye he saw one of the convicts pick up his hoe. He said sharply, 'Leave that!'

The man looked at Dinny who said, 'You heard.' The rebel put the hoe back. Dinny jabbed a thumb at the door and the men went out. He said, 'I must be going now.'

Mary came forward with a little rush and threw her arms round his neck. 'Take care.' She fought down the dread and despair she felt for him. 'May the saints be with you and guard you.'

The old Dinny O'Byrne looked out of the eyes of this martial stranger for a moment. 'Sure, and haven't the saints given me up long ago? But, if a blessed creature like yourself should put in a word for me, who knows?' He turned to Jonathan. 'Now, you look to our girl and take good care of her.' He raised the musket in salute. 'And I'll look to your friend here to take good care of me.' And he was gone.

Jonathan took his wife in his arms. She said, against his chest, 'You wanted to go with him, didn't you?'

He thought for a moment. Then, almost with surprise, he said, 'No. No, I didn't. This is where I'll fight my battles. Here.'

*　*　*　*　*

For the Commandant of Parramatta Barracks it was not, as he had so confidently predicted, a day as uneventful as any other Sunday. On the contrary, he thought, breaking into a light sweat as he remembered the two clear warnings he'd had of the rebellion, it could be the day on which he was cashiered for gross neglect of duty. He strode into his office not long before midnight, buttoning his coatee, with a settler called Joyce at his heels. 'How many convicts entered your home, sir?' he asked crisply. His sergeant placed a lantern on the desk, sat down and picked up a pen.

'I couldn't tell. Half a dozen—a dozen, perhaps. Some were already armed and they took every weapon in the house.'

Abbott indicated a chair. 'So now at least twelve of them are armed.' He went to stand behind his desk.

'Captain . . .' Joyce, looking shaken, settled himself. 'I called in at several houses on the way here. The blackguards have been to every one. There are bands of the villains all over the district shouting "Death or Liberty" —that they intend to attack this town—march on Sydney. . . .'

'Begging your pardon, sir,' the sergeant cut in, 'but would you mind speaking more slowly?' His quill raced over the page as he spoke.

Abbott said impatiently, 'We can dispense with a written record, sergeant.'

The NCO went numb with shock. Dispense with . . .? Slowly, his quill drooped to half mast and he laid it down. Gawd, he thought. Things must be serious. 'I thank you, Mr Joyce,' Abbott said, 'for your prompt and courageous action. The sergeant here will see to your immediate refreshment.'

The settler bowed. As he went through the doorway Greville stood aside to let him pass. Abbott snapped, 'What is the situation, Mr Greville?'

The ensign, for once, had lost his urbane calm. His pale face was flushed and his eyes were unnaturally bright as he said urgently, 'More settlers have arrived in the barracks, sir, seeking protection. They claim that several hundred armed convicts are marching on Parramatta. I gather', the thin smile appeared for an instant, 'the Reverend Marsden has departed the town by water with a number of the ladies.'

There was no bloody justice, Abbott told himself, in the Army. Raise the alarm, and your superiors play the very devil for being disturbed at dinner. Fail to raise it, and they have your tripes for breakfast. He said urgently, 'Greville, take the fastest horse you can find and ride immediately to Sydney. Inform the Governor, and urge him to send Major Johnston with every available man.' He leaned forward on his desk, his face harshly shadowed in the light from the lantern. 'Make it quite clear to His Excellency that this is no mere convict outbreak. This is armed rebellion!'

To oppose it, Captain Abbott had fifty-six men of the New South Wales Corps garrisoned at Parramatta, very few of whom had seen action. The rebels were close to seven or eight hundred strong now, with the servants they had recruited from the farms; they were armed, cloaked in darkness as they moved unhindered in their three groups about the countryside, and they were filled with the invincibility of men who know they are fighting for their lives. By the small hours of Monday morning they commanded a hundred square miles north of the Parramatta River and were marching to unite at Constitution Hill, some two miles north-west of the garrison town itself, and looking forward to their rendezvous with the reinforcements from the Hawkesbury, with each of the three captains hoping to find that General Holt had joined up with one of the other two groups.

But when, several miles short of the rallying point, Dinny O'Byrne's column fell in with that of Phillip Cunningham, the doubts that had been gnawing at the latter began to bite more deeply when he saw that Holt was not with the other party and Dinny said, 'There's no sign of the General?'

'His son claimed he hadn't been home all day.'

'Then, for sure,' Dinny said heartily, 'he'll be waiting for us at Constitution Hill.' When the other man didn't answer he added, 'He's doing what's best.'

'What's best for us,' Cunningham asked, 'or for himself?'

'He's a great soldier, a great man. He'd not abandon our cause with never a word.'

'I want to believe that, Dinny,' Cunningham said quietly, 'and I think you believe it, too. But we may have to face a battle without the General. Will ye follow me?'

Dinny said simply, 'To the death.'

Cunningham gripped his arm for a second, then turned to his followers. 'All right, boys! Forward! To Constitution Hill and liberty!' They cheered and moved off, brandishing their weapons. In the moonlight, their rags and dirt and the pathetic collection of garden implements carried by some were hidden. There was only the cold blue gleam of metal, the muffled tramp of footsteps, the set, determined faces as they advanced like the army of Brian Boru, the High King of Ireland who swept the Norsemen into the sea.

There were others on the roads, too, in the moonlit early hours of that Monday morning, another army whose tramp of boots was machine-like in its precision, whose uniforms were very far from being in rags, whose weapons were the reverse of pathetic. Major George Johnston's column was marching in perfect step, its fixed bayonets flashing, along the moon-bleached highway from Sydney. And marching fast, the tramping boots chewing up the miles. But even so the Major, a formidable figure in the huge black-feathered bonnet he wore, turned in his saddle. 'Mr Laycock, would you force the pace? We must reach Parramatta before dawn!'

In the moonlight, Quartermaster Laycock looked like something out of a legend, his six feet six inches suggesting that a giant had been dressed in the scarlet-and-yellow of the Corps and placed at the head of the column of marching men. And his voice rang out into the night like that of Stentor as he bawled, 'All right, lads, pick it up! Dawdle along like this and there'll be no time for your rum issue! Left! . . . . Left! . . .' The crunch-crunch of boots increased perceptibly in tempo.

Dawdle! Greville thought as he rode at Johnston's side. Good God, his stallion was almost at a trot as it was. At this rate, we'll be in Parramatta by five o'clock. . . .

On Constitution Hill, Cunningham said, 'No sign of Liam Johnston's company. No sign of the reinforcements from the Hawkesbury and . . .' he paused, '. . . no sign of General Holt.'

Dinny stared at the silent countryside. It seemed to him that, already, the moonlight was fading and that the wind on his cheek carried the promise of dawn. 'Unless we move on Parramatta soon,' he said thoughtfully, 'we lose the cover of darkness.'

That was what had been worrying Cunningham. 'If we attack now, without our full force, we risk too many lives. But, if we wait for the others to join us, we're committed to a battle in daylight.' He walked away, then back, thinking. 'We must wait,' he said, 'and hope they get here before dawn. At least the men can take a rest.'

Long before dawn, the column from Sydney had swung, still in perfect step, into Parramatta Barracks and, by the time the sky to the east was streaked with saffron, the men were sitting among their stacked muskets, eating their breakfasts and resting their aching feet. 'Sixteen miles in three hours!' a young private said. 'I don't call that bad, eh?'

'Bloody loafing, we was.' A corporal stuffed bread into his mouth and gestured with a crust. 'Why, I remember once, when I was with the 73rd . . . .'

Major Johnston was also breakfasting, seated at Abbott's desk and wolfing scrambled eggs. He was a Dumfries man, outspoken and impatient of inefficiency of any kind. He was also a professional to his fingertips, ruthless and as hard as nails. He said in his Scots voice between mouthfuls, 'The Governor gave me written orders—badly written, I should add. Might as well have been in Greek. Had to ask him to read them out to me.'

Abbott said drily, 'Did that make them any clearer, sir?'

Johnston gave a bark of laughter. 'Barely—except in one respect. He desires that I fire upon any person who attempts to run away when challenged. I told him that's all I want.' He waved his fork. 'We have martial law, gentlemen.' He turned his head as there was a tap at the door and Greville ushered in Father Dixon. 'Good morning, Father', the Major said briskly. 'Thank ye for coming so promptly.'

'The gentleman', said Greville casually, 'was fully dressed when he opened the door.'

'Was he, now?' Johnston sat back, wiping his mouth with a napkin as he studied the priest. 'Up early to say your prayers, Father, were ye?'

Dixon had been in front of men like Johnston before. He recognised the type—a superbly-trained fighting-machine that, once given a directive, would stop at nothing, literally nothing, to accomplish it. He said levelly, 'Why have I been brought here?'

'I think ye know full well. A battle is imminent between a large party of your countrymen and the military. I must warn ye that my men are ready for blood.' He turned to the huge Quartermaster who was putting away a vast mound of fried ham in a corner. 'Agreed, Mr Laycock?'

'They are that, sir.' Laycock, caught with his mouth full, swallowed. 'Spoiling for a fight.'

'So I look to you, Father, to persuade your misguided countrymen to lay down their arms.'

Dixon had seen the redcoats in the yard. He'd seen the sunrise. He'd seen, too, what had happened in Ireland when an untrained rabble of patriots attempted a pitched battle with a man like Major Johnston in broad daylight. Hooves clattered outside and there were raucous shouts from the yard as he said, 'If I do this, will their lives be spared?'

Johnston stared at him coldly. 'Do not bargain with me, sir! If you wish to remain a priest in this colony, you will do as I say. Is that . . .?' He broke off as the mounted trooper who had accompanied the column as a scout came into the room. 'Yes, Andlesack?'

Andlesack snapped to attention, his helmet under his arm. 'Sir! There's a large force of rebels occupying high ground just beyond the town!'

Johnston was on his feet in a flash, scooping up his huge bonnet and sword-belt. Laycock was regretfully pushing aside the remnants of his feast. The Major said, 'Let's have a look at them, then. Form the men up, Mr Laycock. Trooper, escort Father Dixon.' He gave the priest his cold stare. 'He will be accompanying us.' He turned to Captain Abbott. 'Keep your garrison at their posts, Captain. Detach a party under Ensign Greville to scout for rebel stragglers. The town militia can follow me in support,' he grinned, 'if they can catch me.'

Abbott, relieved beyond words at having the situation taken out of his hands, said, 'Good hunting, sir.'

Johnston paused at the door after Father Dixon and the trooper had gone out. 'I fear my hounds are too ill-tempered from broken sleep and a long march. So it will not be a "good" hunt, Captain. But it should be a quick one.'

Dinny O'Byrne was scouting in the low scrub just outside the town. Crouching, he surveyed the scattering of thatched huts and white houses in the grey light. 'Not a sign of life', he whispered to the man with him. 'We may be in luck yet . . . .'

A rebel, incongruously dressed in a filthy but once well-cut bottle-green coat with torn and dirty lace at his wrists, ran up bent double and threw himself down, gasping with exertion and excitement. 'Redcoats . . . marching out of the High Street . . . heading this way!'

'How many?' Dinny asked.

'Too bloody many.'

'Back to the hill.' Dinny scrambled to his feet. 'Come on!'

*　*　*　*　*

The sunlight, pale gold and tinged with pink, lit Mary's face as she knelt on a chest at the window, looking at the tranquil beauty of the sunrise. Jonathan was washing in a tin bowl at the table. He turned in surprise, water dripping from his chin, as she laughed suddenly. She said, turning to him, 'I was just thinking of the time I met Dinny—when he pricked those two holes in his leg and pretended it was snake-bite so he could come to the house. And the time he stole a pocketful of tarts that Mrs Kemp had just set out to cool.'

Jonathan dried his hands, smiling faintly as he remembered. 'We ate those tarts together in the stable-yard. We were talking and . . .' his eyes misted with memory, '. . . and he said neither of us could ever think of marrying you.' Mary's smile faded. 'He said a convict slave couldn't have anything to offer a girl like you.' He put down his towel. 'My life's changed a lot since then. But his never changed. He thought a lot of you, in his own funny way.'

They were discussing him, Mary thought with horror, as if he was already dead. She said, her voice rising, 'And d'you think I don't care about him? Do you think my heart's not breaking at the thought of what might have happened to him? Jonathan, don't you understand? I want them to win! I want them to crush the redcoats!' She stopped suddenly and the fire went out of her. 'But I don't believe they can. It's a dream that kept them alive but now . . .' her voice faltered, '. . . now, it's going to destroy them.'

Will Price, too, had been watching the sunrise. He pulled his jacket down from its peg and reached for his hat as Polly, yawning and only just awake, came into the tap-room from the kitchen. She said, 'Will! Where are ye going?'

'I can't stand any more of this waiting.' He went to the door. 'I'm going to ride towards Parramatta and see if I can find out what's happened.'

She said anxiously, 'You won't do anything foolish?'

'Me?' He grinned at her reassuringly. 'I'm a very sensible man. Just keep both doors barred and I'll be back as soon as I can.'

*   *   *   *   *

Phillip Cunningham said, 'I never thought I'd be so glad to see your ugly face, Liam!' At least, he'd thought when the lookouts had reported Captain Liam Johnston's men coming up the hill, that's one worry taken care of. The two groups met in the warm morning sunlight, shaking hands, slapping backs and shouting with relief.

'Nor I yours.' Liam Johnston, his breeches wet to the knee with dew, his face dirty and scratched with thorns, said, 'Lord, what a night it's been! Some of my men are still missing. And not a sign of the force from the Hawkesbury, though I had a lookout five miles down the road.' He stopped short and looked about. 'The General? Where is he?'

Cunningham said flatly, 'God or the Devil knows.' He shrugged. 'All this time there's been a doubt in my mind that I've tried to ignore and forget. But no more. He's betrayed us, Liam. So—will you have me as your leader?'

The younger man put a hand on his shoulder. 'None better', he said quietly.

Cunningham said, 'We'll have to move quickly now . . . .'

Dinny and his two men burst out of the scrub below them and came pounding up the hill. Fighting for breath, Dinny said, 'Redcoats! Heading out of Parramatta! This way!'

Cunningham looked at Liam Johnston, then back at Dinny. 'How many?' Dinny shook his head. 'Did ye see who was leading them?' The other two rebels were lying flat in the wet grass, panting. If it's a detachment under Captain Abbott, Cunningham thought, and we attack instantly . . . .

The man in the bottle-green coat said, '. . . Officer . . . in a big Scotch bonnet . . . .'

Cunningham went very still. 'It's their commanding officer. They've brought a column from Sydney.' He was thinking aloud. 'But we still outnumber them. And if we fall back until we meet the men from the Hawkesbury . . . .'

Dinny, squatting and getting his breath back, looked up. 'Fall back? Ye mean turn and run!'

'I mean fall back!' Cunningham snapped. 'You've said you'll have me as your leader and now I'm telling you this: never underestimate a force of redcoats. Believe me, we need every man we can get before we make a stand. Agreed?'

The other two nodded. 'We're to fall back', Johnston shouted to his men, 'to the Hawkesbury road.' The rebels, resting on the grass, looked at him with disbelief. The three leaders went among them, gesturing and shoving. And so, murmuring and reluctant, they turned and streamed down the hill, heading north-west.

Trooper Andlesack saw them go. He reined in his horse beside the Major and saluted. 'The rebels are falling back along the Hawkesbury road, sir.'

Major Johnston showed his teeth in his weather-beaten face. 'They're starting to run.' He half turned in his saddle. 'They'll have to run fast, eh, Mr Laycock?'

'They will indeed, sir!'

'Your best pace, Mr Laycock!'

'Yessah!' The Quartermaster raised his foghorn voice.

'Detaa—*chment*! Muskets at the port—one!' Down the double file of men, right arms snapped across, the movement as precise as the beat of the marching feet. 'Two!' Again in perfect synchronisation, the musket butts swung across the scarlet-and-yellow coatees, the left hands smacked against wooden musket-stocks, the bayonets stabbed out diagonally, exactly aligned. 'At the double! One-two, one-two . . .!' The men with their stony expressionless faces could have been so many life-sized clockwork toys as they began jogging in step along the road.

And the rebel withdrawal was becoming a rout. At first they had walked, puzzled but still full of the impetus that had taken them to the top of Constitution Hill. But someone looked over his shoulder and his mate joked, 'Keep going, Patrick. It's me that's behind ye, and not a redcoat!' Somebody picked it up. 'Redcoats, by Jasus!' Another man began to run. And then they were all running, spilling off into the bush, crashing through it, the panic spreading the more they ran. Cunningham yelled, 'Steady, lads! Keep together!' but they were sweeping past him now so that he, Dinny and Liam Johnston had to run to keep at their head. And, seeing their leaders running, the men ran the faster, some of them throwing their arms away into the bush. 'Take heart, boys!' Cunningham shouted desperately. 'Our brothers from the Hawkesbury are coming to meet us!'

*   *   *   *   *

'It's going to be bad.' Will slid from his horse outside Jonathan's where Mary and her husband were standing under a sky that was now overcast, trying to imagine what was taking place out there beyond the tall trees that shut them in. 'Dinny and the others, they're on the run back to the Hawkesbury with a pack of redcoats after them. I've left Polly at "The Bird" getting some things together—bandages and the like.'

Mary said, 'We'll come with you.'

'Meet us back at "The Bird". I'll stow the horse and we'll cut through the bush to the Hawkesbury road.' He wheeled the horse and galloped away.

* * * * *

Men, drained of stamina by years of malnutrition, were dropping out of the rebel ranks, exhausted. More began to fall out, white-faced and gasping, as they struggled up a hill. They were ten miles north-west of Parramatta and some, Cunningham knew, could not go on. He shouted, 'Halt! We rest here!' As Dinny O'Byrne and Liam Johnston collapsed gratefully on the grassy slope he said, keeping his voice down, 'We must face up to it. There'll be no men from the Hawkesbury.' He gestured at the weary, ragged figures sprawled on the hilltop. 'This is our army. We've been on the march all night and half the morning with nothing to put in their bellies and I can ask them to go no further. This hill is as good a place as any to make our stand.' As his two captains nodded he turned to his men. 'All right, boys! We'll run no more. We face the enemy on this ground!'

They began to stir. One or two even scrambled to their feet. 'I fear that our brothers from the Hawkesbury won't be here before the redcoats. Well, that's their misfortune because, like Liam Johnston here, and Dinny O'Byrne, and you—' he pointed, '—and you—we'll all be remembered as the men who struck the first blow against tyranny on these shores.' Someone gave a cheer. 'This is a proud day, and I am proud to be numbered among you. For you men here today are kings beside those who oppose us and those who choose to spurn our cause. You are loyal. You are steadfast. You are a credit to the land that gave you birth.'

He had them in the palm of his hand, Dinny O'Byrne thought, watching the men climbing eagerly to their feet as if getting out of bed after a good night's sleep, fresh and alive and burning again with the desire for freedom. He could feel the uplift himself. Cunningham drew his sword.

'The honour of leading you has fallen on my shoulders and, again, I give you my pledge. Death or Liberty!' He waved the sword and the men cheered, brandishing their weapons against the morning sky. 'Now, boys, musketmen to the front!' The men, their eyes alight, began to take up their positions. 'Pikemen in support, ready to take the front line for the advance!' He looked across the rolling bushland towards the unseen enemy, O'Byrne and Liam Johnston standing beside him. 'All right,' he said under his breath, 'let them come.'

The column halted as Trooper Andlesack galloped up to the Major who sat his horse like a statue. Father Dixon, on a white cob, was beside him. 'The insurgents', the trooper said, saluting. 'On a hill, sir. About a mile ahead.'

Major Johnston nodded thoughtfully. He took a white handkerchief out of his pocket and handed it to Andlesack. 'Ride ahead of me with this, Trooper.' To the priest he said, 'Father Dixon, you will accompany me. And Mr Laycock. . . .'

'Yes, sir?'

'Bring the men up at the double.' He shook out his reins. After a moment Father Dixon followed him while the trooper spurred his horse on ahead.

They turned off the road through a belt of trees and reined in their blowing, fidgeting horses at the foot of a hill that was hedged with pikes under the overcast sky, a row of muskets levelled ready in the front line. Andlesack waved the white flag. Major Johnston sat back in his saddle, his professional eye assessing the opposition. Devil of a lot of the villains, he thought. He glanced back along the road, leaned across to Andlesack and, out of Father Dixon's hearing, murmured, 'We must play for time.' He turned to the priest. 'Urge them to lay down their arms, sir. It is their only hope.'

Dixon looked at him. There was something going on here that he did not fully understand. But, to save life . . . . He touched his heels to his cob and trotted up the slope.

Major Johnston said, 'Trooper, mark my actions and

149

follow suit.' He drew a pistol from its saddle holster, checked the priming and thrust it under his sash. Andlesack, watching him expressionlessly, did the same.

Dixon halted in front of the rebels. He said, 'My countrymen, I beg you, lay down your arms. It is the only way to avoid bloodshed and destruction.'

In the silence that hung over the still ranks of the rebel army Cunningham said, 'We cannot, Father. We have chosen our course.'

Father Dixon glanced helplessly at Major Johnston and the trooper as they rode up to halt beside him. The Major said in his Scots burr, 'The Governor is on his way here to address you.' Dixon stared at him, astonished. There was a sudden shifting in the rebel ranks. 'In the meantime, I am here to address you on his behalf.'

Cunningham turned excitedly to O'Byrne and Liam Johnston. 'The Governor! Did ye hear that?'

The Major said, 'I call upon your leaders to come forward.'

Cunningham and Liam Johnston looked at one another. Dinny said urgently, 'Don't trust him!'

There was a pause. Then the Major smiled contemptuously. 'Your leaders must have very little spirit if they will not come out into the open to talk with me.'

Cunningham, stung, shouted, 'We'll talk with ye!'

Dinny grabbed his arm. 'It's a trap!'

Cunningham shook him off. 'Let's hear what he has to say. There can be no harm in that.'

'I'm with ye there, Phillip', Liam Johnston said.

'We've had nothing but treachery from these bastards!' Dinny was almost shouting with apprehension. 'Why should we trust them now?'

'Then you stay here with the men', Cunningham said impatiently. 'Liam and I will hear him out.' He and his fellow-captain, their swords in their hands, walked down the slope.

As they approached, the Major urged his horse forward. The trooper did the same. Cunningham and Liam Johnston thought they were being granted the courtesy of being met halfway. As Father Dixon watched, puzzled and uneasy, from the background, the two rebel leaders stared up at the daunting figure of the Major, gigantic in the raven-black bonnet. He said coldly, 'Whom do I have the honour of addressing?'

'Phillip Cunningham.'

'Liam Johnston.'

'I must urge you to surrender. If you do, I undertake to present your case to the Governor as favourably as I can.'

As favourably as would the Devil himself, Cunningham thought. He said unhesitatingly, 'We will not surrender.'

'You pose me a problem.' The Major's horse appeared to become refractory. It reared and, as it swung round, he glanced back at the road. 'I have no wish to shed blood. What is it you require?'

'Freedom to leave this colony in peace and a boat to take us home.'

'That . . .' the horse fidgetted again, this time crabbing and circling round the two standing men, '. . . is quite impossible.'

'Then', Cunningham said flatly, 'it's death or liberty.'

As the Major brought his horse under control he saw what he was waiting for. Laycock and the column was debouching from the trees at the double. He said, 'Death or liberty, is it? Well, I'll liberate you, you scoundrels!' He whipped the pistol out from under his sash and held it to Cunningham's head. Andlesack did exactly the same to Liam Johnston.

Father Dixon saw the column burst out of the trees. He heard Quartermaster Laycock shout, 'Detachment, halt! Right face!' He saw the two rebel leaders disarmed and herded past him into the scarlet-and-yellow ranks that were already checking their priming. In an agony of horror, he shrieked to the men on the hill, 'For the love of God, lay down your arms!'

He heard Dinny O'Byrne scream, 'No!'

Major Johnston said calmly, 'Cut them to pieces, Mr Laycock.'

CHAPTER TEN

To Dinny O'Byrne, accustomed though he had been throughout his turbulent life to a denial of fair treatment, to being always outmanoeuvred by the power of authority, it was an act of betrayal appalling in its enormity. He stared disbelievingly at the scarlet-and-yellow ranks that had swallowed up his friends as if they had disappeared into a quicksand, followed helplessly by Father Dixon. Through a red fog of fury he saw the apocalyptic figure of Quartermaster Laycock, his sword drawn, walk forward and say, his voice deadly quiet for once, 'Front rank, kneel!' Like puppets activated by the one string, the line of men sank onto the right knee. 'Front rank, ready! Aim!' The Brown Besses swung up as one, the red, beefy faces squinting along the barrels. Laycock raised his sword.

It was at that moment that Phillip Cunningham, dazed by the speed with which it had all happened, woke up. He lunged through the ranks towards the huge Quartermaster, his arm extended as if in appeal. 'Stop!' he yelled.

Laycock whirled and, in the same movement, slashed his sword down across Cunningham's head.

It couldn't be, Dinny O'Byrne thought. It was all some hideous nightmare in which his comrade was reeling to one side, his hands clapped to his face and the wet crimson blood spurting through his fingers. He went down, kicking in agony. 'Oh, Jesus!' he screamed. Then, with a final spasm, he was still.

'Murderers!' The others scarcely recognised Dinny O'Byrne's voice. He stood for a moment, his face contorted with rage and hatred. Then he turned to his men. 'Come on!' he yelled, his voice cracking.

As the rebels started downhill in a ragged charge, Quartermaster Laycock called, 'Fire!'

The line of kneeling soldiers disappeared in a bank of white smoke stabbed with orange flame and the crash of the volley was like one gigantic thunderclap. A high wind seemed to hit the rebel front rank as men were blown off their feet under the impact of the one-ounce lead balls. 'Rear rank forward!' Laycock bawled. 'One, two, three!' The men marched through the gaps in the front rank in three simultaneous steps. One of them, hit by the ragged volley fired by the rebels as they ran, flung up his arms and toppled forward, his musket flying. The other ignored him as he lay writhing. 'Kneel!' They dropped as one. What was now the rear rank was already re-loading, their ramrods busy. 'Fire!' Another redcoat crumpled as the line exploded in smoke and flame. 'Rear rank forward!'

Dinny O'Byrne was spun sideways by a sledgehammer blow and the smoke, the screaming, the crack of muskets dissolved into a black silence. As he fell, the rebels halted their charge. They faltered, panic-stricken, as a third volley tore into them. Then they broke and ran. In the fog-bank of smoke that was drifting across the slope, Laycock bawled, 'Cha-a-arge!' The two ranks of redcoats surged forward, cheering—cheers that turned to yells of exultation as the killing-lust took them. 'Cut them to pieces', the Major had said, and they did just that as they caught up with the screaming, terrified fugitives who tripped and fell and begged for mercy as the bayonets flashed in the light, then stabbed until they gleamed red and dripped and shone no more. To the horrified priest it was like a flock of seagulls he'd once seen, their beaks jabbing methodically as they ravaged a colony of frogs.

Mary and her husband saw it all as they stood with Polly and Will Price in the cover of the trees. Too numbed to move or speak, they stood watching as the prisoners, Liam

Johnston among them, were placed under guard. Then they went forward, hesitantly, to give what help they could to the living while Father Dixon moved among the carnage with tears running down his cheeks to care for the souls of the dying. Gently, Jonathan and Will turned their women away from the more terrible of the sights—the boy with his entrails spilling over his hands as he held them to his gaping belly, the man with the bloody mask that had once been his face. Mary stopped beside a tall, black-haired figure that lay curled as if asleep in a puddle of blood. Too cold for fear, she bent and turned the face to the sky. It was a stranger and not Dinny O'Byrne. She went looking for him, stepping over the twisted corpses and calling his name.

But she didn't find him. And when she and Polly had done all they could and could stand no more, they left their men who were helping to carry away the corpses and walked home through the bush. To Mary, it seemed so wrong that the clouds had now cleared to allow the sun to shine with the golden glow of late afternoon, that birds should be singing in the tall gums, the cicadas shrilling like the dry, drowsy voice of summer itself. The heavens should weep, she thought bitterly, for what they had seen this day. All she wanted now was to be home, the door shut and she safe in Jonathan's arms. She began to hurry, almost dragging Polly as she neared the hut. Then she stopped.

The door of the cottage stood ajar.

She seized Polly's arm and pointed. 'Someone's broken in', she whispered. 'And—listen!' There was the jar of a chair being moved. 'They're still inside!' Polly stared at her, her eyes wide with fright. Mary went to the half-open door as quietly as she could. She pushed it further open and peered inside, her heart pounding.

The man with the musket tucked under his left arm snarled, 'Stop where ye are or I'll blow your head off!'

'Dinny!'

'Holy Mother of God!' He collapsed onto a chair.

Polly followed Mary inside. She said furiously, 'Dinny

O'Byrne! And us thinking for sure you were half a dozen red-coated blackguards!'

'And wasn't I thinking the same of you?' Under the smoke-blackened face, the familiar grin broke through as he saw Mary looking at the musket. 'I'm just returning Jonathan's gun.' Awkwardly, he leaned back and propped it against the wall.

Polly was staring at him, her eyes on his filthy, bloodstained shirt. 'Your arm—ye've been wounded.'

'Aye, but not badly. I'm better off than most.' Mary was already filling a bowl with water and tearing up a shirt into strips. 'Better off than Phillip Cunningham and . . . .'

'We saw.' Polly was slicing bread, fetching butter and cheese.

He nodded slowly, his eyes still shocked behind the attempted nonchalance as Mary cut away his sleeve and began on the wound. He said, 'Sure, and it's only a scratch. The ball's not lodged.'

'What are you going to do?' Mary asked. 'If they find you . . . .'

'They won't.' He nodded his thanks to Polly as she handed him a wedge of bread and cheese. 'I'll lie low for a while across the Hawkesbury River.'

They all heard it—the clop of hooves from outside, the clink of equipment, the tramp of boots. They stared at one another, then Mary jumped up and ran to the door. She went out, closing it behind her.

Greville was tossing his reins to a soldier, a sergeant and five more redcoats behind him. Without a word he strode straight for the door. She stood where she was on the threshold. 'You've no right . . . .'

He halted in front of her, so close that she could see the drop of perspiration that trickled down his smooth cheek. 'Under the state of martial law that now exists,' he said harshly, 'following today's mischievous—and misguided— attempt at rebellion, I have every right to search wherever I please.'

'There's no-one in there that you're seeking . . . .'

'Stand aside!'

'No! You've no right . . . .'

Greville jerked his head at the sergeant who strode forward and pulled Mary away from the door. He drew his sword. Then, with two redcoats, their bayonets fixed, at his back, he went into the hut.

Polly sat at the table, daintily eating a piece of bread and cheese. There was nobody else in the room. She said politely, 'Good day to ye, Mr Greville.'

He turned to the sergeant, who pushed Mary inside. He stared for a moment at the fleeting surprise, then relief, that showed in her eyes. He pointed at the musket propped against the wall. 'Whose is that?'

'My husband's', Mary said with perfect truth.

He picked it up and sniffed delicately at the muzzle. 'It has been recently fired.'

'This morning.' To her own astonishment, the ring of truth in her voice remained unaltered. 'He went out into the bush and shot a wild dog that had been at our hens.'

'And left his gun uncleaned.' Greville put the musket down. His eyes went down from Mary's to the sticky brown substance that had come off on to his white glove.

'That's blood', she said quickly. 'Wild dog's blood.'

'And the carcass?'

'He buried it where he shot it.'

'A recently-discharged, blood-stained musket', Greville said thoughtfully. 'Found on such a day as this in the home of an Irishwoman known to have consorted with rebels. I wonder what a magistrate would make of that?' He stared at her while she stood before him, the hatred showing in her eyes. He sheathed his sword. 'For the moment, you are at liberty.' He strode to the door. 'But . . .' he turned back, '. . . these premises and their occupants remain under the strongest suspicion. Sergeant!'

As he went out, Polly said sweetly, 'Good afternoon, Mr Greville.' Her courtesy ignored, she took a bite of bread and cheese. When the clump of boots had gone she said, 'He went out through the wood-hatch.'

It was not, Ensign Greville thought irritably, a good

afternoon at all. First, he'd raided that squalid little tavern where the rebel ruffians had been known to congregate, only to find that the birds, far from being in the barley, had flown. Then that pair of Irish slatterns had behaved damned suspiciously but the evidence, really, wasn't strong enough—not even for the Reverend Marsden—to convict on. He brightened considerably when he encountered Jonathan Garrett tramping along the track towards his house in company with a neighbour, the drunken and dissolute Sam Fitchett, but once again there wasn't enough proof of insurgency about the pair of them to hang a cat, although Garrett had looked most damnably shifty when asked about the wild dog he was supposed to have shot. Greville had been forced to content himself with a few threats and a promise that, if found out after dark, they'd be shot on sight. But, at least, he'd be able to settle accounts—quite literally—with Sam Fitchett before very long.

'I owe him money. Jonas Pike, too.' Fitchett, his eyes bloodshot, his hands shaking, picked at his plate of boiled bacon and corn as he sat at dinner after Jonathan had brought him home after meeting him on his way back from the dreadful events of that day. 'Last December that damned Greville bought my wheat crop. Paid me in rum at two gallons an acre—after he'd bought it off a ship at ten shillings the gallon. It was Jonas-bloody-Pike as done the the deal. Said the rum was worth five pounds a gallon.'

Jonathan nodded grimly. The barter system in rum, by which the rich could profit at the expense of the poor, was an old evil in the colony. It was even said that the pious Richard Johnson, the clergyman who had played a silent role at the *Britannia* inquiry, had built the first church in Australia by paying his convict workmen part of their wages in rum which he valued at ten shillings a gallon after buying it at four shillings and sixpence—although he, of course, was not using the system for personal gain. Others, particularly in the New South Wales Corps, were doing so unashamedly.

'Of course,' Fitchett said, 'when I try to buy victuals

with it, I'm fortunate to get two pounds a gallon. Now it's all gone and the year barely begun. What I haven't bartered,' he shrugged his thin shoulders, 'I've drunk.'

Mary looked at the skinny, middle-aged little man with compassion. He lived alone with his old dog, Nimrod; there was nothing and nobody for him to turn to in the long lonely evenings except the rum-bottle. After she'd invited him to call whenever he chose, Jonathan walked a little way with him, Nimrod, his tail waving, coming out of the shadows to meet his master. Before going on alone, Sam said, a trifle awkwardly, 'I was wondering if I might borrow your rake for a few days, Jonathan? I seem to have mislaid mine and I've some work that needs doing.'

After Sam had gone off with it, Jonathan turned back to the house that always looked so beckoning with the lamplight streaming out through the open door. And Mary waiting for him . . . . Inside the house, he said to her, 'What a long sad day it's been.'

She nodded, putting away the remains of the food. 'And that poor man. So lonely. Jonathan, I couldn't tell you while he was here . . . .' She went to the corner and lifted the sack she'd draped over the musket. 'Dinny came here. He brought back your musket.'

He stared as he went to it. 'It's—there's blood on it!'

'He was wounded, but not badly. Polly and I attended to him. He's gone across the Hawkesbury.'

'He should have taken the gun. He'll need it in the wilderness for hunting.' A thought struck him. 'Lucky he wasn't taken here. I met Greville and some of his men on the track.'

'They were here', she said, trying not to re-live the terror of the encounter. 'I kept them outside while Polly got Dinny away through the wood-hatch.'

He stared at her, the enormity of what she'd gone through hitting him like a blow. 'Oh, Mary!' He took her in his arms and she clung to him desperately.

But, at least, one thing had come out well for Greville. As he was able to announce to Louisa Wiltshire a week later, after the hunt for the rebels had died down and martial law had been rescinded, he was now to be gazetted lieutenant. It took some of the lustre from his announcement when he was compelled to add that the promotion had been purchased and had not, as he would dearly have liked to say, been granted for bravery in action. Louisa smiled. 'The practice by which superior rank is gained by preferment and purchase', she pointed out, 'is the very basis of our military class structure. It is my regret that my dear husband chose to resign his commission in the Corps during his current visit to England. Why he should prefer farming to soldiering I will never understand.'

'Do not despise agriculture, ma'am.' Greville was thinking of certain plans of his own. 'The farmer will yet prove himself to be the very backbone of the colony.'

March gave way to April and an autumn of retribution in which Liam Johnston was hanged in chains, and others with him, while some went into penal servitude at the Coal River settlement. It was an autumn of high winds and icy, slanting rain that buffeted Jonas Pike as he went about on Greville's work. He arrived at 'The Bird in the Barley' one cold wet afternoon, seeking bottles of rum and information. 'Sam Fitchett', he said after he'd grumbled at the price of the liquor and Will Price had hinted that there were those who charged a good deal more. 'See much of him, do you?' He and a 'business partner', he explained, were worried about Sam's drinking habits; it was possible he might have been attempting to sell his assets—tools and so on—in return for grog.

'No,' Will said, 'he hasn't.' Then, after Pike had picked up the three bottles he'd paid for and tossed back the drink for which he had not, Will added, 'The dram you've just had, Mr Pike—I'll charge it to your business partner, should I? I'm sure Mr Greville won't mind.'

Mary and Jonathan, too, were concerned about Sam. They were even more concerned after Jonathan had called on his neighbour for the return of his rake and Sam had informed him, without a trace of shame, that he had sold it to buy the rum that he needed more than food and drink. 'It's stealing, Jonathan', Mary said with indignation. 'Nothing less.'

'Everybody in this colony steals.' He was thinking of the squalor of Sam's house, the overgrown state of his land. He was thinking, too, of the clinking that had come from Jonas Pike's saddlebags as the overseer had passed him on the track that led to Sam Fitchett's farm. The clink that might be made by bottles of rum. 'The big men steal big things—a man's dignity or his freedom or his life. The little man steals little things like his neighbour's rake.'

Or the silver-mounted coach-whip that Sam, half-drunk, tried to sell at the inn a few nights later. Will refused to buy, even after Sam had said he needed the money for food. 'You wouldn't buy food with the money, I'm sure of that', Will said, busily serving drinks.

'Wouldn't I just?' Sam produced one of Pike's bottles from his coat pocket. 'I've all the rum I need. So you can keep yours—and your damned money!'

Will leaned over the bar. 'I'll tell you what I'll do. I'll buy that rum you've got there. Ten shillings!' It was nearly twice its value and Polly, serving beside him, almost dropped a glass.

'Go to the devil!' Sam shouted. He collided with Jonas Pike who was coming through the doorway, stumbled outside, and set a course for his farm. As the cold night air hit him he staggered tipsily and began to sing. To lubricate his throat, he took a swig from his bottle. And another, to ward off the chill. He was quite close to Jonathan's farm when he collapsed into a ditch. Nimrod sat and watched over him as he snored.

Jonathan would scarcely have noticed his caterwauling even if he'd been in the same room, for Mary and he were already in bed and he had been on the point of dropping off to sleep when she'd said, 'Jonathan?'

He grunted. 'What?'

'Nothing.'

He drifted off again.

'Jonathan . . . .'

Jerked back from sleep, he said a trifle testily, 'What is it?'

'Look at me.'

He snorted, threshed round in the blankets and peered at her in the darkness. She was sitting up. She said almost in a whisper, 'I'm going to have a baby.'

He hadn't heard. 'Have a what?'

'A baby. I'm going to have a baby, Jonathan.'

'A baby?' He came awake and sat up as if the bed had caught alight.

She ran her fingertips down his arm. 'Are you pleased, Jonathan?'

It took some time for him to tell her just how pleased he was and for a long time after that they lay in each other's arms, he as delightedly awestruck as if he had just invented the process of human reproduction. They were still wide awake and talking softly in the dark when the faint tapping came at the shuttered window and the voice said quietly, 'Jonathan! Mary! Are ye awake?'

Jonathan lit a candle from the still-glowing fire, tucked his nightgown into his breeches and went to the door. Dinny O'Byrne said, 'It's only meself.'

'Dinny!' Mary, also up and fit to receive visitors, took both his hands in hers as he came inside, holding him at arm's length. Always dark-skinned, he was now weather-beaten almost black, with a short beard that gave him the air of a buccaneer. 'It's wonderful to see you so well—and free!'

'Free?' He gave her the well-remembered quizzical, bird-like glance. 'Aye—free to live with the blackfellows and bolters. The forest's my prison now.'

They gave him food and built up the fire and sat round it drinking mugs of tea. 'I'd have died but for those blacks', Dinny said, sitting back replete. 'They took me in when I was wounded and fed and housed me—God knows why, for they've little enough reason to care for the white men and it's but two years since Governor King sent old Penulwy's head back to London for Sir Joseph Banks to study.' He stared into the fire. 'There's more to them than we think. You've got to live with them to know . . . .' He was silent for a moment. The he stirred himself and laughed. 'Mary, you're looking more lovely every day, and that's a fact.'

Jonathan said, 'Tell him.'

She said, blushing and pretending not to understand, 'Tell him what?'

'Our news.' He smiled at her.

'No. You tell him, Jonathan.'

Dinny looked from one to the other. 'Well, sure now, and somebody'd better tell me before I blow apart with curiosity.'

Jonathan said, 'We're—Mary's going to have a baby.'

His bearded face split in a great grin. Mary said shyly, 'You're the first to know.'

They toasted the future infant prodigy in fresh mugs of tea. And, all too soon, it was time for Dinny to leave so as to be across the Hawkesbury River, the boundary of British authority, by daylight. Mary filled his pockets with cakes of Indian corn. They said they would pray for his safety, that he must come again soon, that he was to watch out for the bloodhound Greville. He gave them his devil-may-care grin, waved a hand in salute and strode off into the darkness.

In his ditch, Sam Fitchett was awakened by the voices. He peered blearily at the light streaming from Jonathan's hut. And he watched with interest as the tall, buccaneering figure waved and went off into the bush. When Nimrod licked his face he staggered to his feet. Then he set off for 'The Bird in the Barley' at a shambling trot.

All the drinkers had departed save Jonas Pike who, mellow and loquacious, was disregarding all Polly's attempts to evict him by sweeping the floor round his feet and blowing out most of the lamps. 'We're closed', she said sharply as the mud-stained, bleary-eyed Sam tottered in.

'It's Mr Pike I want. On a matter o' business.' He looked furtively at Will and Polly. 'Outside, eh, Mr Pike?' In the windy darkness he licked his lips, remembering the empty rum bottle he'd left in the ditch. 'How much', he asked, 'is a bit of information worth to you?'

The sergeant and five privates arrived just after dawn and, under Lieutenant Greville's direction, they pulled the contents of the cupboards onto the floor, emptied the flour-barrel, stripped the very bed from which they had aroused the sleeping couple. 'I'm sure you're both well aware of the penalties for harbouring insurgents.' Greville stood in the middle of the room, tapping a boot with his riding crop. Mary and Jonathan, tousled and in the clothes they'd barely had time to put on, stood side by side, their faces stiff with hate. 'Two men have already received five hundred lashes apiece and been sent to Norfolk Island.'

He turned as the sergeant stood to attention and saluted. 'Nothing untoward to report, sir.'

Greville stood for a moment while the slap of leather on leather became harder, faster. 'This time', he said at last, 'you've been lucky. But, next time, I'll have absolutely irrefutable evidence. A sworn statement by a witness, for instance.' He cast a final cold stare at the shambles he had created before he strode outside.

Sam Fitchett watched the patrol pass him as he stood by the track. Slowly, his filthy, trembling hand went to his mouth as he stared in horror up the hill to Jonathan's hut.

Mary bloomed in health and happiness as the cold autumn turned to winter—a bitter time and one, as Polly McNamara remarked, that the unborn child was well out of. She came to visit these days as midwife as well as neighbour, bringing advice and encouragement—and lemons. 'Lemon juice,' she said, 'to strengthen the baby's constitution. And he'll be needing all the strength you can give him, I'm thinking, if he's to survive the obstacles this place'll be putting in his path.'

For Greville, one obstacle was soon to be removed. He was in the tap-room of 'The Bird in the Barley' on a night when the wind set the inn-sign swinging and howled mournfully in the chimney. There were few drinkers abroad on such a night and he was able to talk confidentially to Will

Price. 'I'll wager', he said, taking a sip from his glass of rum as he stood at the bar, 'you're paying a pretty price for this liquor, landlord.' He held the glass up to the lamp-light. 'And not exactly what I'd call best quality, either.'

Will was polishing a glass. 'I have to take the best that comes my way, sir, things being what they are.'

'Well, now.' Greville leaned a little further across the bar. He put a finger to the side of his nose. 'Things being what they are, I find myself in the position of being able to put the finest spirits in the colony in your way, so to speak.'

'Really, sir?' Will stacked a glass on a shelf. 'In that case, I can't say I'm not more than a little interested. How much were you thinking of?'

'Aha!' The lieutenant sipped his rum, his pale eyes on Will. 'It's not quite as simple as that, my dear fellow. What I had in mind was a rather more personal interest in your establishment.'

Will frowned. 'I'm afraid I don't take your meaning, sir.'

Greville smiled. 'What I'm thinking of is a silent partnership. It could be profitable for both of us. I provide the rum—cheaply; you provide the means of selling it—not so cheaply, eh?'

Under such an arrangement, Will knew perfectly well who would be taking the lion's share of the profit. On the other hand, he didn't wish to thwart Greville directly. He reached for another glass to polish to give himself time to think, and at that moment Jonas Pike came in and Greville's attention was diverted. 'One for Mr Pike, landlord!' The lieutenant raised an eyebrow questioningly at his overseer.

Pike took the drink, shot a glance at Will and pointed to the table in the corner. 'Perhaps, if we could . . . ?' Greville nodded and led the way. When they were settled, Pike took a swig of his rum and leaned forward on his elbows, his voice lowered. 'By my reckoning, Fitchett's all ready to hook and land, Mr Greville, sir.'

'Excellent! When?'

'Tonight. I'll pick up another couple of bottles from here

and get him good and fuddled. He's so far gone in debt he'll sign it all over to us—he must.'

'Indeed he must, or he goes before the magistrates.' Greville smiled happily. 'Is there any possibility of landing another couple of fish on the same hook?'

'Sir?'

'That night Fitchett claimed to have seen the rebel O'Byrne leaving the Garretts' hovel—do you think he'd sign an affidavit to that effect?'

Pike grunted. 'I doubt it. Fitchett and the Garretts have been pretty thick again lately.'

'But, if we offered Fitchett a proposition—the opportunity of having his debts alleviated if he swears a statement implicating the Garretts with O'Byrne?' Greville sipped his rum. 'We would, of course, foreclose in any case.'

Pike said doubtfully, 'I'll do my best, Mr Greville.'

Sam Fitchett, his face sickly pale, his eyes bloodshot, came to the Garrett house next morning. 'I've done it', he said as Mary put a mug of hot tea into his shaking hand. 'Last night I signed away me farm. He tricked me into it— Pike did, working for bloody Greville. He got me drunk and I signed, cancelling all my debts. Otherwise they'd have hauled me into court.' He drank his tea, his head hunched into his shoulders, looking at them over the rim. 'But I didn't let you down. You've been good to me.' His thin shoulders shook in a sob. 'I couldn't do that, thank God, no matter how drunk I was.'

Jonathan said, 'What do you mean, Sam?'

He didn't answer. Instead, he put down his mug and up-ended an old calico bag he'd brought with him. A rusty rake-head fell to the floor. 'I found me old one after all', he said. 'You have it. But you'll have to cut a new handle for it, Jonathan.'

He came again the following morning. But this time he was driven in a cart, dead drunk. Jonas Pike booted him off the tail of the waggon and threw his few pitiful possessions after him while Nimrod sat by his unconscious master and whined. 'He wouldn't get out,' Pike said, 'so I had to evict him.' He climbed back into the driving seat and picked up the reins. 'I'm your new neighbour', he said with a grin. 'Managing Fitchett's farm for Lieutenant Greville.'

That night in the tap-room Will said, 'Mr Greville. That proposition you were mentioning the other night . . . .'

'Ah, yes.' The lieutenant nodded. 'Given it some thought, have you?'

'I've a counter-proposition, as you might say.'

'Have you indeed?' Greville smiled blandly. 'What have you in mind, landlord?'

'Fitchett's farm. I thought—that is, me and Polly thought—we might take over his debt. Give him a chance to start afresh and work it off.'

Greville laughed. 'Save your money, my dear fellow. I could never allow it.' He leaned forward confidentially. 'Let me tell you something—a word of business advice. The courts are full of scoundrels like Sam Fitchett. Debtors. Drunkards. Forfeiting everything they possess. And, as for those neighbours of his, the Garretts, why, they're birds of a feather. Shiftless. They'll go the same way, mark my words. Only a matter of time.'

When Sam was able to walk, Jonathan and his wife watched him from the doorway of their house as he trudged away along the track to Parramatta and Sydney Town, his belongings tied in a bundle on a stick on his shoulder, his dog Nimrod trotting at his heels. Jonathan said quietly, 'They'll never do that to us, Mary. They'll never force us off our land.' With one arm round her shoulders, he touched her stomach gently with his other hand. 'It's our child's. He'll be part of it and this is for him. Or . . .' he smiled, '. . . or her.'

She held his hand and pressed it to her, her eyes moist as she looked up at him. Unnoticed, the lonely figure of Sam Fitchett disappeared with his dog into the tall trees and out of their lives for ever.

CHAPTER ELEVEN

'A Government and General Order!' At the sergeant's
signal, the young New South Wales Corps drummer who
had drawn the midday crowd to the end of the High Street
in Parramatta gave a final banging flourish, crossed his
sticks and stood at ease. The red-faced NCO, tall and
imposing in his plumed shako, cross-belted high-necked
coatee and white breeches tucked into half-boots, cleared
his throat self-consciously and looked down at the paper in
his hand. 'From the unlawful meetings lately held in the
colony,' he bawled, 'and the numerous depredations of
various kinds committed on the public, patrols from the
New South Wales Corps are directed to visit the different
parts of the towns of Sydney and Parramatta and their
environs at indeterminate periods from sunset to daylight.
The inhabitants are therefore cautioned to attend to the
following instructions!' He paused for breath. In the crowd
Polly and Will, dressed in their best to come into town for
supplies on this warm January day of 1805, looked at one
another resignedly.

'First! Not to suffer lights to be kept in improper houses
after tattoo beating! If such houses should be lighted after
that hour and improper persons, not resident, found
therein, they are to be confined and the proprietor's
conduct to be reported!'

Polly dug her man in the ribs. 'We'll be saving on

candles, then,' she hissed, 'in that improper house of yours.'

He grinned a chubby wicked grin. The sergeant yelled, 'Second! All idlers found loitering about the towns or environs after sunset to be imprisoned! Third! . . . .' Will took her arm. They eased out of the crowd and walked away. '. . . Convicts taken up by the guard or patrol at night . . . .'

She snorted, 'Sure, and they'll be after making government regulations on breathing next.'

Will was still grinning. 'If we're all to be locked in at night, Polly, the midwife business should be booming.'

'And how will I be getting to the poor women?' she asked. His grin faded and he looked at her, this slim woman of his with the temperament as fiery as her hair. Aye, he reflected for the thousandth time, it had been a lucky day for him when her spool of thread had rolled across his path. And a lucky day for others, too, for Polly was a skilled midwife and had delivered most of the babies for miles around, the government midwife being far more dangerous when she was sober than when she was drunk. But how, if a curfew was to be imposed, was she to get about?

'Sixth!' The bull-like roar followed them down the street. 'Persons of whatever description making use of abusive or insulting language in the guard house or gaol . . . .'

'Abusive language!' Will grunted. 'The gaols won't be big enough to hold all the folk who'd like to abuse and insult the government.' They went back to where they'd left their cart.

Mary, in the ninth month of her pregnancy, seemed more beautiful to Jonathan than she had ever been. Her chestnut hair had a sheen that caught the light like silk as she moved, her creamy skin glowed with health, her hazel eyes had a new softness, a maternal mystery, that filled him with awe. He never ceased to wonder at the miraculous new life that had sprung into being within her like the seed he sowed in the fields and that lay waiting beneath the ripe curve of her belly. He stood behind her, stroking it possessively as she placed a bowl of dough before the fire. 'I can't feel him moving', he said.

'He's been quiet.' She turned in his arms to kiss him over her shoulder, her face flushed with the heat of the day, the fire and the exertion of the kneading she'd been doing. 'Or *she* has.'

'She?' It was fascinating, this not knowing whether he had fathered a son or a daughter. 'Mary, you mean.'

'I don't think we should call her Mary.' They'd talked of little else but naming the infant for months now. 'It'd be too confusing. What if there was work to be done, and "Mary!" you'd be calling, and she hiding behind a haystack and saying later she thought you were calling myself?' He laughed with her, still holding her. 'No. She can be Catherine, like her grandmother.' She was suddenly silent, moving out of his embrace as she thought of the pleasure her mother was being denied at this time. Letters took so long. The child would be six or nine months old by the time her parents even knew of the birth.

He said, 'What if she's a boy?'

She turned to him, the brief sadness gone. 'Now, that's Irish, if you like! If she's a boy!'

*   *   *   *   *

The 'horde', or food-gathering sub-section of the tribe, had put up their bark wurlies on the western bank of the river they called Deerubbin, at a point where the Hawkesbury flowed through sandstone gorges interspersed with river flats—all part of the tribal territory of the Gandangara people. Smoke from the damped-down fires drifted, white as steam, into the blue sky and hung sharp-scented on the hot afternoon air. This was a good place for the men to find fish and meat, for the women to gather plants and roots. A lush, fruitful place, where a man had time to sit in the shade and repair a broken spear, or to play the riddle game, or simply to sleep.

But Ngilgi's man was doing none of these things. He was squatting idly, she observed, and staring thoughtfully into the white ashes of the fire, as he so often did. As she came up to him with the coolamon containing the lily roots she had been collecting, he looked up. 'Mizzled off while I was asleep, did you?' Dinny O'Byrne said. He was wearing a pair of canvas trousers cut off at the knee, and the upper part of his body and his face were burnt so brown that, with his bushy black beard and hair, it was only this garment and the shape of his nose and forehead that readily distinguished him from the other men who sprawled about the camp—the men who were now his kinsmen. He said, 'You were after yelling in your sleep last night.' He put his head sideways on his joined hands, closed his eyes and made jerky grunting noises, pointing at her. He could understand most of what she said to him but the blackfellows' language, like most of the other things he'd discovered about them, was far more complex than he had ever imagined. He still found it hard to make up speech for himself.

She said in the nasal staccato of her own tongue, 'I dreamed of a child. A child to be born. I dreamed of a bad thing. Death.'

He picked that up. 'A baby?' He pointed. 'Your baby?'

An expression of fear came across her chocolate-brown face and she shook her head violently. 'The child to be born of a ghost woman. A woman of your people.'

He stared at her. She watched him out of her dark, expressionless eyes for a moment while someone began to sing in a low monotone. Soon, someone else joined in with the brittle clatter of rhythm-sticks.

*   *   *   *   *

Jonathan, alarmed, ran out to scold her and take the two pails of water Mary was carrying to the house. She smiled fondly at him. 'I always carry two at a time. I've been doing it since I was so high.' She held up a hand at waist height.

'It's too close, Mary!' He had carried the pails indoors, still making disapproving noises, when she saw Polly and Will trundling up in their cart which was stacked with barrels and boxes. Polly was prodding professionally at Mary's stomach when Jonathan came outside again. 'You're just a bit early, Polly', he said, grinning.

'Day or so there yet, I think.' She gave Mary a hug.

Will was tugging a freshly-sawn plank off the waggon. 'See this? I'm making a cradle.' His speech was very slightly slurred and his face was flushed. It was apparent that he'd been sampling his purchases to some extent.

Jonathan said, 'Just don't try to saw a straight line today, Will.'

'What are you talking about?' Will had put back the plank and was now dragging a demijohn from under the seat of the cart, watching Polly go into the house with Mary. He proffered the jar and watched Jonathan take a small swig. 'It'll be a great day when people in this country find out that it's better for them to drink beer than rum.' He took the demijohn of rum back and tapped it. 'Now this is all right for cleaning brass but I've been to the government brewery run by Thomas Rushton at Parramatta and they're making a fine brew there—and I should know, for I've always taken an interest in brewing. Twelve thousand gallons, Rushton hopes for this year, made from maize.'

Jonathan nodded. 'There's your beer, then.'

Will shook his head. 'They're finding it an expensive procedure. Besides,' he shrugged, 'there are certain people in the colony—Greville, for instance—who want us to drink rum, not beer.'

In the house, Polly was saying, 'Some time in the next two days, I think.'

'You only think?' Mary, lying on the bed, looked up at her.

'Week, maybe. Babies have minds of their own. They come when they're ready and not before.' She put out a hand and helped Mary to struggle off the bed.

'And there's nothing wrong?'

Polly laughed. 'Of course not. The head's down, and that's the main thing. You're a picture of health . . . .'

From outside, Will shouted, 'Come on, woman!'

Polly sighed. 'He went to the brewery this morning. They wouldn't sell him any but they didn't object to him sampling the product.'

As the women came out of the house, Will said, 'Polly, if we're not home soon we'll be locked up as improper persons.'

She looked at his flushed face. 'The only improper person present is yourself, Will Price.' She turned to Mary. 'In the towns it's all curfews now and locking decent people up for being out at night.'

'A curfew?' Mary thought of Rathcurran. 'Then how will you be able to come to me if it's at night . . .?'

'Oh, we won't see a patrol out here. Too far from the Mess and their misses!' She climbed up beside Will. 'Let's be off. And all I can say is, it's a good thing the horse is sober.'

*   *   *   *   *

Dinny O'Byrne knelt to drink at the river. Behind him, the fires glowed more brightly as the day cooled; there'd be a corroboree that night—sure, and weren't they all working themselves up to it already, with the sticks clicking and his brother Boolyal bringing out his didgeridoo? By the saints, he'd have them all dancing reels and jigs before long . . . .

He stood up, the cool clean water running down his chest. Ngilgi was a little way off, drawing in the sand with a stick. He went to look.

It was a house on a hill. The drawing was like that of a child, without perspective and out of proportion. A small hut with two windows and a door between them. A house he knew well, crudely represented though it was.

But how could Ngilgi have seen Jonathan's house?

He thought for a moment, then said in her language, carefully pronouncing the sounds, 'Where did you see that?'

She looked up at him, her eyes with that strange blank look they'd had before. 'In my dream. There is birth in that place. And death.'

He stood, the Celt in him telling him to listen, the man of the nineteenth century jeering that it was nonsense, that one settler's house was much like another and she could have seen one somewhere and remembered it in her dream. Angrily, he kicked his foot through the drawing. 'That's enough!' he said in English. 'Enough of your heathen superstitions!'

*   *   *   *   *

Next morning, Jonathan had finished milking the goat and had carried the pail into the house when he discovered Mary scrubbing the table with an energy that vaguely disturbed him. He put down the pail of milk and said, 'Mary, love! What are you doing?'

'What d'you think?' She flashed him a smile, the brush going harder than ever. 'Scrubbing!'

'But there's no need . . . . Look, I'll do it . . . .'

'It's all right! It's such a beautiful day and I feel so alive! I could scrub a hundred tables!'

He went out to work—or so she thought. In fact, he ran as hard as he could to 'The Bird in the Barley'. 'What does it mean?' he asked Polly.

She was already fetching from the kitchen the bag she kept for occasions like this. 'Goodbye, Will!' she called.

Jonathan said as she opened the door, 'You mean—it's coming?'

'Of course it's coming, you great lump! Now, d'ye want to be there or not?' He ran after her.

When they reached the house, Mary was lying on the bed; even as they went in, she was seized with a contraction and her face screwed up in pain. Polly said, 'How long has it been?'

She gasped for a second. 'Just after Jonathan left.'

Polly sat on the bed. 'Have you been counting between them, like I told you?'

Jonathan was bewildered and scared at the pain in his wife's face. 'Between what?'

Polly whirled on him. 'What are you doing here? It's women's work. Out with ye!' As he turned to go she added,

'If you want to make yourself useful, get some water. And leave it outside the door.' She turned back to Mary. 'How many between the last two?'

'Three hundred,' Mary said. Polly nodded.

* * * * *

She had dreamed again in the star-filled night, moaning and jerking in her sleep, then sitting up with a shriek that made Dinny's blood run cold. He'd soothed and comforted her like a child, her head on his shoulder; afterwards he'd lain awake for hours, resolving in his mind what he must do. And, early next morning, he went to the river. There was a place they'd shown him where, at this time of year at high summer, a man could wade most of the way across; it was only in the middle that he'd need a small log to cling to while the gentle current carried him into the shallows on the other side. He stared up and down river cautiously. There was always the chance that some adventurous lads from the Green Hills settlement might come exploring. There were, however, no craft of any kind in sight, so he slipped into the cold water with his log and set off. On the far bank he climbed out, shivering. To warm himself, he trotted briskly as he made his way through the trees, but without undue noise and with an ear cocked for the footfalls of others.

For he was now in enemy territory.

* * * * *

It was mid-afternoon. Having been ejected by Polly, Jonathan had decided to sit against a tree close to the house and whittle a spoon for the baby from a bit of wood to calm his nerves. There had been a terrible scream some time ago—about midday, he thought—and he'd run to the door in a panic only to have it slammed in his face. Now, the spoon was well-nigh finished and still there was no sign. He'd carve a design for the handle—a duck's head, perhaps. He was well into it when the door opened and Polly came out. He dropped the spoon and jumped to his feet. Boy? Girl? He didn't really care because, thank God, it was over at last. He ran to Polly and the joy drained out of him in a sickening rush when he saw her face. She said, 'Get a horse! Go to Parramatta and fetch one of the government surgeons!'

He was suddenly more frightened than he'd ever been in his life. 'What are you saying?'

She shouted at him, her fear as great as his own. 'We could lose Mary and the baby both! Get the surgeon!' She watched him race off, then she went back to where Mary was lying, her face clammy with sweat, her hair plastered to her scalp, her eyes wide with fright. Polly tried again. 'Bear down, lamb', she said, trying to keep calm. 'Bear down.'

She tried again, but more weakly. 'I can't', she gasped. 'Polly, I can't.'

There was silence in the hut apart from Mary's panting. Then Polly said, 'We're going to rest ye now. Rest, love. So that when the surgeon gets here you'll be ready.' She felt sick at the thought. Under his knife, Mary would need all the strength she possessed. She took a cloth from a tin bowl and began to sponge the clammy face, almost as worn out as her patient by the long ordeal.

At the inn, Will tightened the girth on his horse. 'When you reach Parramatta, go to George Champness at the smithy. He'll provide a change of horse for the return journey.' He gave Jonathan a leg up into the saddle. 'And, for God's sake, be clear of the town by nightfall. There's a curfew and patrols out.'

'I'll be all right.' Jonathan said impatiently. 'I'll have the surgeon with me.' He kicked the horse in the ribs and tore off. Will's animal was a long way from his first youth and he was more accustomed to the shafts than to the saddle but, as if some of his rider's terror communicated itself to him, he put his shaggy head down and ran like a rabbit. A crossroads came up; Jonathan swung onto the road to Parramatta. He was too frantic with fear to notice Lieutenant Greville's mounted patrol that trotted out of a side road and he was moving much too fast to be recognised. As the dust of his passing hung and drifted in the late afternoon sunlight, the lieutenant turned in his saddle. 'Fellow's in the devil of a hurry, sergeant. Expect the husband came home a little too early, eh?' The men guffawed dutifully.

Polly stood at the door of the hut, the red glow of sunset lighting her tired, anxious face. She wiped her forehead, pushing back a strand of auburn hair and turned as Mary said, 'Polly?' She went back to the bed where the sheets were stained with the sweat of Mary's efforts. 'If I don't get the baby out,' Mary said unsteadily, 'we'll die, won't we?' Polly opened her mouth to lie but Mary had already closed her eyes. 'I can try again, I think.'

'He'll be in Parramatta by now.' Polly took her hand. 'We'll have the surgeon soon.'

In Parramatta High Street Jonathan said, breathing hard, 'The surgeon! Where can I find him?'

The soldier was using his flintlock to ignite some tinder. He ignored Jonathan, blowing gently until the flame caught and flickered yellow in the dusk, illuminating the man's face as he lit his pipe. He said, 'Who's asking?'

'My name's Garrett. I'm a settler. My wife—she's dying.' He had to restrain himself from jumping off his horse and seizing the idiot by the throat. 'Where can I find the surgeon?'

'The *assistant* surgeon.' The private took the pipe out of his mouth and used it as a pointer. 'Turn right. Fourth house down.' As Jonathan wheeled his horse he added, 'There's a curfew, Garrett.'

There was a light outside the house. A smart little mare was saddled up at the rail. Jonathan fell out of his stirrups and beat on the door. It opened in his face and an elegantly-dressed middle-aged man came out, pulling on his gloves. Jonathan stood back. Despite his agony of mind, the years of servitude had their effect when he saw the lace, the beautifully-cut velvet coat, the gold thread on the waistcoat. 'Sir,' he said humbly, 'I'm looking for the assistant surgeon.'

The man hardly looked at him. 'I am he.' He began to check his mare's girth.

'I'm Jonathan Garrett, sir. I'm a settler out at the Hills, and my wife's . . . .' He faltered. The man looked over his shoulder impatiently. 'Sir, the midwife says she'll die if she doesn't have a surgeon.'

'I'm on my way to Sydney.' He swung up into the saddle.

'Sir, the midwife says she'll die!'

'Yes, I'm sure she does.' He turned his horse's head and began to move off.

'Sir! She needs you!' Perhaps, Jonathan thought, he hadn't been plain enough in his anxiety. He began again, 'Sir, my wife's in childbirth and the midwife . . . .'

'Garrett!' The man stopped his horse. 'What you must do if you wish to help your wife is not to pester me but go where you should have gone in the first place—to the government midwife.'

Anger, stronger than anxiety or servitude, began to take over. 'That's woman's a butcher!'

'The government midwife', he shook his reins, 'is the person you require.' In desperation, Jonathan lunged forward and grabbed his boot as he began to move off again. The elegantly-dressed one turned in his saddle, lashed at Jonathan with his riding crop and cantered away.

'Curfew, brother!' The soldier who'd directed him had walked up, his pipe glowing as he puffed. Jonathan didn't even hear him. He led his horse away. The smithy . . . . fresh horse . . . . home . . . . home to Mary . . . .

Lieutenant Greville was enjoying himself. Barely dark, and he'd blooded his hounds already. Not that that particular fox had given him much of a run—at the view-halloo he'd merely scampered off into a field where he'd been grabbed and bundled off to Parramatta Gaol at the tail of a horse. But, doubtless, there'd be other curfew-breakers to provide better sport. He led his patrol at a canter through the silent darkness away from the town, the hooves thudding softly in the dust, the harness clinking rhythmically. Abruptly, he cocked his head and said, 'Halt!' He sat listening. Yes, by God! A distant thud-thud from the direction of the town. And coming at the devil of a clip, too. He wheeled his horse. 'Into line!' His five men turned their horses also and stood in a solid barrier across the road from ditch to ditch. The sound of a horse at full gallop grew louder, the chink of metal on metal, the heavy snorting . . . . Suddenly, the horseman was upon them, materialising out of the darkness like a phantom. Greville smiled. Ambushed, by God!

It dawned on him only at the last moment that the madman had no intention whatever of stopping. He clutched at his shako with one hand, his reins with the other, too astounded even to curse as the dark figure tore straight through the line of plunging, rearing horses and was gone, the road filled with choking dust. Greville brought his mount under control and wheeled it in a fury. He jabbed savagely with his spurs and screamed, 'I want that man!'

Polly was warming milk in a saucepan at the fire. She turned at the moan from the bed. 'I'm cold—very cold.' Mary moved her head from side to side on the pillow, her face deathly pale in the lamplight. 'Is that you, Jonathan?'

'It's me, love.' Polly straightened the blanket over the humped figure in the bed. 'I'm making you a drink.' She went to the fire, poured the milk into a mug and supported Mary while she drank.

'I'm cold,' Mary said again. 'And the ship—it's so dark, Polly. Captain Dennott . . . .' Her voice sank to a murmur.

'That was nine years ago, love.' Tears were welling in Polly's eyes and running down her cheeks. After enduring so much, after so much endeavour, so much sorrow, was it to end like this? 'Jonathan'll be back soon.' When, almost immediately, she heard the footsteps outside and saw the latch lift, she thought it was he. Instead, to her utter amazement, it was Dinny O'Byrne who came in.

He said simply, 'I've come to help.'

'Help? How did you know?' Suddenly, the relief at having someone—anyone—to share the strain she'd endured through the last few hours flooded through her. She stood up, mechanically adjusting the covers over Mary who was moaning softly and whispering to herself in delirium. 'I don't know what to do', Polly said helplessly. 'Jonathan's gone for the surgeon. . . . It's been going on for so long.'

'Easy, girl. Easy.' He put an arm round her shoulders. Even in her distress, she found time to think it strange that this great peace, this tranquillity, should be coming from a turbulent creature like Dinny O'Byrne. She rested her head on his shoulder, drawing strength from him.

More composedly, she said, 'I lost one like this, once. I couldn't bear it if Mary . . . .'

'Hush, now.' He went to the bed, sat down and took Mary's hand.

Polly said again, 'How did you know—to come?'

'Ngilgi told me. Me woman. From the tribe.' He had a hand on Mary's hot forehead. 'She dreamt of trouble here.' She'd dreamt of death, but he wasn't having that. Trouble he could deal with—and hadn't he been doing it all his life? He saw Polly's expression. 'Back home in Ireland,' he said quietly, 'did ye never hear of someone having the Gift?'

She nodded slowly. 'Me Auntie.' She crossed herself. 'She taught me herbs.'

'Well, then.' Dinny turned back to Mary. 'Had a cow like this once', he said thoughtfully. 'Saved her. Saved the calf, too. Fine bull it was he turned into.' He looked up at her and, for the first time in hours, she smiled. 'So now let's see if you with your witch's blood and me with me cowman's hands can't be coaxing this little bull out of her.'

'Watch your language, Dinny O'Byrne', Polly said primly. 'And go and wash your hands this very minute, you rascal!'

Lieutenant Greville was in such a state of cold fury that he could scarcely think rationally. Not only had that pox-ridden peasant on horseback galloped straight through his detachment; he'd gone off the road somewhere, damn his soul to hell, and vanished into thin air. 'I give you my word, Sergeant,' he snarled as his terrified troopers prodded at the bushes and peered helplessly into the gloom, 'if you don't find where he turned off, you'll wish you'd never been whelped.' In his turn, the sergeant began to bawl threats at his men until, thanks be to God, Trooper Sedgwick found the hoofmarks in the dust where the bastard had turned off the road and taken to a bush track. 'Very good', said Greville bleakly. 'Now follow me.'

Mary came out of a cold, clammy darkness to find Polly and Dinny O'Byrne leaning over her. 'Dinny!' she said, and then, 'Where's Jonathan?'

Dinny stroked her forehead. 'The fever's down.'

'It'll be all right now', Polly said soothingly. 'And Jonathan'll be here soon.'

'Ah, it's been fine all along,' Dinny said, 'what with Polly praying and me with me medical knowledge . . . .'

'Polly?' Mary managed a weak smile. 'Praying?'

'Now shut your mouth, Dinny O'Byrne!' Polly was grinning with relief. 'You come in here with your heathen mumbo jumbo and . . . .'

'Polly?' Will Price pushed the door open. 'I was getting worried so I thought I'd . . . .'

Mary gasped suddenly. 'I've got the pains back!'

'. . . come to see what was taking so long.' Polly flew at Will, shoved him through the door and slammed it in his face. She rushed back to the bed and seized Mary's hand. 'Hang on to that. And when it's over, start your counting!'

And, a little while later, at the first cry of the new-born infant, Dinny said, grinning all over his bearded face, 'By the saints! I told ye we had a little bull!'

When Jonathan arrived, they were grouped round the bed where Mary, pale but smiling, lay with the baby. He didn't see Dinny or Will Price. He didn't hear Polly when she said, 'Ye missed the whole thing, ye great gossoon!' He went to the bedside and knelt as if he was in church. Mary put out a hand and he took it, staring at the child. 'So little', he said wonderingly. 'So small a thing.' He put his head down, his cheek against his wife's. 'Oh, Mary, I thought tonight I'd lost you.' She stroked his hair, murmuring softly to him.

'And the surgeon?' Polly asked. 'What about the surgeon?'

'He wouldn't come.'

Dinny said tightly, 'Wouldn't come?'

'I promised myself I'd kill him if anything happened to Mary.' Jonathan looked up. 'Dinny!' On the point of asking how it was that his friend was there, he nodded, accepting everything; he was almost as exhausted as Mary. Nothing really mattered, anyway, except the fact that she was safe. He straightened, still kneeling, and held out his big, work-calloused hands. 'Can I?' Polly leaned across and placed the bundle in them. 'So little', he said again, marvelling. Then, very quietly, he began to laugh with the joy of it all.

'Beauty and the Beast', Polly said. In relief and happiness, they all began to laugh, gently, at the sight of the tiny fragment of humanity in the huge hands with Jonathan's dirty face peering down at it.

From outside, Lieutenant Greville shouted, 'In the King's name, surrender!'

There was a silence in which nobody moved. Greville called, 'The house is surrounded. If you do not give yourselves up directly, you will be fired upon!'

Mary said in alarm, 'It's Dinny! How did they . . .?'

'It's all right', Jonathan said. He gave the baby back to her. 'I broke curfew to get back and a patrol chased me.' He stood up. 'If I give myself up, they'll take me to Parramatta and lock me up for the night. I'll be back in the morning.' He raised his voice. 'I'm coming out!'

Dinny said, 'If they find me here . . . .'

'They won't. Polly, come out with me and we'll tell them about the baby. Even soldiers are human.'

'Not Greville.' There was a trapped look on Dinny's face as he looked round the hut. 'They'll want to see the baby.'

'We'll take it out to them. You stay here . . . .'

'They'll be after searching the hut, man! Ye know what they're like! And d'ye realise what'll happen to you and Mary if they find ye harbouring me?'

'It's the only way.' Jonathan already had his hand on the latch. 'I'll talk to them and keep them out. I tell you I'm the one they're looking for, not you.' He opened the door and walked out, his hands raised. He went towards Greville who was standing, his sword drawn, with his sergeant.

There was a shout from the back of the hut. Greville cursed and sprinted for the corner, Jonathan and the sergeant with him. In the light from the window they saw the trooper down on one knee, a little distance from the house. They saw the dim shape, running for the bush. Then the night was split by the flash and the explosion that echoed back from the hills. There were more shouts and boots pounded as the troopers closed in but Jonathan was already running, to drop to his knees in the grass. 'Oh, God, Dinny,' he said, 'why didn't you stay?'

He was trying to fight his way to his feet, sobbing with the effort of struggling against the vast warm drowsiness that was pulling him down. 'Came here because she dreamt of death . . . thought she meant the baby or Mary . . . or you. But it was me all along . . . .' Two troopers took him under the arms and lifted him to his feet. Another ran up with a lantern and he hung there in the yellow light with his head lolling and a crimson trickle oozing from the corner of his mouth into his beard, his right side and the front of his breeches soaked wet and gleaming with blood. He looked at Jonathan and, for a moment, his eyes lit up with the warmth and the humour and the defiance that had been Dinny O'Byrne. 'By all the saints,' he said, the blood bubbling in his throat, 'I've got me certificate of freedom at last!'

Greville stared at the black mop of hair, the tangled beard, the wild brown face. 'Who are you?' When there was no answer he raised his voice. 'In the King's name, who are you?'

Dinny's eyes were already glazing as he stared back at Greville, his mouth open with the white teeth showing as he gasped for breath. Suddenly, with a strength that took the troopers by surprise, he tore himself free. 'To hell', he snarled, 'with your King!' He surged forward, his big hands reaching for Greville's throat. And a thick gout of blood gushed out of his mouth as he died, his impetus carrying him on so that it was a dead thing that Greville caught and held in his white-gloved hands. For a moment the dead face seemed to stare into Greville's before it fell forward and the lieutenant lowered the body to the ground.

In the hut he said, 'Who was he?' The anger had gone out of his voice; it was almost as if he was inquiring about a man killed in action whom he had respected. Nobody answered. They stared at his blood-soaked gloves, at the stain splashed across the front of his tunic. He said again, 'You were harbouring him. Who was he?'

'Just a poor wild man', Polly said, 'out of the night. He came to help.' She indicated the baby in Mary's arms. 'Born tonight. To make amends for the one you've killed.'

'Yes.' To their surprise it was said without the satisfaction they might have expected from Maurice Greville. He walked to the fire and stood staring into it. 'You called him a name. Dinny.' He peeled off the gloves and dropped them onto the glowing ashes. As they caught he turned. 'Dinny O'Byrne. The rebel leader.' When they didn't deny it, he said, 'Why did he run? If he'd surrendered he'd have had a trial . . . .'

'And you'd have hanged him just the same.' Will spoke out of the tight group that had placed itself, as if in defence, around the mother and child.

'Not now. The example has already been made. Norfolk Island, perhaps. And surely that would have been better than . . . .' He gestured.

'Not to Dinny O'Byrne', Polly said. 'A Dinny O'Byrne can be free or he can be dead. Free or dead, and that's all the choice he has.'

He looked at her for a moment. Then he nodded to Jonathan and the two of them walked out into the darkness where the men were tying the corpse on to one of the horses.

* * * * *

Ngilgi knew. In the bark wurlie on the far side of the river that flowed silent and placid under the glory of the night sky she woke, screaming, for while her spirit had been absent from her body in sleep it had been touched, briefly and tenderly, by something that swooped past like a great bird and was then gone on its way to the place of shades. The screaming gave way to a sobbing, keening wail and, as she keened, she was already composing in her mind her song for the dead.

* * * * *

Polly was dozing in a chair by the grey ashes of the fireplace when Jonathan returned late that morning. Will had gone to attend to the inn; Mary and the baby were asleep in bed. As Jonathan went to the hearth to start the fire and make a pan of tea, Polly came awake in a flash, her fingertip going to her lips, but Mary, too, had awakened, her face lighting up when she saw him. He kissed her, then stood for a moment looking down at his son.

Polly said, 'What happened?'

'No charges of harbouring.' Jonathan was still looking at the baby. 'I don't know why. But Greville was—well, different, somehow.' He thought of the night journey to Parramatta with Dinny's body and the lieutenant not sneering and triumphant as he'd have expected but strangely quiet and preoccupied. 'I made a deposition and they let me go.' He was not to know that Lieutenant Greville, who had never seen action in his life, had been shaken more that he would have cared to admit by the bloody corpse that had died reaching for his throat. And strangely moved by the baby lying there with its mother. . . . As Jonathan himself had said, even soldiers are human.

Jonathan reached down and placed a finger in the tiny hand that had escaped from its blanket. Fingers like tendrils closed over it with surprising strength. He said, 'I know the name for him now.'

Mary nodded. 'Dinny', she said softly.

CHAPTER TWELVE

'Heaven alone knows how we'll find this new martinet, "Bounty" Bligh.' Lieutenant Greville smiled ingratiatingly at John Macarthur with whom he was enjoying a drink in the Mess at Parramatta Barracks. 'Have us all walking the plank, I'll wager!'

Macarthur did not look as if, for his part, he was particularly enjoying the barley water that he, as a non-drinker, had ordered. 'Governors come,' he said briefly, 'and governors go.' He, too, had gone—to England, four years previously, to face a trial for the duel in which he had severely wounded his commanding officer, Lieutenant-Colonel Paterson. But, after being acquitted and resigning his commission, he had recently come back again—in spite of Governor Philip Gidley King's scathing comment to his superiors that 'if Captain Macarthur returns here in any official character, it should be as Governor, as one half of the Colony already belongs to him and it will not be long before he gets the other half'. And, although Macarthur had not returned in any official character, he had brought with him six merino sheep from the Royal Stud and permission to acquire five thousand acres of the best land in the colony. His choice of the rich, highly-desirable spread of country at Cowpastures had certainly done nothing to alleviate Governor King's tendency to gout.

Now, in December 1805, Macarthur was once again a

force to be reckoned with in New South Wales—which was exactly why Greville thought it his duty to give the former captain the benefit of his company. Not, Greville thought, that the man looked particularly grateful. In fact, it seemed to be with some relief that he rose to his feet when his fellow-civilian and landowner Charles Wiltshire came into the Mess. 'A good ride down, Charles?' Macarthur asked after Wiltshire, with his usual affability, had greeted them both.

'Yes, indeed.' Out of force of habit, Wiltshire stood with his back to the empty fireplace. 'The country is looking superb.'

'Good ripening weather', said Greville, the up-and-coming agriculturalist.

'Indeed it is.' Wiltshire took from the steward the drink that Greville had been quick to order for him. 'The crops are the best I've seen. From here to the Hawkesbury is a veritable granary.'

'An open, smiling land,' Greville said sardonically, 'patiently attended by an industrious, smiling peasantry.'

With a slight lack of enthusiasm, Wiltshire said, 'Something like that.'

Macarthur nodded. 'Before this season is over, the stores will be bursting with best quality wheat and barley.'

'All owned by us', Greville murmured happily. 'Purchased on our terms and our conditions.'

Even if true, it was expressed much too baldly for the taste of the others. Macarthur said curtly, 'Quite.'

Wiltshire raise his glass to try to shift the conversation onto a less frankly commercial level. 'Gentlemen,' he said, 'your health.'

'And . . .' Greville lifted his own glass, 'wealth, eh?'

*　*　*　*　*

'It's a fitting reward for all your back-breaking industry, Jonathan.' Polly McNamara, on her way with a basket of scones to visit Mary and the eleven-month-old Dinny, shaded her eyes to look at the rippling waves of light and shade on the field of wheat as it moved in the warm breeze. 'It's a beautiful crop!'

'Aye.' Jonathan looked down at the heavy golden ear of wheat he had plucked. He rubbed it between his hands, blowing away the chaff to leave the plump grains lying on his palm. 'It's a good crop, right enough. And the barley will be even better.' He offered the grains to Polly and put on in his mouth. 'But a ripe crop in the field's only so much dry forage. I've still got to bring it in.'

'You'll manage.'

'Aye, maybe. But this crop is twice the size of any I've had before. I shall need labour, and where am I to obtain it? And the means to transport it to the government stores at the Hawkesbury?'

She said again, 'You'll manage, Jonathan. The way you and Mary have always managed everything you've set your mind to.' As she walked towards the house, however, her thoughts were not so much on Jonathan as on whatever it was that Will Price had set his mind to of late. For he was behaving most oddly, smiling to himself and not answering when spoken to. Even her scones that he'd always been so fond of . . . .

'He seems to have gone off them a bit, lately.' She spread them with butter and jam while Mary poured the tea. 'In fact, he seems to have gone off a lot of things. Like keeping things about the place in a bit of order. Some of the hitching posts outside the inn are ready to give way—but d'ye think he'll do anything about it?' She sat down at the table and put sugar in her tea, stirring it absently. 'He's been doing a lot of figuring.'

'Figuring?' Mary raised her eyebrows as she sipped her tea. 'Keeping his accounts, you mean?'

'No. Scribbling away on scraps of paper and putting them out of sight if he thinks I'm watching him. And hoarding bottles.'

'Bottles?'

'Old bottles. Hoarding them for months, he's been. And

he won't tell me a thing.' Polly put her mug down firmly. 'He's up to something, that I do know.'

It was the same thing when she returned to 'The Bird in the Barley' an hour or so later—the piece of paper slipped out of sight, the guilty air. 'You're back early', he said. 'How's the Garrett family?' He took a perfectly polished glass off a shelf and began to polish it, humming to himself.

'Well enough.' Polly looked at the folded paper sticking out of his pocket, at the smile he was trying to suppress, and wondered briefly if her man was becoming slightly deranged.

'Good. Good.' Will caught her eye and coughed. 'That's good. And Jonathan's crops?'

'The wheat's almost ready to harvest. It'll be a fine crop—if the fine gentlemen who run this colony let him get it in, or even sell it.' She dumped her empty basket on the bar. 'The fate of poor Sam Fitchett is a bitter memory in the Garrett household, you know.'

'Good', Will said, still polishing vigorously. 'And the barley—how's the barley?'

'Still standing.' He grinned vacantly at her and held the glass to the light, staring at it as if it was a crystal ball. 'Which is more', Polly snapped, 'than can be said for those hitching posts out there.'

'Eh?'

'Hitching posts', she said loudly. 'Posts for hitching horses to. They've been in need of attention for weeks— along with a lot of other things.'

'Hitching posts.' He nodded wisely. 'Ah well, you see, Polly, it's all a matter of priorities. Putting things into their natural sequence and correct order. Their ordained position in life, you might say.'

She stared at him in amazement before she went into the kitchen and began to slam the pans about.

Jonas Pike, too, considered Will's behaviour a little odd when he called in for a tot of rum on the following afternoon. In fact, he wondered whether the blasted fellow might not be trying to make a fool of him when, after Pike had commented on the excellent quality of the spirits, Will

188

said, 'And so it should be, seeing as how the good gentlemen officers of the Corps take upon themselves the onerous task of buying and selling spirits within the colony exclusively. So it should be.'

Pike had been so busy trying to catch a note of sarcastic sedition in Will's voice that he had lost the thread. 'Should be what?'

'Good quality. Good quality rum. Stands to reason, the keen, law-abiding gentlemen of the Corps wouldn't be letting no inferior-class spirits past their eagle eyes and discriminating palates.'

Pike drank some more rum, watching Will closely. 'No', he said. 'That's right. They wouldn't.' He hadn't the least idea why Will Price was putting on this display of sycophantic loyalty, but there had to be a catch in it somewhere.

'Couldn't be anyone better qualified to control the trade, as you might say.'

'That's right.' It was high time, Pike thought, that this ale-draper was put in his place. 'Not', he said heavily, 'that there aren't villains enough doing their damnedest to upset the legal and legitimate order of things by dealing in low-grade rotgut, threatening the health and stability of the colony, as it were.'

'No!' Will said. 'But where are they getting this stuff from, if I might ask? Not through official channels, surely?'

Pike leaned across the bar, exhaling rum-fumes into Will's face. 'They're distilling it themselves. Malting the corn and distilling it. Irish riff-raff, mostly.'

'Ah!' Will said, as if that explained everything. 'Well, that's a tale that'd bring a blush to the cheek of many a fine old inspector of excise, and no mistake.'

'Aye.' Pike gave up wondering what was afoot. Most innkeepers were rogues and this one was merely putting on a show of virtue to keep a valued customer, most like. 'I better be going. I've some business to transact before dark.' He drained his glass, paid up and went to the door.

'Distilling it themselves, eh?' Will said. 'Well, I never! Wonder how it'd sell?'

'I wouldn't be trying, if I was you', Pike said grimly, his hand on the latch. 'It's an offence.'

'Of course not', Will said earnestly. 'My interest was purely theoretical, as you might say.' But, when Pike had gone, he was wearing his secret smile again as he washed the dirty glass.

Pike's business was with Jonathan, whom he found chopping wood. 'Bit of a business proposition, as you might say.' It was a hot day and Pike licked his dry lips as he glanced at the house. 'Thought we might discuss it somewhere cooler.' Jonathan was not at all anxious to have him anywhere near his home, much less inside it, but he found it difficult to be churlish even to the man who had evicted Sam Fitchett. Reluctantly, he led the way indoors. Mary, on her way out to visit Polly with the baby Dinny, recoiled as if she had seen a snake at the sight of the squat, detestable figure following her husband through the door. Ignoring Pike's loutish bows and hat-touchings, she swept out with her head averted as if to avoid some noxious smell. And, indeed, in the heat of the day, Pike's aroma of stale sweat was very apparent in the small house. 'I'm here representing Mr Greville', he said when, instead of the rum he'd hoped for, he was given a mug of tea. 'He's prepared to make you an offer for your wheat crop.'

'How much?' Jonathan stared with dislike at the fat, pallid face.

'It's a fine crop—at the moment . . .'

'How much?'

'. . . though a sudden cold spell . . . .'

'How much?'

'Seven pounds ten shillings an acre', Pike said at last. It was well below the current value.

'Paid in cash?'

'No. In goods.'

'What sort of goods?'

'Household goods. General merchandise.' When Jonathan sipped his tea and looked at him, Pike said impatiently, 'Look, I haven't time to be beating about the bush. Seven pounds fifteen shillings an acre—in goods. That's our last offer.'

Jonathan stood up. 'I'm selling it to the government stores.'

'How are you going to get it there? And labour . . . .' Pike saw that he was being shown to the door. He hauled himself to his feet. 'Labour's very hard to come by these days.'

'I'll manage.'

'The men will require payment in advance. You can't manage that.' He gulped the rest of his tea. 'You sell to us', he said ingratiatingly. 'Next season we'll most likely arrange a horse for you. You can double your acreage.'

'I tell you I'm not interested.'

Pike's thick lips curled upleasantly. 'You will be.' He went out and turned as he put on his hat. 'When the time comes.'

In bed that night Mary said, 'You were right, Jonathan. The less we have to do with Jonas Pike and Greville, the better.'

Jonathan was lying on his back, his hands behind his head, staring at the moonlight that streamed through the shutters. 'A crop won't wait, though, Mary. When it's ready to harvest . . . .' His voice tailed off. Then he said, 'We could end up with nothing if we wait too long. A sudden storm, and that could be the end. Perhaps Pike *is* our only hope.'

'There must be some other way.'

'Perhaps I could try for convict labour from the government farm?' There was a long pause before he said, 'I don't know. I just don't see myself as an overseer of convicts. It goes against the grain, somehow.'

'I know.' She reached out and stroked his hair. 'But they'd be a lot better off working here than in a lot of places.' There was another long silence. 'Anyway, Greville isn't the only officer-gentleman prepared to buy a crop of wheat.' She came up on one elbow. 'Mr Wiltshire. Maybe he'd help. He's a fair man.'

But Wiltshire couldn't help. 'It's not a matter of what I

want to do, Garrett', he said, after Jonathan had been accorded the privilege of being received in the Wiltshire day-room. 'I would, in fact, very much like to buy your excellent grain. But I am unable to do so. You see, your farm does not lie within my—er—my "territory". It's in Lieutenant Greville's.'

Jonathan felt out of place in this quiet room where the clock ticked unhurriedly and his shabby, weather-beaten reflection stared back at him from the polished, glass-fronted bookcase with its rows of leather-and-gold bindings. He felt even more out of his depth with Wiltshire's explanation. 'What's Lieutenant Greville to do with it? It's my crop. Grown on my land.'

'Of course. But, you see, a number of us have entered into an agreement not to compete by way of trade. We have divided the settled parts of the colony into areas of exclusive rights, as it were.'

'And my farm's in Lieutenant Greville's area?' Jonathan felt a slow fire of anger at the thought of his farm, his hard-worked acres, being appropriated in whatever way by Greville. It seemed to cast a blight on his crop, like rust. 'So therefore I'm not at liberty to deal with anyone but Lieutenant Greville?'

'No, no!' Wiltshire looked slightly uncomfortable as he stood in his habitual manner, feet apart and hands behind his back. 'You are free to trade with whom you wish . . . .'

'Then I wish to trade with you.'

'Except that each and every member of our—ah—combine is honour bound to respect all other exclusive rights . . . .'

'You mean,' Jonathan said slowly, 'I may only do business with one man?' Accustomed though he was to the way in which the colony was run as a profit-making concern for the privileged few, he was awe-struck at the brazen banditry of this arrangement. Sharing the spoils, he thought. Aye, that's what brigands and the like called it.

Wiltshire smiled—a fatherly smile, as if he was dealing with a son who did not yet know the ways of the world. 'Of course not. If you wish to deal with someone outside our combine then that, naturally, is your right.'

'And who else is in this "combine"?'

'I'm not sure I can tell you that.' Wiltshire looked slightly embarrassed. 'I may have explained too much already.'

Jonathan said quietly, 'All the officers in the Corps, I'll wager. And a few magistrates and rich men like yourself. Which would leave precious few who'd be in any sort of position to buy my crop, I'll be bound.'

'I'm sorry, Jonathan.' There was sincere regret in Wiltshire's voice as he moved to the door. 'I'd help you if I could. But I cannot. It's a matter of honour, you see.'

Honour among thieves, Jonathan thought as in the glaring sun he trudged the ten miles from Westbury to Castle Hill prison farm, only to find that, even there, the rules of the "combine" held good. 'The few men not required for our own purposes', the Commandant said, smiling as indulgently as the Governor of the Royal Mint would smile if some harmless lunatic asked for free samples, 'are already spoken for.'

'Spoken for?' Not so long ago, there'd been convict labour and to spare for any who wanted it—as Jonathan himself knew only too well.

'Long since. By certain gentlemen farmers who have long-standing arrangements with us.' Again he was politely but firmly ushered towards the door. 'It's a matter of precedence, you see, Mr Garrett.'

Dusty, weary and footsore, he tramped the five miles to 'The Bird in the Barley'. Labourers went there—free men, who were not bound by considerations of honour or precedence. They were, however, bound by considerations of payment; furthermore, their combine was as tight as that of the rich. In the smoky, riotously noisy tap-room, he was told that they had their rates and that they expected payment the moment the work was completed—a thing he could not possibly promise. When Will Price poured a drink for him and told him it had been a good day, with good ripening weather, Jonathan merely swallowed his drink miserably and went out. It had, in fact, been a disastrous day and the weather had merely been a source of trouble in his walking.

Polly shot Will a murderous glance. 'He's in trouble,' she hissed, 'and all you can do is discuss the weather.' A few minutes later she found him grinning his inane grin and re-reading a letter that a traveller had brought in for him earlier that day. She had purposely refrained from asking what it was about. Now, however, she said bleakly, 'Aren't you going to share your good news?'

'Surprise', he said. He winked and she could have struck him. 'But I can tell you that I must go to Sydney soon.'

And if he's waiting for me to ask why, he'll wait a long time, she thought. She began serving customers as if they were dying of thirst.

Christmas came and went—an anxious time for the Garretts, a time of frustration for Polly, with her Will acting so strangely, and a very festive season indeed for those who were hoping to make high profits from the harvest. For January of 1806 came with clear, cobalt-blue skies, a sun that warmed but did not burn, and winds that never rose above a gentle breeze. Jonathan's wheat was now fully ripe, hanging heavy and full in the ear, and he knew the time had come. In the middle of a sleepless night he said aloud, 'We'll have to accept Pike's offer. There's no other way.'

In the morning he went down to the inn. 'Where's Will?'

'Blessed if I know.' Polly gave him a mug of ale and refused payment. 'Off seeing that wild mob that own the broken-down farm out past the government cattle yards.'

'The Irishmen? What's he want with them?'

Polly shrugged. 'Who knows? I've given up asking meself what he's about these days. A man of mystery.' She wiped the bar. 'That's Wilberforce Price, these days.'

He nodded, drinking his ale. 'Seen Jonas Pike lately?'

She stopped wiping, knowing why he'd asked. 'Not today.'

'When you do, tell him I'd like a word with him, will you?'

He came that very afternoon, smirking and humming to himself as he rode up to the house. Without bothering to dismount, he said to Jonathan who was waiting at his door, 'Me and Mr Greville knew you'd see it our way sooner or later.' He grinned down at Jonathan. 'Pity you left it so late, though.'

Jonathan felt a stab of premonition. 'You mean you won't . . . ?'

'Oh, we'll buy it.' Pike laughed his grating laugh. 'But the price has dropped, see?' He paused, enjoying the play of expression on Jonathan's face. 'The original offer was seven pound ten an acre, if I remember . . . .'

'Seven pounds fifteen shillings.'

'Aye, well, now it's six pounds an acre. For latecomers. Payable in goods.' When Jonathan didn't speak he said, 'I'll have the men here within the week.'

Jonathan nodded. What else could he do?

The time had come, too, for Will Price's mysterious journey to Sydney. 'A day to travel there, a day in the town and a day home. I should be back by Saturday.'

She said, her manner cool, 'I don't know why you have to be going off like this.' For a while she'd even entertained the horrid thought of another woman. That would certainly account for the day-dreaming, the secret smirks, the letter she wasn't allowed to see. He was of an age, too, for that kind of foolishness with some twenty-year-old dolly or other. But she'd rejected the idea. She knew her Will.

Or did she?

'I told you, Polly love. Business.' He was smiling that bloody smile again as he clambered into the seat of the cart. If there *was* some doxy in Sydney, she'd choke him with her bare hands and so she would . . . .

Jonathan and Mary worked harder than the hired hands to bring in the harvest, scything, sheaving, threshing. And at last it was all in. 'All done and finished', Jonas Pike said as the last bag was stacked onto the waggon. 'Four acres of wheat at six pounds an acre. That's what we agreed.'

'Aye.' Jonathan was physically exhausted. All he wanted was to be paid and to be rid of Pike.

'Less six pounds for labour.' As Jonathan opened his mouth he said, 'Six pounds is what I've agreed to pay these men. And it's your wheat, after all. You got the cartage gratis, didn't you?' He climbed onto the cart and picked up the reins. 'That's eighteen pounds due to you. I'll drop it by later.'

That afternoon he returned with six small kegs of rum. 'Six gallons', he said, stacking them on the ground in front of the hut. 'Current market value—three pounds a gallon. That's eighteen pounds in all—full payment for your crop.'

Knowing it was hopeless, Mary said none the less, 'You said "goods".'

Pike grinned. 'Rum is goods, ma'am.'

'And what do we want with six gallons of rum?'

'Do what you like with it. It's yours. Trade with it. Drink it, if you wish.' He tapped a keg with his boot. 'Better nor money in the bank, that is. Leastwise, in this colony. A man'll work harder for a pint of rum than he will for any worthless promissory note. Keeps your assets liquid, so to speak.' Guffawing, he drove off.

Later that evening he met Lieutenant Greville in their secluded corner of 'The Bird in the Barley'. They drank healths to each other with the satisfied smiles of toilers whose labour has been well rewarded. Greville said, 'Do you know how much those six gallons of rum cost me? Three pounds four shillings, all up and landed.' He chuckled, raising his glass to Pike. 'Four acres of prime quality wheat for exactly three pounds and four shillings. Now that's what I call a capital bargain!'

Jonathan's thoughts, too, were on rum. He was sitting at the table in his house, staring at the six kegs that were stacked neatly against the wall. Six months' work. The back-breaking clearing of the land there'd been. The digging—four acres with a spade. The sowing. And then the waiting for the weather, wondering if he'd have a crop at all. The final wonder of it waving in the wind like a girl's hair, soft and rich and full of promise. He laughed suddenly, went to a keg and tapped it, drawing off a dram. He drank and made a face. It was just about the worst rum he'd ever tasted. None the less, he drank it down. Then he tucked the mug into his pocket, put the keg under his arm and went out into the cool golden evening.

Mary was hanging out washing on a line. She watched him walk away without a word, down to the creek at the foot of the hill.

He woke up to bright moonlight with his head splitting and a tongue like saddle-leather. Groggily, he groped for the keg, then stared. The bung was out. The rum had flowed to waste, the earth about him wet and stinking of it. His mug had gone God knew where. He heaved himself to his feet, cursing, went to the creek and drank, scooping up the cool water with his hands. Then, with the world heaving about him like a rough sea, he staggered back to the hut.

It was something that neither of them, later, wished to remember, his falling over the furniture and causing the child to wake in terror and scream, his attempting to make love to Mary with the fumes on his breath that made her feel sick. She was frightened, disgusted, angry and yet filled with compassion for her husband who had tried to make himself unconscious so as to forget the terrible iniquity that had been done to him. Finally, when he collapsed onto the bed and was instantly asleep, she cradled his drunken head in her arms and wept.

'I'm worried sick, Polly', she said next day in the kitchen of 'The Bird in the Barley'. Will, returned from Sydney, was in the tap-room; Polly was nursing the small Dinny. 'After he woke he hadn't a glance for me or the baby. He seems broken, utterly without hope. I'm terrified he'll open another keg and start all over again.'

'I know what I'd do', Polly said. 'I'd take the kegs and hide them.'

Mary shook her head. 'I don't want to start doing things like that. Not with Jonathan. We've never hidden anything from each other.'

'Then trade with . . . .' She stopped. 'Will!'

He ducked his head to peer between the shelves of bottles that separated the tap-room from the kitchen. Polly said, 'That scoundrel Pike has paid Jonathan for his crop in rum. We could buy it from him, couldn't we?'

He came into the kitchen looking doubtful. 'I don't know. Perhaps not at his price . . . .'

'Will!' Polly said indignantly.

'But I do want to see Jonathan, and as soon as possible. On a business matter.' He turned to Polly. 'Why don't we invite him and Mary to supper this evening? I'll open a bottle of that French cognac I brought from Sydney.'

'Cognac?' Polly said in horror. 'It's the drink that's one of Jonathan's problems at the moment. Mary doesn't want you filling him up with cognac.'

Will said slowly, 'Drink a problem, is it? Aye, well, maybe it is. But it can also be a solution. You wait and see.'

He met his guests outside the inn as they arrived, the baby Dinny on Mary's hip. 'Hello, Jonathan', he said. 'My, but you're looking well.' Jonathan and Mary exchanged a puzzled glance; Jonathan, with the marks of lack of sleep and his recent dissipation upon him, looked far from well. 'Come and see what I have in the stable,' Will said, 'before it's too dark.' He led the way to the building attached to the side of the inn and pulled aside a tarpaulin to reveal a number of packing-cases, each with 'W. Price, Esquire, c/o Tarbuck & Grant, Sydney, New South Wales' lettered on it. He lifted a lid and took out a coil of copper tubing that gleamed dully in the light. 'There! D'you know what that is?'

Jonathan shook his head. Mary said, 'It's part of a still. I remember seeing one in Ireland.'

Will, his surprise spoilt, said, 'Part of a still? There's a whole still there. I had it sent out from England.'

Mary took the coil from him, looking at it. 'But isn't it illegal?'

'Illegal if you're caught. Highly profitable if you're not.' He looked at Jonathan. 'You have a barley crop to harvest, haven't you?' He patted the coil. 'We'll distil it. Turn it into whisky and beat the Grevilles' at their own game. It's as good as minting our own sovereigns. And it'll be good whisky, depend on it. I know my trade.'

Jonathan said, 'It's a bit risky, isn't it?' With spirits being used to a very large extent as currency in the colony, illegal distilling ranked in infamy with forgery—minting one's own sovereigns, as Will had said. And, since the Corps controlled the currency, they would be striking a blow at the military that would hurt their pockets deeply.

Will said, 'Aye. There'd be the devil to pay if we were discovered. But, if things go well, you could pay off your debt to the government, buy implements, maybe a horse. Put more acreage under crop, extend your house . . . .' He looked at them. 'What do you say?'

Jonathan harvested his barley himself, working like a slave but with the deep satisfaction of knowing that there was no profit for Lieutenant Greville this time, no triumph for Jonas Pike. And, on a day in late February, they all went together to the ravine, a cunningly chosen spot, where Will Price had set up his still. He drew off the first sample, holding the glass up to the light critically. 'It's clear', he said. 'Perfectly clear.' He sipped judicially. 'Proof, too, I'll be bound. The flavour's excellent.' He poured some into three more glasses.

Polly sipped daintily. Then she looked at her man and smiled. '*Uisce beatha*', she said softly. 'The water of life, as we say in Ireland.'

He raised his glass. 'The spirit of enterprise,' he said, 'as we say in New South Wales.'

CHAPTER THIRTEEN

It was inevitable that John Macarthur, who had already fought two duels with men placed in authority over him and who had quarrelled in turn with Governors Hunter and King, should cross swords with Governor William Bligh The two men were too alike; to put them together in the small isolated community of New Sòuth Wales was like putting two matched fighting cocks in the same cockpit Both were Devon men, of Drake's stubborn, self-willed temperament; both had had stormy passages in their lives for which they had faced courts in England and been exonerated—Macarthur for his duel with William Paterson, Bligh for the *Bounty* mutiny; both had become public figures by virtue of the many fine qualities each possessed; and both were devils incarnate when crossed. The running battle continued for almost eighteen months from the date of Bligh's arrival in the colony in August 1806, the Governor using as ammunition not only his own causes for dispute with Macarthur but some of his predecessor's as well, until, on 25 January 1808, Macarthur was put on trial on a charge of 'deceitfully, wickedly and maliciously abetting and contriving' against His Excellency the Governor.

The hearing was to take place before the Judge-Advocate, Richard Atkins—the man who, acting in that capacity, had conducted the inconclusive inquiry into the state of the *Britannia* eleven years previously. He was an old enemy of Macarthur's. They had written abusive letters to one another and Macarthur had tried to sue Atkins for libel. Even as the trial began, therefore, the accused denounced his judge as biased, malicious and a liar, whereupon Atkins left the courtroom in a fury and Captain Anthony Fenn Kemp, a friend of Macarthur's on sick leave from Port Dalrymple and the senior of the six officers remaining, granted Macarthur bail.

'You have called His Excellency's bluff!' Lieutenant Greville said enthusiastically. He and Charles Wiltshire were among the crowd of supporters who had gathered at Macarthur's house in Sydney on the morning following the abortive trial. 'He is on the run, sir!'

'The battle is yet to be won, Mr Greville.' Macarthur, elegant and unruffled, sat in his chair basking in the warmth of their admiration. 'So far, His Majesty's chosen representative has taken great pains to observe the letter of the law. Justice, so-called, has been seen to be done. A trifle more provocation, however, and he may over-step the mark. We can then right the scales of justice for all to see.' There was a murmur of approval. 'And, mark my words,' Macarthur smiled grimly, 'ere long he'll wish he was back on the *Bounty*—or rowing to Timor!'

There was a roar of laughter—a roar that was cut off abruptly as fists pounded on the street door. In the silence they all looked at Macarthur, who stood up and nodded coolly to Greville. The lieutenant went out into the hallway, gratified at being chosen to play the part of butler; Macarthur followed him. Greville shouted, 'Who is it?'

'Constables! Open up!'

Greville glanced back at Macarthur, who nodded. He opened the door and the two burly men pushed inside. One of them said, recognising the tall, dark-haired figure with the prominent nose, 'Are you John Macarthur?'

'I am.'

'Sir, I have here a warrant for your arrest. I must ask you to accompany me from this place to another.'

The men who had spilled out into the hallway after their leader looked at one another in consternation. In the forefront of the group, Wiltshire said, 'What is the charge?'

'It's an escape warrant, sir. Mr Macarthur is charged with escaping from legal custody.'

'Preposterous!' Wiltshire snapped. A growl of agreement came from the other men in the doorway.

'Constable.' Macarthur was as calm as ever. 'There has obviously been some error. Yesterday I was remanded on bail. Why should I bother to escape?'

The constable looked ill at ease before this man whose power in the colony was something to reckon with. 'With respect, sir,' he coughed nervously, 'you were not remanded by a legally-recognised court. Without the presence of the Judge-Advocate. . . .'

'But he left and refused to return!' Wiltshire pushed forward angrily. 'Is Mr Macarthur supposed to languish in gaol indefinitely?'

'Begging your pardon, sir.' The constable was beginning to sweat. 'I'm merely executing my orders.'

'Yes, of course.' Wiltshire checked himself. 'Who signed the warrant? Let me see.' He glanced at the document the constable handed over. He looked up. 'I'm afraid it's valid, John. Information sworn by William Gore, the Provost-Marshal.'

'Very well.' Macarthur moved towards the street door.

It was an excellent opportunity for Maurice Greville to make a public gesture of loyalty at no possible risk to himself. He drew his sword. 'You shall not', he said theatrically, 'be taken against your will, sir!'

Macarthur stared at him. This Greville was, of course, a servile idiot but this was an excellent opportunity for making a public gesture that would stir things up a little. 'Stand aside, man!' he said. 'I must obey the law. That's what we're all fighting for here—the finest traditions of English law. No man,' he half-turned to his followers, 'no matter what his cause, should set himself above it—as His Excellency has done so blatantly!'

He went out, leaving behind him the uproar he had intended.

*　　*　　*　　*　　*

'If the court finds him guilty of sedition,' Will Price said, 'he has to abide by the verdict.'

'*If* they do.' Jonathan, sitting beside Will on the driving seat of the cart, took a swig from the water-bottle as they lumbered along the road to Sydney in the sweltering January sunshine. 'And then there's still the Corps to deal with. Will they abide by the verdict?'

'Don't see what else they can do.' Will, holding the reins, turned to check that the tarpaulin was securely lashed so that it protected—and hid—the load of one-gallon casks of whisky they were carrying. The still had made them prosperous during the past two years; both men wore smart town clothes nowadays for expeditions like this, and could look forward to comfortable board and lodgings overnight in Sydney. Their women, too, were better dressed, their homes more comfortably furnished—Jonathan's now had an additional room—and the small Dinny, three years old, was better provided for in the way of playthings. And their whisky—poteen, Mary called it—was, if highly illicit, of an excellent quality and much sought after in Sydney. They were, as Will said, beating the Corps at their own game.

Thinking of them, Jonathan said, 'Look at it this way: Macarthur's not only their brains; he's being made an example of. Whatever happens to him could happen to the rest of them. So who's going to enforce the verdict?'

'Bligh, of course', Will said.

'He's only one man, Will.' Jonathan was thinking of the 'pipe' or political pamphlet that had been slipped under the door of the inn only the previous night, attacking William Bligh. *O tempora! O mores!* it had said, and then, referring to the *Bounty* mutineer, 'Is there no *Christian* in New South Wales to put a stop to the tyranny of the Governor?' Will had said that Greville was behind it and that it was obviously an attempt to offset the New Year address signed by 833 settlers thanking Bligh for his improvements to colonial conditions.

'He doesn't mind taking on the Corps', Will said confidently. 'He's done it before. And he's done a lot to stamp out the trade in spirits.'

Jonathan shot him a sideways glance. 'Hasn't stopped us.'

'That's different. We're only doing it because we have to. When the Corps stops, so do we.'

Mary wasn't so sure that it was different. At 'The Bird in the Barley' where she and Dinny were staying with Polly, she said, 'Somehow, I can't get used to the idea of . . .' she lowered her voice, '. . . making our own poteen.'

Polly, wiping down the bar, stared at her. 'After two years of it?'

'I can't help it, Polly. It was the way I was brought up. I know in my bones it's wrong.'

'But, Mary love, what'd we do without it?' When Mary didn't answer, Polly leaned her elbows on the bar. 'Well, I'll tell you. You'd have your Jonathan out there in the fields breaking his back for six pounds an acre. And Greville and Pike taking all the profit out of your farm.'

'I know. But . . . .' Mary sighed. 'Sometimes I wish I were you, Polly. You always seem to enjoy life, no matter what happens.'

Polly smiled. 'Sure, and I like a bit of a laugh, I must confess.' She began wiping again vigorously. 'Come on, love. Things won't go on like this for ever. Bligh's the man to clean up the colony.'

* * * * *

'The whole thing', said Charles Wiltshire indignantly, 'is a travesty of British justice!' He and the rest of Macarthur's supporters had remained in the house all morning, keeping their ranks closed, as one of them put it, and awaiting further intelligence to be brought by Lieutenant Greville.

'Of course Atkins is prejudiced! How can John possibly obtain a fair hearing when the Judge-Advocate owes him money? Governor King distrusted Atkins; even Bligh himself considers the man to be a flabby drunkard. The whole thing's quite absurd.' He swung round to the door as Greville, now acting as messenger-boy, came in. 'Well?'

'The Court has been re-convened.' Greville, suave and beautifully-tailored as ever, went to take up a nonchalant pose at the end of the mantelpiece, conscious of the attention he was getting. 'But without the Judge-Advocate. And without Macarthur.'

'Without . . .?' Wiltshire looked stunned. 'What?'

'Atkins is apparently advising His Excellency at Government House, along with the infamous George Crossley.'

'Crossley? That perjurous attorney?' A fifty-nine-year-old solicitor, George Crossley had left an incredible trail of jurisprudential villainy behind him that extended to the other side of the world. Twice convicted for perjury in England, he had finally been transported for seven years for that offence and, on the way out on board the *Friendship*, had somehow contrived to purchase a cargo of goods at the Cape of Good Hope, paid for in bills that were later dishonoured. Even more unbelievably, he had set up a shop on his arrival in Sydney, running up more debts until his creditors, unable to take legal action against a convict, actually petitioned Governor King to pardon him so that he might be sued. This was done but Crossley, using all his legal skill, never paid over a farthing. It was said of him that he had once put a fly in the mouth of a dead man so as to be able to swear on oath that there was life in the body of the testator when he witnessed the forged will. 'A transported convict', said Wiltshire above the shouts of protest, 'has been elevated to the position of Governor's counsel!'

Greville said, 'And Macarthur remains in prison—on the escape warrant.'

'Obviously,' Wiltshire's ruddy face was almost puce with indignation, 'Bligh does not want the trial to proceed!'

'The officers of the court have written to the Governor

requesting him to appoint an acting judge-advocate and to restore Macarthur to his former bail. But', Greville shrugged, 'to no effect.'

Wiltshire swung round to the others. 'Gentlemen, loath as I am to say this, it may be necessary to take the law into our own hands.'

'That's not what Macarthur advocated.' Greville had failed to see beneath his leader's oration about law and order in the hallway.

A stout New South Wales Corps lieutenant asked, 'Is it possible to get a message to him?'

Greville nodded. 'Nothing easier. The keeper of the gaol happens to be an old friend of Macarthur's.' He shrugged. 'In fact, if we're patient, I expect he'll make his wishes known.'

Macarthur had never been one to delay in making his wishes known, and the note arrived an hour or so later. 'He suggests', Wiltshire said, studying it, 'that Major Johnston be sent for.'

'I thought', the stout officer asked, 'he was inconvenienced with a wound?' Soon to be gazetted Lieutenant-Colonel, Major George Johnston had been in charge of the detachment that had routed the rebels after the Castle Hill rising four years before.

'It's nothing', Greville said impatiently. 'A scratch, no more.'

Wiltshire hadn't been listening. He was staring at the note, a look of shock on his face. When he became aware that they were all waiting for him to continue he looked up at them. 'He also suggests that Bligh be placed under arrest.'

Nobody spoke. It was a thing they'd talked of, threatened, said ought to be done. But to do it . . . to seize His Excellency the Governor and lock him up! Why, it was like laying hands on His Majesty himself . . . . 'If we take such a step,' Wiltshire said quietly, 'there can be no turning back.' Fletcher Christian, he thought, had probably used similar words to his men.

Even Greville had a pang of uneasiness. Then he

shrugged it off. 'What other choice have we?' As on board the *Britannia*, he could always say afterwards that he had merely carried out his orders.

'The court has decided to take steps against William Gore, the Provost-Marshal, for swearing out a false deposition. If the escape warrant can be quashed then Macarthur must be released—on bail, at the very least.'

'To what purpose?' Greville asked. 'To stand trial again—under Atkins? It will resolve nothing.' There were murmurs of agreement from the others. Wiltshire walked to the window and stared out.

He turned. 'I will abide by the majority decision. But I think each of us should be aware that detaining His Majesty's chosen representative will have repercussions far beyond this colony. It is not a course to be embarked upon lightly.'

Again, nobody spoke. One or two turned to study the faces of their friends to see how it stood with them. With a sense of irony, Wiltshire remembered that that day, 26 January, was the twentieth anniversary of the hoisting of the British flag in Sydney Cove by Arthur Phillip, the first Governor of the colony.

Greville's voice broke in. 'Very well, gentlemen. What's it to be?'

*   *   *   *   *

It was hot in the streets of Sydney that Tuesday evening. Will and Jonathan had spent the afternoon in alleys and back streets, exchanging kegs of whisky for provisions, household goods, little luxuries for their women. Now they were free to stroll and enjoy the excitements of the little town—the 'sink of iniquity', as Bligh called it, that was 'improving in its manners and in its concerns'.

There was certainly plenty of excitement afoot. The streets were filled with groups of evening walkers who were busy exchanging rumours. John Macarthur, sword in hand, had fought his way out of gaol only to be recaptured after a pitched battle with a party of constables; he had challenged Governor Bligh to a duel; he was at that very moment in irons and likely to be hanged. 'Excuse me, friend, but we've only just arrived in town', Jonathan said for the tenth time, hoping for a sensible answer. 'Can you tell us what is happening?'

'Dunno.' This passer-by, at least, was an honest man. 'But you can wager it's trouble. Listen!'

Down the street they saw a crowd scattering and they could hear yells above the squeak and thump of a drum-and-fife band playing 'The British Grenadiers'. Then the scarlet-and-yellow of the Corps swung into view in column of route, colours flying and bayonets fixed. At their head rode Major George Johnston in his black bonnet, his right arm in a sling and his drawn sword in his left hand. Greville rode immediately behind him. Will said, 'They're heading for Government House!'

'Told you', said their acquaintance with satisfaction, 'it was trouble.' He vanished as the crowd surged back to allow the troops to pass in a storm of mingled cheers and cat-calls. On the other side of the street Jonathan caught a glimpse of a face he recognised. 'Macarthur!' He seized Will's arm. 'Look, he's urging them on!'

That evening, the streets were filled again—with drunken soldiers, and patrols went from house to house compelling the residents to illuminate their windows to show their appreciation of the 'glorious victory'. It was the only one the Corps had ever had, so they made the most of it.

At 'The Bird in the Barley', the women found out about it on the following day. Polly, sitting in the back room with the three-year-old Dinny on her knee, had been confiding in Mary how much she missed Will, and Mary had asked whether she and Will wouldn't like a child of their own. For several years now, Polly had made no secret of the fact that she and Will were sharing the shelf with the possum rugs in the back room. They'd even talked of marriage, but there was no hurry for that—they knew how they stood with each other. Now Polly laughed. 'Too long in the tooth to be a mother all over again,' she said. A customer came into the tap-room so she handed the child back to its mother. When she returned she was pale with excitement. 'There's been a rebellion! The Corps has arrested Bligh and locked him up in Government House!'

'Oh, no!' Mary looked scared. 'Are you sure? Is it another rumour, do you think?'

Polly jerked her head at the tap-room. 'He's just from Sydney. There's been no bloodshed, but Johnston's declared himself Lieutenant-Governor and proclaimed martial law.'

'Jonathan—and Will! I pray they're safe.'

'Safe as houses', Polly said reassuringly. 'They're not ones to go seeking trouble.'

And they returned safe, if weary, on the Thursday. After being suitably welcomed and having given a brief recital of their adventures, they all gathered at the bar in the tap-room so that Will and Jonathan might quench their thirsts. 'Well, it's good to have ye home again', Polly said. She turned to Will and, practical as ever, asked, 'What did ye bring me?'

Will grinned. 'Wait and see. First things first—it's a long and dusty ride from Sydney Town.' He went behind the bar to get the drinks. As he did so, the front door opened and Jonas Pike walked in.

He said, 'Been looking for you two.'

Will recognised the hated croaking voice. Without turning round he said shortly, 'Well, now you've found us. State your business.'

'Sign this.' Pike slapped a paper on the bar.

'What is it?' Will turned, his hands full of tankards.

Jonathan said, reading it, 'It's an address to Major Johnston, urging him to arrest the Governor. It's dated two days ago.' He looked at Pike with loathing. 'If Johnston was acting on behalf of the citizens, as this claims, it should have been drawn up and signed before he arrested Bligh.'

'There was no time and he'd have been forewarned. Anyway,' Pike tapped the paper, 'never mind the debate. Are you going to sign or not?'

'No,' Jonathan said.

'Lieutenant Greville won't like this. I warn you, Garrett, you'll become a marked man. You run the risk of being deported.'

He looked at Mary. When she shook her head he said, 'That's a risk I'm prepared to take.'

Pike glowered at him. Then he turned to Will. 'What about you, Price?'

Instantly, Will disappeared into the back room, came back with a pen dipped in ink, and signed his name. The others stared at him as he handed the paper to Pike and said, 'Now be on your way.' Pike, sensing division, smirked at them and went out.

Conscious of the silent accusation on the faces of his friends, Will said as the mutter of conversation from the other drinkers in the tap-room started up again, 'I had to.' He gestured with the quill. 'Don't you see? If I hadn't signed, they'd take away my licence. Then what would we do, Polly and me?' Still nobody spoke. He went on, 'You mark my words. Before long, they'll have their men in every official position in the colony, with Macarthur as the power behind the throne. And there's nothing we can do about it. You'll see.'

Mary said coolly, 'I'll just collect Dinny. I think it's time we went home, Jonathan.'

At home, they discussed Will's action and Mary brought up again the matter of the poteen that was making her so unhappy. Jonathan agreed with her; they were no better than the rum traffickers while they ran the still that was hidden away in the bush. But he also agreed with Will Price. When, a day or so later, they were preparing the still for a fresh run and Jonathan talked of giving it up, Will said, 'Talk sense, man. I doubt if I could make a living for six months if I had to pay what the rum traders ask for their rotgut. And how long d'you think you'd last with Greville paying you whatever he liked for your crops?'

Will was correct, too, in his political predictions. Lieutenant Greville, Captain Kemp and others who had supported Macarthur were sworn in as magistrates;

Macarthur appointed himself Colonial Secretary. Richard Atkins, of course, lost his judge-advocacy, William Gore the Provost-Marshal was sentenced to seven years at the Coal River penal settlement, and the 'perjurous attorney' George Crossley to two years in gaol.

Jonathan was thinking about all this one morning in mid-February when he was on his way to the still with a sack of barley on his shoulder. He had almost reached the place where it was hidden when he stopped, listening. The crashes in the undergrowth and the loud curses he had heard stopped too. He went on, but very quietly, and looked out at the still from the cover of the thick bush.

Jonas Pike was there. He had been trying to catch a strayed calf and now he stood examining a brass measure he had picked up from near the still. A measure that, Jonathan knew, had the words 'The Bird in the Barley' stamped on it.

Without a sound, he withdrew. He ran back to the house. 'I'm going to warn Will', he told Mary. 'Come to 'The Bird' with Dinny and we'll see what can be done.'

Will groaned. 'Damn me for a fool for leaving that measure lying about!'

'We could say it had been stolen', Polly said.

'They'd never swallow that.' Will shrugged fatalistically. 'Ah well, we had a good run for our money.'

She turned on him. 'Ye're not just giving up?'

'What else is there? I'm no woodsman—I can't take to the bush. Besides, what would happen to you if I did? Pike's reward for informing on me is the licence of "The Bird".' He put an arm round Polly. 'Sorry, love. I've made a right hash of things.'

'What will happen when . . .?' Polly didn't finish.

Jonathan said flatly, 'Will and I will go to Van Diemen's Land for three years—Port Dalrymple or the Derwent River.'

'Oh, no!' She threw her arms round Will.

He said, over her shoulder, 'The measure connects me with the still, but not you. You're safe enough.'

Jonathan shook his head. 'We're in this together, Will.'

'No sense in us both going.'

'We shared the profits. We'll share the penalty.'

Polly said, almost weeping, I don't want either of you to go! Can't you think of anything before . . . oh, Mary!' She ran to her friend as, carrying her son, she came into the kitchen. 'These two are both after giving themselves up and they'll both end up in Port Dalrymple or some other hell-hole for the next three years! Will ye talk some sense into them, for I can't!'

Will held up a hand. 'Look, if you don't mind, I'd like to say something first. As you all know, I've always been a one for taking the least line of resistance and, with a bit of luck, I've always got what I wanted that way. I've avoided fights and principles and managed to get a few things through the side door. Well, I think it's time I made up for all that. The still was my idea. I talked Jonathan into it—although I never quite managed to convince Mary.' He smiled at her. 'It's my fault it's been discovered and nobody else's. As far as I'm concerned, I'm the one to blame—the only one.'

Jonathan said, 'Now wait a minute . . . .'

'Let me finish. I'd be a lot happier serving my time knowing that I have friends who'll be looking after Polly for me. After all, there's no sense in leaving two helpless women instead of one.'

'Mary's not helpless', Jonathan said.

'No, I'm not.' She shook her head. 'But—managing the farm, Jonathan. It's man's work. I don't know if . . . .'

'Then it's settled then.' Will paused. 'My only regret is that we won't be able to keep "The Bird".'

'It doesn't matter.' Polly was rummaging for a handkerchief. 'We can start again . . . .'

'Wait a minute!' Suddenly, Will punched one fist into the other. 'I've got it! The law says that whoever informs is awarded the licence.'

They stared at him. Polly said, 'Well?'

'Don't you see? If somebody else went to a magistrate before Pike, the licence would be awarded to him.' He paused, looking at Polly. 'Or her.'

She gaped at him. 'Me? I couldn't do that.'

'But I'm going to lose the licence anyway. Better for it to go to you than to Pike. Then we'll still have "The Bird" when I've done my time.'

As Polly turned to her, Mary said, 'It makes sense, Polly. If it'll work.'

She said unhappily, 'What would I have to do?'

'Tell the magistrate . . .' Will began.

'Captain Abbott,' Jonathan cut in, 'not Greville.'

'. . . of the terrible corrupt thing I've been doing. Distilling illicit spirits. And how do you see it your duty to have me brought to justice.'

'I don't think I can.'

'Polly,' Will said gently, 'you're a born actress if ever I saw one. You'd have no trouble convincing Captain Abbott of the purity of your intentions.'

'Purity?' she said. 'Me?'

'You can do it, love. For me. But you must reach the magistrate before Pike.'

Mary stayed behind to attend to her child and to the inn. Jonathan drove, with Will and Polly hanging on for dear life as the cart bounced along the Hawkesbury road towards Parramatta in a pall of dust as if being pursued by bushrangers. Outside Abbott's office, Jonathan said, 'No sign of Pike. Which means we've beaten him or . . .'

'. . . he's beaten us,' Polly said. In one way, she hoped he had.

'Only one way to find out.' Will jumped down from the cart. 'Come on, girl.'

She didn't move. 'I don't think I can do it, Will.'

He reached up and pulled her down gently from her seat. 'You can.'

'You think so?'

'Sure of it.' He grinned at her encouragingly. 'And you have to—for us.' He shoved her towards the magistrate's door.

Captain Edward Abbott, the Commandant of Parramatta Barracks, had been a magistrate since 1796 and was a member of the committee that had deposed Bligh. It had, in fact, been suggested that he should take up the post of Judge-Advocate lately vacated by Richard Atkins. 'Your name?' he said.

'Polly McNamara, Your Honour. It's about my—er—my husband.'

'His name?' Abbott was making notes.

'Price—Wilberforce Price. He's the inn-keeper of "The Bird in the Barley".'

When the magistrate looked up at her, Polly decided that all was lost; Pike had already made his accusation. She felt sick and cold at the thought of the inn—their inn—falling into those flabby toad-like hands.

But Abbott was merely querying the difference in surnames. He said, 'Are you his common-law wife?' When she nodded he made another note. 'And what have you come to see me about?'

'Sure, and it isn't easy for me to do this, Your Honour.' That much was true, at any rate. She drew a deep breath. 'But I know my duty. I know right from wrong, sir, and . . . .'

'Yes, yes.' When they started like this it was always some damned domestic fight or other, Abbott thought. 'Go on.'

'Well . . . . I was checking the account books the other day and it seemed to me we were selling more spirits than we were buying.' Abbott sat up. 'So', Polly was warming to her work. She became confidential. 'I kept an eye on him. And I found . . . .' She paused dramatically for effect. 'He's got a still out in the bush.'

Abbott's eyes narrowed. 'This is a very grave allegation to make.' Why was she doing this? One never knew, with women. Had another man, possibly, and wanted her inn-keeper fellow disposed of . . . . 'The penalty is a fine and three years' imprisonment.' When she nodded gravely, he said, 'You are to be commended for bringing this matter to our attention. And, if this information results in a conviction, you will be rewarded with the licence of the inn and £56 in goods.'

'Oh, Your Honour!' Polly managed to look totally surprised. Crafty little doxy, Abbott thought. Doesn't fool me, though. She'll take the inn and have her next lover move in. Then, when she tires of him . . . . 'Where is your—er—husband?'

'Outside. Shall I bring him in?'

It was Abbott's turn to look surprised. 'Won't you need a constable?'

'Oh, no, sir.' Polly smiled sweetly. 'I've persuaded him to give himself up.'

Good God! Abbott thought. Like those wretched female spiders who eat their mates when they've fulfilled their function. No, he'd never understand women. Never.

In Jonas Pike's case, however, he was more like the fly who has been entangled in the spider's web. Jaunting along the road, thinking happy thoughts of the inn he would soon possess, of the commendation he would receive from Lieutenant Greville, of the discomfiture of the Price-Garrett faction, he decided there would be no harm in calling, very briefly, at the house of a lady he knew. After all, he merited a small celebration.

And so, when he met Lieutenant Greville in Parramatta, he was full of good spirits. So much so that he had to clutch his horse for support as he fell off it and said, 'Good day to you, Mr Greville, sir! I have made a discovery of . . .' he hiccoughed, '. . . some significance.'

'You're drunk.' Greville stared at him with distaste.

Pike waved away that detail. 'Wilberforce Price', he said, leaning comfortably against his horse's rump, 'has an illicit still in the bush.'

Greville said nothing. Pike peered at the three lieutenants and addressed the middle one. 'You seem to entertain some doubts, sir.' He wagged a finger reprovingly. 'But I have proof positive of his complicity.' He groped in his saddle-bag and tugged out the brass measure he'd found. 'See? We can take his licence from him with this.'

Greville seemed singularly unimpressed. 'When', he asked coldly, 'did you make this significant discovery?'

'Smorning', Pike said smartly.

'Then what took you so long to get here?'

'Some light refreshment.' Pike waved a hand carelessly. 'Along the way. With a lady of my acquaintance who shall be nameless but who stocks a fine three-month-old whisky . . . .'

'You fool! Polly McNamara has already informed on Price—to Abbott. It's his case now and there's nothing I can do about it!' Greville gazed at his manager with disgust. 'You'd better appear before Abbott directly—and put forward a damned convincing case!'

Abbott, however, was not convinced. As soon as Pike entered his office he recognised him as the fellow who'd brought him intelligence of the Castle Hill rebellion four years previously. And, even though the information had turned out to be true, the man had acted as if crazed, babbling about half-witted Irishmen on inn-roofs who intended to walk to China. 'There you are, sir!' Pike, propped against Abbott's desk, waved the brass measure under his nose. 'What more damning proof could you wish, eh?'

None at all, Abbott thought, wrinkling his nose at the smell of three-month-old whisky and sweat of a similar vintage that now hung in his office like a fog. This time, there was proof positive that the blackguard was as drunk as Chloe.

But Polly was suffering the pangs of remorse, even though when she and Jonathan returned to the inn without Will, Mary assured her she'd done what was best. 'But what's going to happen to him now?' Polly asked, hunched in a chair in the kitchen. 'Shut up for ever in Port Dalrymple or on the River Derwent. There's not many that come back from Van Diemen's Land. Will's not a strong man. . . .' She began to sob with the reaction of what she'd done.

Jonathan slipped out to attend to the horses and left the women together. Mary put an arm round her friend. 'If only there was something we could do . . . .' She thought for a moment. Then she said, 'If you'll look after Dinny for me, there's someone I could ask to help.'

She asked Jonathan to take her to Westbury. While he

waited outside with the cart, she stood in the quiet hallway of the Wiltshire home thinking of all the things that had happened to her in this house. Of that strange first night when she'd been told she couldn't stay, of Jonathan coming to claim her in the kitchen, of Dinny O'Byrne stealing tarts. . . . A maid she'd never seen before led her into the day-room where she didn't know whether to curtsey or not. But Wiltshire was as kind as always—severe when she told him about the poteen but sympathetic when he learned that Will was to confess all and throw himself on the mercy of the court. Wiltshire seemed curiously interested when he discovered that the whisky had been extremely palatable. She came away with his promise that he would do what he could.

In the next few days Greville had his men smash the still to pieces and he himself went to the inn to try to implicate Jonathan as Will's accomplice. At the trial, he annoyed Captain Abbott very much by interrupting the proceedings with a demand that the accused should name his associates. 'Order!' Abbott smacked his gavel down indignantly. 'I remind you that this is my court, Lieutenant.'

When the time came for sentence to be passed, Captain Abbott said, 'The penalty for illicit distilling is three years' imprisonment with hard labour at Port Dalrymple.' Polly closed her eyes, then opened them as the magistrate continued, 'However, in this case, there are other aspects to be considered. It has been brought to my attention that the accused has a specialised knowledge of brewing as well as of distilling. This colony is markedly short of such skills. The Court therefore sees fit to assign Wilberforce Price to the brewery at Parramatta for a period of three years.' Polly sighed with relief. Parramatta! Why, she might even be able to see him every now and then. . . . She listened to Abbott's concluding remarks. 'As to the licence of "The Bird in the Barley", I award this to Polly McNamara who, at considerable personal cost, brought forward information to the public good.'

Greville gave Pike a look that did nothing for the farm-manager's peace of mind. Polly smiled demurely at Captain Abbott as he dismissed the court.

Outside, Polly said to Mary, 'Thank you, love, for talking to Mr Wiltshire. If it hadn't been for that . . . .'

Mary said, 'He's always been very kind.'

Jonathan smiled grimly. 'He's also got an interest in the brewery. Thomas Rushton's leaving to build his own brewery at Brickfield Hill in Sydney; Wiltshire's been looking for a practised brewer for some time.'

CHAPTER FOURTEEN

For Polly McNamara there now began a hard and bitter time. The work of managing the inn was arduous enough in itself with no-one to take the brunt of serving in the tap-room while she cooked and washed up, nobody to chop the firewood, keep the accounts, fetch supplies from Sydney or mend a leaking roof. But, worst of all, there was no-one at the end of the long, tiring days, no Will to cheer her with a joke and a chubby grin and care whether she was well or ill. The high bunk with the possum-skin rugs had never seemed so cold or so lonely, and there were times when, had it not been for the support given by Mary and Jonathan, she would have rushed out weeping into the bush and abandoned it all.

It was on one such occasion, on a wet, blustery evening in the July of 1809, that Jonathan came into the inn, a loaf freshly-baked by Mary tucked under his oilskin cape. A customer had just left in a huff because his meal was too slow in coming; a pair of redcoats were making nuisances of themselves with their pawing and lewd suggestions; and Jonas Pike, now wearing the black caped coat and hat of a constable, had arrived to tell her that her spirit licence had not been paid for and that it would be tranferred to another applicant if the money was not forthcoming directly. 'Start collecting your pennies, mistress', he said, showing his yellow teeth at her. 'The duty must be paid before the general muster of settlers next week. I'll see you there.' He turned to Jonathan who had entered behind him. 'You too, Garrett.'

Jonathan shook the rain off his oilskin, 'You won't see me there.'

Pike stared at him. Attendance at a muster was a matter of compulsion, not choice. 'Then', he said grimly, 'that'll be the finish of you, boy.' He pushed past Jonathan and went out.

Jonathan looked at Polly's flushed face and dishevelled hair, at the strain in her eyes behind the smile as she took the loaf he'd brought. 'It's after taptoo, gentlemen', he said, looking round the room. 'The house is closing.'

In the kitchen, when the customers had gone, Polly said, 'Did you mean what you said to Pike? About not going to the muster?' He nodded. She looked worriedly at him as she put the bread away in a crock. 'Have a care, Jonathan, do! Jonas Pike and the Corps are not to be crossed with impunity.'

'Jonas Pike's nothing more than a jumped-up pickpocket from Cardiff. And the Corps—the so-called government—has given him the opportunity of continuing to be a criminal—him and a hundred like him.' He looked out of the tiny kitchen window at the rain beating down out of a lowering sky. 'I thought about joining Dinny O'Byrne in the rebellion', he said. 'I thought about going to prison with Will—and I still don't know if I made the right choices. But I know this time. I'm not going to attend the muster and nothing's going to change my mind.'

*   *   *   *   *

Lieutenant Maurice Greville, however, was more convinced than ever that all his choices had been the right ones. He said as much to Charles Wiltshire when, calling so unexpectedly as to put Louisa into a flutter, he next visited Westbury. 'Stirring times, Charles', he said, joining his host at the fireplace after kissing his wife's hand with so much complimentary charm that she floated out of the room, entranced. 'Prosperous, profitable times, what?'

'Disappointing, I'd call them', said Wiltshire curtly. He, evidently, was not nearly as entranced with his unexpected guest as Louisa had been. He stared stuffily out of the day-room window, his hands tucked under his coat-tails, an irritable frown on his handsome face.

Greville raised his eyebrows, eyeing his host. 'In what way, sir?' he asked mildly.

Wiltshire made an impatient gesture. 'Oh, we're getting nowhere. I'm growing weary of this endless squabbling among the officers of the Corps. Too many lieutenant-governors. Too many axes to grind.' This was true enough, for in July 1808 Lieutenant-Colonel Joseph Foveaux had relieved Major George Johnston of his gubernatorial duties; after another six months, the sick and aging Colonel William Paterson had arrived from Van Diemen's Land to take over Government House; and, as an added complication, William Bligh had not, as he had promised, returned to England but was still hovering menacingly off the Australian coast in HMS *Porpoise*.

'You surprise me, Charles.' There was a slight edge to Greville's voice when he said, 'I would have thought your grant of five hundred acres was—a mark of progress?'

'Dammit, sir, I didn't help depose Bligh just for a grant of land! I looked for better government!'

Maurice Greville's yellow eyebrows went up a little higher. This was a new Charles Wiltshire—a very different man from the bluff, easy-going pastoralist of the pre-revolutionary era who hadn't seemed to give a fig whether the colony was run by Macarthur or Mephistopheles provided his supply of convict labour was assured. 'But', the lieutenant said reasonably, 'surely we have that? All our situations are vastly improved. You have more than doubled your land, you have all the convict labour you need, stock from the government herds. What more can the government do?'

'It can govern!' snapped Wiltshire. 'My farms are doing splendidly—as are yours, no doubt. But the colony is falling apart like a foundered bum-boat. Look at the public buildings! Look at the roads . . . .'

'Look at them indeed!' said Louisa, making an entrance with her hair re-arranged. 'They're a disgrace! Only a few days ago my carriage became bogged on the road to Sydney. I ruined a pair of satin shoes!'

Greville bowed. 'My profound regrets, ma'am.'

'Oh, it is not *your* fault, Mr Greville', she said, smiling languishingly at him. 'No-one could blame *you*.'

'No-one', said her husband, 'could blame Mr Greville for anything. That's the secret of his success.'

'Charles!' said his wife sharply. 'That is most . . . .'

'Please, ma'am.' Greville held up a placatory hand. 'I think I understand how Charles must feel. To have devoted so many years to the Corps and now, at the zenith of its power, to find himself no longer a part of it . . . .' He shrugged. 'It must be like looking through a window at a dinner-party to which one has not been invited.'

Wiltshire said nothing. But he reacted again with uncharacteristic irascibility that evening at dinner, Louisa having invited Greville to stay in spite of her husband's lack of enthusiasm. The lieutenant was in the middle of a discourse on the waywardness of certain settlers who had resolved not to attend the muster when Wiltshire reached for the port decanter and found it almost empty. 'Damn ation!' he said, cutting off his guest in the middle of a sentence. 'I must fetch another bottle. Excuse me.' He left the room.

Louisa pouted prettily. 'I must apologise for Charles's ungracious behaviour', she said. 'I can't think what has inspired it.'

'I can think of two explanations.' Greville moved towards her a little in his chair. He had a capital dinner inside him, he had been responsible for most of the havoc wreaked on the port-supply and just then Louisa seemed particularly attractive with her blonde hair shining, her blue eyes soft and admiring, the curve of her bosom rising and falling entrancingly. He lowered his voice, creating an atmosphere of intimacy in the warm, candle-lit room. 'One of them being that he left the Corps at the wrong time . . . .' He let his voice tail off, looking down at his empty glass as he toyed with it.

'And the other?' She, too, leaned forward so that they were very close.

'Quite simply that . . . .' He looked at her with a directness that made her catch her breath. 'Charles is jealous of our friendship . . . Louisa.'

It was the first time he had spoken her name. She felt as if she would swoon with pleasure as she stared at him, wide-eyed.

He said, 'We have, I believe, a . . .' he paused fractionally, '. . . a special regard for each other.'

She placed a hand on his arm. It trembled slightly, he observed with gratification. 'We have indeed', she breathed.

'And Charles cannot but be aware of it. Therefore . . . .'

The footfalls of her spouse in the hallway, bringing up the port reinforcements, made Louisa snatch her hand away and sit up primly. Greville lounged back in his chair. Wiltshire said, as he came in, 'This was a present from Macarthur. I suspect it came from Bligh's cellar.'

Louisa's cheeks were as pink as if she, too, had been party to the rape of the late Governor's wine-bins. 'I shall retire', she said, with forced calmness, 'and leave you to your port.'

Greville rose and bowed, as cool as ever. Louisa gave him a look that indicated clearly what her plans for retirement would have been under more propitious circumstances. Wiltshire appeared to notice nothing as he uncorked the bottle.

* * * * *

On the day of the general muster of settlers, Jonathan took advantage of the cool July sunlight to spend the day on a picnic with his family. Warmly wrapped, they lunched by the creek, played Blind Man's Buff, and the five-year-old Dinny and his father climbed trees and ran races. And on the day following, Constable Pike came to the Garretts' house while Jonathan was repairing the thatch. 'You're always looking for trouble,' Pike said, 'and this time you've found it.' Grinning triumphantly, he held out a folded paper. 'This is a summons, Garrett. You're to appear before the bench of magistrates in Sydney on Saturday next at nine in the forenoon.' He chuckled as he looked up at the thatching. 'You'd be advised to get this finished by then. Because you won't be coming back for quite some time.'

Other settlers were of the same mind as Jonathan and they, too, had been served with summonses. There was even some wild talk of armed resistance, but both Mary and her husband knew from bitter experience what would come of that. Some protest, however, just had to be made. 'It's come to the point', Jonathan said, 'where I won't be pushed back any further. All I want is to speak out about this illegal government that's slowly bringing the colony to ruin.' He stared at Mary in frustration. 'If only somebody would listen to us!'

She said, 'They'll have to listen to you in court.'

'But how much will they let me say? It'll be a pack of redcoat officers. They'll shut me up the way they've shut up everybody else. You know what they did to Isaac Nichols.'

Suddenly Mary's eyes lit up as the idea struck her. 'Write it, then! A letter, Jonathan! To the Lieutenant-Governor! Colonel Paterson wasn't party to the rebellion. He'll listen.'

It was not, however, an idea that appealed to Polly when Jonathan read his missive to her the following day in the kitchen of 'The Bird in the Barley' while Mary, aglow with pride at her husband's literary achievement, stood at his side. It was she, after all, who had taught him to write in the first place. 'Tear it up!' Polly cried in alarm, staring aghast at the pair of them. The letter not only stated Jonathan's refusal to obey the orders of 'this so-called government'; it praised William Bligh, referred to those who had displaced him as criminals, accused the administration of oppressing the many for the good of the few and, for good measure, castigated the 'greed and power' of the military. In Polly's opinion, Jonathan might just as well have scribbled a note announcing his intention of placing a bomb in the Government House privy. 'Father of pity!' she said in horror. 'Your wits need mending, Jonathan, and what's got into you, Mary, I don't know for the life of me.'

Jonathan merely smiled and folded his epistle while his fellow-conspirator fetched a burning twig from the fire for the sealing wax. 'Well, don't be thinking I'm going to send it to Sydney for you. Somebody's got to save you from your lunacy.'

'You'll send it, Polly.' Mary watched the dripping, flaring wax.

'Now look.' Polly tried to reason with them. 'You must think what this means. You', she pointed at Jonathan, 'might go to gaol. And', she turned to Mary, 'that'd leave the two of us on our own and God knows how we'd get by.'

Mary handed her the letter inexorably. 'Send it, Polly', she said calmly.

*   *   *   *   *

Maurice Greville was already beginning to repent his port-induced flirtation with Louisa over the dinner-table. That she was only too ready to play the ace against the jack was blatantly apparent and, once so engaged, Louisa Wiltshire would be a damned difficult female to get rid of, he knew. At her age, she'd want more than a mere flirtation. She'd talk of her honour being impugned and how it was his duty, etc. etc. In the small confines of the colony she could cause a scandal that would ruin everything he'd worked so hard to achieve. Other men's wives, as he knew from past experience, could be the very devil. So, prudently, he avoided Louisa Wiltshire like the plague.

She, for her part, let matters lie for a week. Then, when Greville made no move, she said to her husband one evening, 'Charles, I have been thinking. We really should invite Mr Greville to dinner again.'

Wiltshire, working on his accounts, grunted. 'It's barely a week since he was here.'

'Yes, Charles. But', she placed another stitch with delicate precision into her embroidery frame, 'I fear we may have been less than gracious hosts on that occasion.'

'I don't see why.' Wiltshire turned a page in his ledger. 'He drank half my port.'

'Charles, if I might speak plainly, you seemed quite peevish on that occasion.'

'I'm sure it had no effect', said Wiltshire grimly. 'But, if you wish it, I shall invite him. Not', he added thoughtfully, 'until next week, however. He'll be in Sydney all weekend.'

'Oh.' She frowned slightly. There was a long pause. Then she said with apparent irrelevance, 'We never seem to visit Sydney now that you have left the Corps.'

'Oh, come now, Louisa. That's not altogether true.'

'And Sydney is becoming such a gay town while we seem to be growing quite provincial.'

This, he well knew, could continue until dawn if necessary and, in the meantime, he had these damned accounts to do. 'Very well, my dear', he said resignedly. 'Would you like to go to Sydney for the weekend?'

'Oh, Charles!' She beamed at him. 'When do you plan to leave?'

'I hadn't planned at all.' He shrugged. 'Tomorrow?'

'Charles, dear, what a lovely surprise! But what am I to wear? I must inspect my wardrobe immediately.' She fluttered from the room. Wiltshire watched her go, an odd blend of exasperation and pity on his face before he turned to his ledger again.

The visit to Sydney was not, however, an unqualified success. True, Louisa tracked her quarry down, as she had surmised she must do sooner or later in so small a place if only she could drag Charles on a sufficient number of promenades about the streets. And it was on one of these excursions that she did, in fact, encounter Maurice Greville. The sun shone, she was dressed to kill, and when she saw him in the crowd she experienced all the joy of Diana tracking down a particularly handsome stag.

Until she observed that, on his arm, he had one of the most strikingly beautiful girls she had ever set eyes on. In addition, the Miss Stoddart who was introduced to her by the perfidious and totally unabashed Greville possessed the advantages of being unmarried and a good twenty years younger than poor Louisa, and no amount of frigid snubs, no number of disparaging stares at Miss Stoddart's clothes, shoes and bonnet could get rid of those horrid facts. But Louisa bore up well under the blow. 'I thought', she said after the introductions, 'Charles said you were in court today, Mr Greville?'

'Indeed I was, ma'am. As a matter of fact, I dealt with a former servant of yours. Garrett. Remember him?'

'Yes. A surly young man.'

'Well, ma'am, he has six months in which to mend his manners, you'll be pleased to hear. He's one of those wretched fellows who refused to attend the muster.'

Wiltshire said suddenly, 'I see congratulations are in order, Maurice.'

For a moment, Louisa could think only of engagements to be married, and her blood ran cold. But her husband, who had been eyeing Greville's uniform coat, said, 'Maurice has been promoted Captain.'

'And, indeed, Mrs Wiltshire,' said Miss Stoddart with what Louisa considered to be a most unjustifiably proprietory air, 'the promotion was not purchased. It was a token of recognition from the Lieutenant-Governor.'

Louisa addressed Greville as if the silly wench was not there. 'Our best congratulations', she said warmly. 'We must have a celebration! If I recall, it is your birthday next month. Let us make it a double celebration. A party at Westbury, with you as the guest of honour.'

'Delightful idea', said Wiltshire in the tone of one remarking that it had begun to rain. He glanced at Miss Stoddart.

But, before he could make the mistake of including her in the invitation, Louisa took his arm. 'Then it's settled. Come, Charles. *Au revoir*, Maurice. And goodbye, Miss Stoddart.'

* * * * *

Jonathan's letter had all the effect that Polly McNamara predicted. His defence in court did nothing to mend matters, either, since it consisted solely of a complete refusal to acknowledge the legality of his trial. The net result was that, while the other recalcitrant settlers received a month's imprisonment apiece, Jonathan was awarded six, plus a fine of one shilling. Polly thought he'd got off lightly. But that did little to help Mary, who was left with all the work of the farm as well as that of the house and the care of her son. The two women joined forces to keep the inn and the farm going, but it was uphill work and before many weeks had passed they were driving themselves to the point of exhaustion.

'You're looking a little tired, Mrs Garrett', Jonas Pike remarked one afternoon as he encountered Mary on her way home from a particularly gruelling day at 'The Bird in the Barley'.

'Don't waste your sympathy', she said coldly. 'I'm perfectly well.'

'Big job for a woman, trying to run a farm.' Pike rubbed his hands together. 'Already I see the weeds sprouting in your fields. They'll be rank as grass by the time your husband gets out in the summer.'

'I'll manage.' Mary urged the young Dinny on but Pike kept pace with her.

'I don't like to see a woman on her own. Lot of bad characters roaming the district. Now, if you were to move down to the tavern with your friend and I undertook to manage the farm for you . . . .'

'I'll look after myself and my child *and* the farm without your help', she snapped.

'I wish you luck.' Pike's wide mouth split in an unpleasant grin as he watched her go.

It was on the following morning Dinny ran into the house, his face white. 'Ma!' he shrieked. 'Come quick! Some men are taking our cows!'

There were two of them, big hulking brutes that Mary had never set eyes on before, armed with cudgels. 'Get away from those cows!' she screamed, running with Dinny at her heels.

They ignored her. 'Stop it!' she shouted desperately as she saw the cattle disappearing into the bush. Dinny picked up a stone and threw it.

At that, one of the ruffians turned. 'Hang onto that boy, missus,' he snarled, 'or I'll crack his skull!'

She gathered the lad close to her. 'Why are you doing this? Those cows—they're all we've got.' She swallowed. She wasn't used to begging. 'Please', she said, trying not to cry. 'Please don't . . . .'

The lout said jeeringly, 'Run and tell the constable about it, why don't yer?'

Then she saw how it was. As the men, guffawing, drove the cows away she turned and went back to the house with her son. She sat by the fire after putting him to bed that night and it was only then, with a letter from Jonathan in her hand telling her of his love for her and how he was counting the days until his return, that she allowed herself the luxury of tears.

*　　*　　*　　*　　*

Louisa Wiltshire said, 'Charles, I am growing quite concerned. What can have happened to Captain Greville?' The celebratory party at Westbury was in full swing. The punch-bowl was being emptied rapidly, the hired violinist was playing assiduously for those who wished to dance and the day-room was ablaze with candles and filled with the chatter of those who passed for gentry in the colony. Only the guest of honour was missing.

'I shouldn't worry.' Obviously, Charles Wiltshire did not share his wife's concern. 'None of the officers are here yet. Probably celebrating in the barracks. It *is* his birthday, you know.' He moved off to discuss his own stud with a neighbour. Louisa, beautifully gowned and managing to look fractionally closer to the age of the Miss Stoddart of evil memory, switched on a brilliant smile for the benefit of a guest across the room.

Mrs Kemp appeared at her elbow. 'Mum,' she said in a sepulchral whisper, 'the patties! Be dried to a crisp, they will, if we don't serve 'em up soon.'

Maintaining her fixed smile, Louisa hissed, 'Cook, we cannot serve supper before the guest of honour arrives. Make some more.'

'More, mum?' Mrs Kemp's jaw dropped.

And, at that moment, a loud voice from somewhere in the crowd said, 'Good Lord! What's happened to Greville?' The whole room fell silent.

For a moment, Louisa couldn't see. Her view was blocked by the throng at the door. But then, as it parted, she saw him.

She found herself looking at a stranger. The smooth suavity had gone. The impassive face was frowning with embarrassment, the arrogant stare had turned into a shifty glance about the room. And Greville's long blonde hair had been cut almost to the skull. Somebody whispered, 'Good God! He looks like a convict!'

His bow and smile for Louisa were a mockery of his former style and charm. 'Ma'am,' he muttered, 'I . . . .' He broke off.

Wiltshire said, 'Maurice, are you quite well?' Fellow's rolling drunk, he said to himself. Somebody else's port this time, though, thank God.

'Thank you.' Greville nodded. 'I am.'

Louisa could not restrain herself. 'Maurice, your hair! What on earth have you done to it?'

Greville hesitated. Then he squared his shoulders. 'It has been cut off, ma'am. On the orders of Captain Cameron of the 73rd Regiment of Foot.'

Wiltshire stared. 'Who the devil's he? And what right has he to do that?'

'Every right in the world, sir.' Greville gave a bleak smile. 'For his commanding officer happens to be the new governor of New South Wales.'

There was a sudden chorus of astonishment above which Greville said, 'Governor Lachlan Macquarie is already at sea. And, when he arrives, the entire New South Wales Corps is to return to England.'

And so, for Louisa Wiltshire, the party was to be no more successful than the visit to Sydney. Moreover, when all the guests had gone, all her dreams of romance with Maurice Greville came to an end. He was lying dead drunk on the day-room sofa when she and her husband found him.

'Maurice!' she shook him gently. 'You must wake up!'

'I should leave him be, my dear', Charles Wiltshire said. 'Heavens knows, he will have little peace of mind from now on.' He went into the hallway. 'I'll get his cloak.'

Louisa followed him. 'He seems to be taking the news very badly.'

'Small wonder. I shouldn't care to be in his boots. He may be going back to face a court-martial. If not, the regiment will be sent off to fight the French.'

'But then he would lose his land—everything he possesses. Surely he will resign his commission and stay rather than that?'

'He has no option, my dear. Some of the NCOs and other ranks may be allowed to remain, but the new governor will not want anyone here who participated in the late rebellion.' He smiled thinly. 'And they thought they'd be here for a lifetime.' He stood with Greville's cloak in his hands. 'Does my departure from the Corps seem so ill-advised now?'

She said nothing. He went on, 'Of course, with Maurice there is something else. His reason for coming to New South Wales.' He shrugged. 'They say he ran away from a duel.'

'Maurice?' She stared at her husband in dismay.

'Some shabby affair involving another man's wife.'

She said, more badly shaken that she would have cared to admit, 'But why didn't you tell me?'

He smiled at her gently. 'Because you wouldn't have wanted to believe me.' He turned, went into the day-room and draped the cloak over the sleeping, strangely pathetic figure of Captain Maurice Greville, one-time landowner, magistrate and merchant.

So, as the year of Our Lord eighteen hundred and ten came in, so did a new era for the New South Wales Colony. On New Year's Day, Colonel Lachlan Macquarie in his Black Watch tartan plaid was sworn in as Governor by the new Judge-Advocate, Ellis Bent, with a twenty-one-gun salute and a parade by the feather-bonneted Highlanders of the 73rd. He read his proclamation: 'His Majesty, having felt the utmost regret and displeasure on account of the late tumultuous proceedings in his colony, has been pleased to appoint Colonel Lachlan Macquarie as Captain-General and Governor-in-Chief of the Territory of New South Wales and its dependencies, requiring him to reinstate William Bligh, Esquire, as Governor of this colony for twenty-four hours.

Furthermore, all appointments, grants and leases made since the arrest of Governor Bligh are immediately declared null and void. All investigations and trials held in this period are deemed to be illegal and are declared to be of no effect whatsoever in law or equity.'

Three days later, Will Price and Jonathan Garrett were released from prison. They met by chance on the Hawkesbury road with much grinning and back-slapping—a reunion that was as nothing compared with the reception they had from their women when they arrived unannounced at the inn and at the farm. Polly, weeping and laughing at the same time, coated Will thickly with flour as she hugged him and he was so overcome with emotion that he asked her to marry him. Characteristically, she asked, 'Whatever for?'

Jonathan, Mary and their son met in an equally-ecstatic whirl of tears, shrieks and embraces but later, when Dinny was asleep, they sat in front of the fire in a quieter, more reflective mood. Mary said nothing of the hard labour she herself had endured. There was no need, for Jonathan could read it in the lines of strain round her eyes, the calluses that had formed on her hands. He said, 'I suppose it was Pike who arranged for the cows to be stolen.'

She nodded, remembering that dreadful day. 'But it doesn't matter now. He won't trouble us again. He's gone.'

'He'd have been murdered if he'd stayed.'

'He was like a dog that's lost its master. He left on the day of the new governor's proclamation. They say he was seen in Sydney, drunk and trying to board a ship for Van Diemen's Land.' She stared at the fire. 'I wish I could have saved those cows. And done more to keep the farm going.'

He put a finger to her lips and she took his hand and held it tightly as if afraid he would vanish if she let go. He said, 'It's all my fault, love. Not yours. I was the one who wanted to make a stand. Well—I did. And much good has it done us.'

She shook her head. 'No, Jonathan. It's been hard, true enough. But all the time I knew you'd done something we both knew was right. No-one can ever take that away from us. So don't say it was all for nothing.'

But all the same, after five months' neglect, the farm was falling into ruin and for the rest of that summer they worked like slaves to put it to rights with even young Dinny doing his share of the raking and weeding. It was on a Sunday in early March that Charles Wiltshire rode over Jonathan's land to where the owner was repairing a broken fence. 'Not having a day off, Jonathan,' Wiltshire said as he dismounted, 'even on the Sabbath?'

Jonathan grinned tiredly. 'Not with five months' work to catch up on.'

'You seem to be making progress.' Wiltshire looked thoughtfully at the sunburnt, powerfully-built farmer who had once been his convict groom and whom he'd once sent to the magistrate for a flogging. 'I spent yesterday with Governor Macquarie', he said abruptly.

Jonathan nodded politely but without great interest. 'A remarkable man', Wiltshire went on. 'He has already studied the affairs of the colony in amazing detail. Even the documents concerning your trial.' He paused. 'Including the letter you sent to the Lieutenant-Governor.'

Jonathan went very still. Surely it wasn't going to start all over again? 'I thought that was over and done with', he said slowly. 'All I want now is to be left in peace to farm my land. I served my sentence—five months of it, anyway—so . . . .'

Wiltshire laughed. 'Jonathan, you misunderstand me. The Governor is very impressed with the stand you took— with your courage for daring to speak out. His words to me were: "Here is a former convict with a greater sense of loyalty, integrity and justice than some of those who

233

governed this colony during the last two years".'

Jonathan shrugged. 'I wanted to say what I thought . . . .'

'He believes that emancipated convicts should be allowed to play a part in the public life of the colony. Now, I have been appointed a magistrate and His Excellency asked me . . .' he paused, studying Jonathan, 'if I would have you sit with me as an honorary magistrate—a justice of the peace.'

Jonathan gaped at him. 'Me?'

'I have already spoken highly of your character to His Excellency and told him I would be more than happy.'

'A justice of the peace?' said Jonathan incredulously.

Wiltshire took a letter from his pocket. 'The Governor wishes to meet all the civil officers of the district, and their wives, at Government House next Wednesday.'

'Government House?' It was all too much. Jonathan took the invitation, looking from it to his former employer. 'But I can't do that, Mr Wiltshire!'

'I believe you can, Jonathan.' Wiltshire swung up into the saddle. 'And I look forward to meeting you and Mary at Government House next Wednesday evening.' He raised a hand, wheeled his horse and rode off.

'He's mad', Jonathan said later that Sunday afternoon when, with the invitation standing on the mantelpiece of his cottage, he and Will and Mary and Polly were sitting in an awe-struck semi-circle in front of it, eyeing it as if it was a bomb that might explode at any moment. 'Quite mad, Mr Wiltshire must be—and this new governor's worse. How in heaven's name can I be a justice of the peace? I mean—what do I know of the law?'

Polly grinned. 'You've been tried three times, Jonathan. That's more experience than Mr Wiltshire's had—or the Judge-Advocate himself, for that matter.'

Mary smiled as she stood up to place a pillow under the head of her son who, tired out after his day in the fields, had fallen asleep on the floor. 'What do any of the magistrates in this colony know about the law?' she said.

'Some of them are about to find out', Polly said.

234

'Greville, for one.'

Will nodded. 'Aye, they've all gone—or are about to go. Johnston and Macarthur already in England to plead their case—with Johnston to be the scapegoat, I don't doubt. The former Judge-Advocate Atkins sent packing after changing sides; Abbott and the whole of the Corps' officers to sail for England in a month or two.'

'Some of them weren't so bad', Polly said. 'Captain Abbott, for instance . . . .'

'Of course.' Will nodded. 'But we're in a new century now, with all sorts of new things being discovered and invented in Europe—new ideas, too, about government and the rights of ordinary people like us. Governor Macquarie can see that. But those others—they were living in the past.'

Jonathan said doubtfully, 'Mary, do you think I can do it?'

She said unhesitatingly, 'I know you can.'

'Will?'

The little innkeeper stood up and went to the window, looking out at the dying light of sunset. 'It's all in a mess', he said. 'It'll take a lot of pulling round.'

'We're doing the best we can', Mary said defensively. 'You'll have seen that the fences are mended and . . . .'

'I didn't mean your farm.' Will turned from the window, his face shadowed. 'I meant the whole colony. It's had a bad time of it in the short span of its existence. Since I came here twenty-odd years ago I've seen pestilence and famine, battle, murder and sudden death in this place and I reckon it's time for a change. I think this governor's the man to make that change, and anybody who can give him a hand ought to step forward. That's why I not only think you can do it, Jonathan lad. I think you must.'

He turned to the window again where already the sun had gone down and the first stars were beginning to shine softly in the night sky. 'You know,' he said quietly, 'it's going to be like a new dawn for this colony if we go about it the right way. We've got all the space and all the riches we need here and I can see the time coming when all that', he pointed out into the darkness, 'is all inhabited and filled with farms and new towns springing up all over the place, with people living in happiness and prosperity. And who knows but one day this land might even be like America, free and independent, with men like Jonathan doing the governing of it and nobody caring if a man's father was a lord or a convict?'

In the darkness behind him Polly laughed softly, remembering the dreamer she'd ridden with on horseback from Sydney long ago. She said, 'Oh, Will . . . .'

'I'll go further. Maybe even the blackfellows'll come to live alongside us one day and have the same rights.' He paused. 'As they allowed Dinny O'Byrne to live alongside them and share what little they had.'

There was a silence in the darkened room while, for a moment, a fifth friend joined them, his laughter whispering in their memories. 'Aye', Jonathan said. 'But we'll not see those things, Will.'

'Oh, we won't see them.' Will Price was now only a head and shoulders silhouetted against the night sky. 'We're part of the past, too. But we owe it to the future to, well, to lay the foundations, so to speak.' He pointed into the gloom to where the sleeping boy lay curled up on the floor. 'And there's the future of this colony, Jonathan. Your son.'

A flame flared as Mary lit the lamp. The room bloomed with golden light so that, from outside, the house on the hill seemed to shine out like a beacon into the vast and sleeping land.

Finis